WRANGLEST❄NE

WRANGLEST❄NE

DARREN CHARLTON

stripes

STRIPES PUBLISHING LIMITED
An imprint of the Little Tiger Group
1 Coda Studios, 189 Munster Road,
London SW6 6AW

www.littletiger.co.uk

A paperback original
First published in Great Britain in 2020
Text copyright © Darren Charlton, 2020
Illustration copyright © Jana Heidersdorf, 2020

ISBN: 978-1-78895-121-0

MIX
Paper from
responsible sources
FSC® C020471

The Forest Stewardship Council® (FSC®) is a global, not-for-profit organization dedicated
to the promotion of responsible forest management worldwide. FSC defines standards based
on agreed principles for responsible forest stewardship that are supported by environmental,
social, and economic stakeholders. To learn more, visit www.fsc.org

10 9 8 7 6 5 4 3 2 1

For Shaun

LAKE WRANGLESTONE

N
W · E
S

EAGLE'S REST

MOOSE'S REACH

KESTRAL'S WATCH

STONE'S THROW

NORTHERN TRAIL

THE RIDGE

CABINS CREAK

OLD PAPPY

WATCHTOWER

BOATHOUSE

BEAR ISLAND

SIX LITTLE FISHES

THE WHISTLES

WRANGLESTONE FALLS

BOULDER

EXTRACTION POINT

SKIPPING MOOSE

RIVER WRANGLESTONE

THE PLAINS

THE SHARK TOOTH MOUNTAINS

1

Peter was born into a world of unwelcome visitors. And winter on Lake Wranglestone sure as hell was one of them. Just when the bears had started to leave for higher ground, those damned dark clouds came down off the mountains, carrying something far worse inside.

Peter drove his axe into the woodpile and looked out across the water. The lake, tucked in between the Great Glaciers to the north and the Shark Tooth mountains of the south, was among the most remote of all the refuges built for the nation's National Park Escape Program. A dozen little islands, all peaked with pine, dotted the deep blue eye of the forest.

His island, Skipping Mouse, on account of it being the smallest, was down one end. Eagle's Rest, where Cooper lived, was all the way up at the top. On a clear day, you could watch him skimming stones in nothing but his undershorts, but not this morning. Fingers of icy cloud hung so low over the water that the islands disappeared inside them. Peter steadied himself on the grip of the axe. The lake took on a special eerie feel now that the year was dying, and the air was thick with log smoke and bull elks grunting. But there was something else.

A loon bird wailed like a wolf in the night.

A canoe broke through the mist.

A moment later, it came.

"No," Peter whispered. "Not yet. Please go away. I'll be real good, I promise."

A single snowflake bobbed over Peter's head and settled on the blade of the axe. He chewed the skin around his fingernail and the snowflake dissolved to nothing. But it wasn't nothing. It just wasn't. Soon more snow would be on its way. More than just the snow too. Soon *they* would come.

Peter swung round, furiously scanning the shoreline. Over on the mainland, yellow leaves shimmered down from silver branches like sunlight on water. The lake clapped the rocky shore. He sighed. At least there was no sign of the ice forming yet. Their clawing hands couldn't get to the islands for now. But the big freeze was coming and it was coming fast, and no one was going to dig out their box of sleigh bells and Christmas stockings for First Fall. Not any more. Not ever.

Peter turned back. Above him, candlelight twinkled from inside the island's piney chamber. They were safe in their little timber tree house. The six wooden stilts that held it up there in among the pine cones and black squirrels were built to withstand a heavy knock, even a herd. That's what his dad had always promised him anyways. Not that it made much difference. Nothing stopped those stilts from looking as flimsy as matchsticks at this time of year. But then winter was the one season every Lake Lander feared. Not because Montana was about to get colder than a bald eagle's gaze, but because the Dead could make it across the lake's frozen waters.

2

"First Fall, huh?" came a gravel voice from behind.

Peter swung round and watched the canoe approach the island. It was a stranger's. An old man lifted up the wooden paddle and sliced it back down through the water. The flaps of his trapper hat swung about his face like the ears on Bud's old bloodhound, Dolly. He looked just as harmless too. But he'd got a good pace going and hadn't asked for permission to come ashore yet, so Peter made his way down to the water's edge.

"Who goes there?"

"Permission to land?" said the old man, hoisting the paddle out of the water. "Yes, yes. Permission to land."

Peter glanced back up toward the tree house. He shouldn't really be letting strangers anywhere near the island on his own. But his dad was nowhere to be seen.

"Bah!" bellowed the old man. "You can make up your

own mind, can't ya? You're a big boy."

"Yes," said Peter, without convincing himself. "I'm nearly sixteen."

"And you're real handy with an axe too."

"You think?"

"Sure."

Peter shrugged. "I s'pose."

"No suppose about it."

"Well, I'm trying my best."

"Better than trying."

"I'm trying real hard."

"I can see that. Broad shoulders n'all."

Peter creased the corner of his mouth into a half-smile and looked down. Darlene had told him that if he wore extra-thick knit it'd fool the eye into thinking he had the same broad shoulders as Cooper in a T-shirt. But he was nothing like Cooper. Nobody was. Peter braced his hand across his bony collarbone and wondered if he'd be lucky enough to spot him out on the lake today. He hadn't seen him for a few days now, three and a half to be exact.

The old man rested his paddle across the width of the canoe, smiling broadly.

The canoe glided into the shallows under its own momentum and grazed the shingle below.

"No," said Peter. "I'm skinnier than an aspen mauled

by beavers. But I patch up all our socks, and I know how to make a quilt out of old shirts and sweaters big enough to cover a king-size bed *and* make sure all the colours match up and complement real nice too."

The old man pulled off his trapper hat in an *I'll be darned* kind of way and used it to wipe the sweat off his bald head. "Well, fancy that," he said. "And a good thing too. We all need a use, a trade in this world. But I gotta admit, it is kinda unusual for a boy. You must take after your ma."

"No," said Peter quietly. "She's dead."

"Too bad. Then who do you get it from?"

Peter shrugged. He didn't know what made him this way any more than anyone knew why the planet had become a walking graveyard all those years ago, just before he was born.

A moment passed in awkward silence. The sun broke behind a passing cloud and dazzled across the water like starlight.

"Anyhoo," said the old man. "I take it I got permission to land?"

Peter looked up, embarrassed that he'd forgotten his manners, and rushed down to yank the nose of the canoe on to the shore.

"Oh sure! Sorry."

The old man wiped his hand across his thigh and

thrust it forward. "Ben."

"Peter. "Nice to meet you."

The old man nodded as if to say *likewise* and whipped an old blanket off the front of the canoe to reveal a big pile of stuff. He was a trader. The lake was full of them in the summer months. Whether it was rare essentials like cooking pots and flare guns, or novel trinkets from the old world like CDs for shaving mirrors, there was nearly always something to find if you rummaged deep enough. And, just as long as Peter didn't dwell on how traders had to raid dead people's homes for these items, he always looked forward to their visits.

"Anything take your fancy?" asked the old man. "We got pairs of boots in all sizes, a Swiss army knife complete with a corkscrew and some good old titty porn with all its pages intact."

Peter pushed the bundle of magazines aside and started to rifle through the rest.

"Oh, they were so sure the internet had killed off print," the old man went on. "But then the world blew its fuse and look who's laughing now!"

"I guess," said Peter, none the wiser. "Do you have a needle and thread?"

"You're a right little homebody, ain't ya?"

"It doesn't matter what colour it is."

"Well, I'm not too sure we do, Peter."

7

"I mean, it does matter. You don't want to mend a pair of white socks with black cotton if you can really help it, but anything will do really."

The old man looked up into the pines toward their tree house. "And what have you got to trade anyhoo?"

"We got a freshly hung deer," said Peter, distracted by a neatly stitched gingham oven glove.

"Uh-huh."

"And I made a dreamcatcher out of some twigs and eagle feathers."

"Right."

"I can show it to you if you like."

"Bet you got it looking real nice in that there tree house of yours."

"Yes," said Peter. "Dad felled trees for a bunch of logging companies before the world went dark. The cabin's made out of solid pine. Real good grain apparently. And he made the roll-up rope ladder too. The Restless Ones can't climb up it, but the bears will have a good go."

"Is that so? Well, I bet it's real cosy."

"Oh yes. It's just the one room with an outhouse round the back. But we've got a log burner and some old deer hide in the middle of the floor to make it soft underfoot."

"Well, lucky ol' you."

Peter continued to rummage through the pile. A few things caught his eye, but he'd made serious mistakes before by trading hard-hunted meat for things his dad decided were frivolous. He put the oven glove back on the pile because nobody had ovens any more and kept looking. After a while, his fingers came across something small and plastic, and he pulled out a toy animal. Peter turned the black and white striped horse over in his fingers and wondered how such a thing was ever possible out there in the world.

"Aha!" said the old man. "Zebra."

Peter looked into his eyes and smiled. "Wow."

"Yeah. Zee used to be for zebra, on kids' alphabet charts, I mean. But now zee just stands for—"

"Yes."

Peter held eye contact with the old man for a moment and a silent understanding passed between them. Nobody knew what was worse: being too young to remember what life was like before the world was turned upside down or being old enough to have to live with the loss. But this wasn't the first time Peter had felt someone look inside him and wish their memories were as short as his.

Tears welled in the old man's eyes. Peter noticed just how bloodshot and tired they were and wondered if he should invite him in to sit by the fire.

Snow drifted over the canoe. Heavier now.

"Suppose you'll be battening down the hatches if the snow keeps up like this," said the old man, clapping his hands together to warm them.

Peter looked out toward the islands where the other thirty or so Lake Landers lived, and nodded.

"Yes. Once the lake's frozen over, we're in for the long haul."

"How d'you even manage to defend yourselves? I know you've got a tree house n'all, but if a herd of Rotters came toward ya, I mean."

"The watchtower mainly," said Peter, pointing at the middle of the lake where the vast wooden structure stood. "The military built it when everyone had to abandon the towns and cities, and they turned all the national parks into refuges."

"Yup, I remember. And you're the lucky few who get to live here, huh? I heard Yosemite and Yellowstone damn near bust they were so full."

"I don't know," said Peter. "Why, which park have you come from?"

"You must all be scientists and neurosurgeons the world can't live without."

"I s'pose." But the truth was Peter had never really given it much thought.

The old man held eye contact. "Well, fancy that."

Peter smiled. An awkward silence passed between them so he quickly filled it.

"We don't even let the Restless Ones get this far. As soon as one of them breaks cover from the woods, we shoot on sight."

"Just like the old infomercials told us to do, before our television sets went dark."

"I heard," said Peter. Except it was hard to imagine how TV even worked, or the internet, or planes or electricity or anything.

"Yup. *IF YOU SEE SOMEONE WHO DON'T LOOK RIGHT, CLOCK IT. KILL IT—*"

"*RID THE WORLD OF IT!*" said Peter, nodding. "My dad taught me it was better to forget my pants in the morning than ever to forget that."

The old man's eyes narrowed, but he wasn't smiling any more. "Uh-huh. We all got told a lotta things back then."

"So people use the watchtower for fishing and diving in the summer months, but in the winter, we're scanning the shoreline like hawks on the wind. They don't stand a chance."

"I see. And what about others approaching the lake? Not the Dead, I mean, just good clean folks looking for sanctuary."

"There's a strict vetting procedure. All newcomers

have gotta report to Henry over on Cabins Creak."

The sun disappeared behind a cloud and the water dulled to a murky grey. Peter became aware of just how much cooler the air was when, all of a sudden, he felt a searing, stinging pain in his side. He looked down and watched the old man yank a bloody knife out from inside him.

"I'm sorry, boy," said the old man as if he genuinely meant it. "But who are you people? I brought my wife here on good faith we'd both be taken care of and you're not even wearing the snowflake."

Peter's legs gave way beneath him. He grabbed on to the nose of the canoe for support. It was only then that he realized the old man wasn't alone. Another blanket stirred at the far end of the canoe.

"It's gonna be OK, Martha," said the old man. "This nice boy was just being careful we were who we said we were. He's gonna let us up now. I'm sure our ol' knees can manage the rope ladder."

Peter fell forward on to the canoe all woozy. The air was suddenly so cold. He stared into the man's eyes, but there was no menace or evil hiding inside them, just the most practised look this world knew: need. Peter tried to push himself free of the canoe, but the old man clapped his hands down on top of Peter's to keep him there.

"It'll be over for you in seconds," he said. "I promise."

He wiped the bloody blade across his leg. His eyes scanned Peter's body, deciding where to stick it next. They glanced at his chest. Settled on his neck. But before the blade could find its way there, Peter heard a sudden *swoosh* and the knife fell from the man's hand.

An arrow jutted sharply from the old man's face. Peter watched gore seep out of his punctured eyeball and ooze down toward the quill. His life left him in seconds. Peter felt his own consciousness leave him, but his dad's footsteps pounded across the ground behind him and he fell backward into his arms.

"He said I was good with an axe, Dad. I'm sorry."

"Damn it, Pete," said his dad, helping him up. "You don't need a stranger to tell you that." He saw the blood and gasped. "Shit, Jesus. Darlene's got our first-aid kit. We've gotta get you over to her place quick."

Peter felt his body being lifted up, then lowered down into the canoe. His dad tossed the old man's body overboard, then scrambled in too. He was barefoot and hadn't even changed out of his white long johns yet. For some stupid reason, it crossed Peter's mind that his dad's black stubble was too thick now, too thick for Darlene to take any interest in him anyhow. Before he had time to mention the old man's wife, Peter felt

13

the canoe push away from the shore. He drifted off to the sound of the paddle cutting sharply through open water.

3

Peter woke behind his eyelids. He couldn't have been unconscious for more than a moment or two, but it was so quiet he thought he'd come round at Darlene's place. But he hadn't.

The canoe rocked gently from side to side, and he realized they were still on open water. He listened for the sound of the paddle cutting a quick course across the lake. But it didn't come. They weren't moving any more. Peter felt the cold kiss of snow on his face and slowly opened his eyes.

Snowflakes tumbled out of the low-hanging clouds, luminous somehow against the dark grey behind them. Peter blinked to clear them from his eyelashes and listened to a loon wail somewhere further off across the lake. But something wasn't right. He went to move and a searing pain bit into his side. Then he remembered the attack.

"Dad?" he cried, clutching the bloody wound. "*Dad!*"

There was no answer. He hoisted himself up on to the heel of his hands, falling back against the nose of the canoe. His dad was nowhere to be seen, but Peter wasn't alone.

The old woman was leaning over the side down the other end of the canoe. The blanket that had hidden her before was now crumpled at her feet. A powder-blue nightgown patterned with maple leaves fell across her bony frame. Tresses of long grey hair spilled into the water obscuring her features so Peter couldn't tell if she was alarmed or not. She didn't appear to be.

He clutched his side again and swung round to face the direction of travel in case his dad had gone ashore to fetch the first-aid kit from Darlene. But they were still some distance away from her island. He turned back round. The paddle had drifted away from the canoe, too far out to reach. However, the old woman was unconcerned by any of this. She ran her fingers dreamily through the still water, seemingly unaware of his presence or her missing husband even. Peter looked out toward the mainland, scanning the trees for movement. His dad was still nowhere to be seen.

"Where's my dad?"

The old woman didn't speak.

"Martha, isn't it? Please tell me."

The snow fell thickly now, forming fluffy clumps on top of the old woman's grey hair. But her focus stayed on the water and she said nothing.

"Martha," he said. "Miss Martha, please."

Peter pressed one hand to his wound, ready to stand, then stopped. The skin on the woman's legs was blotchy, like moss on stone. Her shins were black and mottled where the blood had stopped circulating and dropped with the weight of gravity. But this wasn't because of old age. It was a result of her death.

Peter froze. His unblinking eyes burned. The horror of what occupied the very same space as him forced them even wider and they glassed over with tears. He shuffled back into the nose of the canoe, quietly tucking his knees up under his chin so as not to alert the thing, suddenly aware of the surrounding water and just how much distance it placed between him and safety.

He looked down at the thing's black legs and felt the warmth of his own piss seep into his groin, helpless to do anything about it. Only that didn't matter now. He was completely alone out here with one of them and he had to do something. He parted his lips to let his breath escape and looked up. But a pair of black eyes were already on him.

He'd seen eyes like that up close once before. His earliest memory was of his dad showing him a weasel.

He'd held the animal up by the scruff of its neck and asked Peter to say what he saw. When Peter said he saw a 'fluffy wuffy' and reached out to cuddle it, his dad dropped the weasel into the middle of the livestock pen and watched it tear a rabbit's throat out. The life bled out of the animal in seconds. When his dad held the weasel up for the second time, with its bloodied torso twisting in his fist to break free, its black eyes bored right through Peter. There was no connection passing between one creature and another. Nature was cold and it was harsh and it didn't give a damn about your being there.

And so it was with the Dead. The creature at the other end of the canoe might have looked like an old woman – it carried her flesh, it wore her skin – but it was no such thing any more. It was a monster hiding in an old-lady costume.

The Restless One watched Peter through strings of grey hair. The whites of its eyes were so dark both eyeballs appeared to be all pupil.

Peter recoiled. "*Clock it*," he muttered. "*Kill it. Rid the world of it. Clock it. Kill it. Rid the world of it.*"

He fingered through the pile of stuff for a sharp object, something to stab it with. But before he could find anything, something slapped the surface of the water.

The Restless One's head turned back toward the lake. Peter scrambled to his knees and peered over the side.

One of its hands was still absent-mindedly stirring the surface of the water. The other was holding a foot. Peter stared at the body floundering in the darkness beneath the surface of the lake and his dad's pale face burst through, gasping and spluttering for life.

"Pete!"

His dad's hands slapped the surface of the water. He tried to break free, but this only made the Restless One tighten its grip further. His dad gulped. Water flooded his mouth and his head disappeared back beneath the surface. The Restless One lunged forward, pulled down by the weight of the body dropping into the depths below. The canoe bucked. Water breached the side, swilling across the vessel's wooden ribs at Peter's feet. But the thing still didn't let go.

Peter swung round. He needed to find a weapon and he needed one fast. The paddle was still out of reach. He looked at the bundle of magazines sloshing at his feet. If only he could find something heavy enough, he could dash the thing over the head and push it overboard. If that'd work. Even then it might not let go and end up dragging his dad under with it.

Peter dropped down to his hands and knees, frantically scrabbling through the sodden pile. There was nothing. Nothing at all and he couldn't believe this was even happening and he didn't have a clue what to do. He'd never set foot off the islands, let alone dealt with one of *them* before. But, before he was able to come up with anything, anything useful at all, another canoe rammed right into the side of theirs and flung Peter backward.

Someone jumped aboard, their boots landing squarely inside the canoe. They didn't even rock it. There was only one person who could do that. Peter couldn't even balance on a beached log in a summer breeze, but this wasn't the way with Cooper. They were roughly the same age, give or take a year or two, but while Peter's dad still hadn't let him anywhere near a rifle, Cooper could pop a row of tin cans into the air simply by smiling at them.

Peter scrambled up on to his elbows.

"I'm fine, Cooper," he said. "I was just about to do something."

But Cooper had it covered. Ropes of matted blond hair swished forward, covering his face. His muddy fingers popped the knife sheath secured to his belt, but his eyes never left the Restless One once. His fist took the handle as easily as someone would grip a door handle and he drew his machete clean out.

Cooper swung the blade above his head.

It sliced through the air.

The Dead One's head toppled off its shoulders and plopped into the water. It was so much heavier than

Peter had expected, more like a boulder than a ball. He scrambled backward, panting wildly, and his dad broke the surface of the water. There was a gasp and his white fingers clenched the lip of the canoe. But Peter never saw his head emerge. The world started spinning and he passed out.

4

News of the incident would spread fast. Cooper's dad, Bud, said as much when he stormed up the steps to Darlene's place, cursing the boy who'd have his son digging two burial holes deep enough for the whole community to shit in so early of a morning. *One unexpected witness with a hot tongue and the whole lake'll be buzzing like flies round a rotting carcass.* And he was right. Nothing scared folk more than a weak link in their system. Not even the big freeze.

Peter drew a blanket tightly round himself and paced the length of Darlene's porch while his dad and Bud argued inside. He leaned over the wooden railing and watched fat snowflakes tumble over the lake like feathers after a pillow fight.

Darlene's island, Boulder, was barely even an island at all. A single grey rock rose out of the water like the hump of a whale. A timber plinth to store firewood and canoes had been built on top. Perched on that, its four corners sticking out either side, was a tiny wooden chalet. With its porch, wind chimes and rocking chair, the chalet looked so impossible balancing there it was as if it had dropped clean out of the sky. But it was perfect.

On those long summer nights, when the stench of dead flesh wasn't carried across the lake by the wind, it was hard to imagine the world was anything other than bobbing fireflies and leaping salmon. Except, if the shouting inside was anything to go by, that was everyone's problem with him. Peter was nearly sixteen and yet he was practically the only Lake Lander never to have set foot on the mainland.

"He needs to wise up, Tom!" barked Bud. "He needs to get his hands dirty. He needs to get his hands real dirty real quick and wake up to the fact that no stranger's ever dropping by for warm milk and cookies—"

A chair scraped violently across the floorboards.

"Bud, he knows that," said his dad, cutting in.

"Does he?"

"Of course."

"Bah! He didn't check the back of the canoe, let alone have the wherewithal to kill that thing. Hell, he didn't even check for a trader's permit. He's too darn nice."

"He's fifteen."

"Yeah. More or less the same as Cooper. He's gotta learn."

"He's fifteen, Bud."

"He's a liability is what he is," Bud growled. "He coulda got us all killed."

Peter slumped into the rocking chair and pushed it back and forth. Bud was right. As the truth of the matter bubbled up inside him, Peter pictured his dad's pale face staring up at him from the black water below and tears ran down his cheeks. He leaned forward. His side was still hurting, but the wound wasn't as deep as it could've been. Darlene was out hunting on the mainland when they finally got to her place, but Bud had done a good job stitching him up. The pain had now numbed to a kind of dull ache that was somehow less painful than all the feelings he had crashing around inside him. Peter pulled the cuff of his sweater over his fist to wipe his face and looked at the bundle of old bones and saggy brown skin splayed out at his feet.

Bud's bloodhound, Dolly, was so old that when she lifted her chin up off the floor at the sound of her master's voice, her skin struggled to follow. But she must have heard him ranting a hundred times before. The tips of her droopy ears didn't even make it off the floor before she let out a deep huff and slumped back down to sleep again.

"That's it, old girl," said Peter, patting her gently. "You're better off dreaming about your good old hunting days."

Dolly sighed a deep sigh and the arguing went on. Peter pushed his foot down, rocking the chair to and fro, to and fro, and looked out over the lake while his dad and Bud decided what to do about him.

The wind chimes tinkled gently from the wooden beam.

The snow kept tumbling.

On the mainland, snow had started to settle across the rocky shore and pines, making the boughs droop. A squirrel scampered from one branch to another, causing a shelf of snow to catapult on to the rocks below. Peter leaned forward in his chair. He looked beneath the row of pines lining the shore and stared deep into the shadows to places in the woods where the world grew dark.

Up in the forest canopy, the animals were free to come and go as they'd always done. A network of branches for miles around gave them passage through the wilderness and kept their homes safe. The forest floor was an entirely different story, however. Sure, the Lake Landers had made paths through the woods lined with hanging tin cans and cutlery that clinked like an alarm bell whenever anything went by. But the dense undergrowth of pine needles and dead branches always crackled to the sound of a hundred shuffling feet. The forest belonged to *them*.

Peter looked away and not for the first time tried to picture his mom's face where there wasn't any memory of one. He hated them for that. He hated them so much. The Lake Landers came from all walks of life and they didn't always have much in common with each other, least of all with him. But if the end of the old world had done one bit of good, it was that it had brought peace, uniting everyone against the monsters that had driven them here. Peter drew his blanket tighter round his body and the unfamiliar sound of clacking heels hit the steps up to the porch.

Darlene flopped a rabbit carcass over the railing and stood there, adjusting her red hair back over her shoulders.

"Darlin'," she said. "What are you doing lurking around my porch like a racoon in winter?"

"Hey, Darlene."

"Now I'm not saying that hearing a bunch of men arguing about me doesn't bring back a lot of fond memories, but what the hell's going on in there?"

Peter looked down at Darlene's heels. "Tell me you didn't go hunting in those."

"No," she said, kicking them halfway across the deck. "Found them on some dead thing back in the woods and for a moment there it took me right back to Saturday nights at Randy's Rusty Spur. Now you might think that was just the name of some no-good bar, but you'd be wrong. God, that boy got around."

Darlene leaned back against the railing, gazing at the shoes wistfully. But the thought didn't linger. She drew a knife from her belt, stabbing the wall next to a set of deer antlers she kept above the front door, and proceeded to hang the shoes heel up criss-crossing each other.

"But that girl's long gone."

Peter placed the blanket over the back of the rocking chair and held out the bottom of his sweater so Darlene could see the bloodstains.

"Jesus," she said. "What happened?"

"Me and dad just had an accident."

"Looks like more than an accident. You both OK?"

"Not really. Dad and Bud are inside arguing about it now."

"Arguing about what?"

"An old man pretended to be a river trader."

"OK," said Darlene. "But he asked for your permission to land, right?"

"Course."

"And you made him keep his hands up in the air while you checked for his permit?"

Peter glanced sideways and said nothing. He'd gone

over this with Bud enough times already.

"Dang it, darlin'," said Darlene, putting her hands on her hips. "You can't be too trusting."

"I get it."

"In the winter, we watch the Restless Ones. The rest of the year—"

"We watch our own," said Peter. "Yes, I know."

"I dunno, maybe serving greasy grills and whatnot in some low-rent diner stood me in good stead for this life, but I ain't never had cause to trust a single soul unless they gave me a reason to. The only difference now is we've got the ones without a soul to watch out for too. Either way you look at it, people are people, Peter, and here we are still fightin' each other."

Peter looked down. He didn't have it in him to tell Darlene about the Restless One. Besides, she'd find out soon enough anyway. The chalet's screen door swung open, breaking the silence, and Bud stormed out, his thick silver moustache twitchier than a squirrel's tail.

"You're real lucky Cooper takes after his ol' man and takes an early morning piss in the lake," he said, twanging his braces back over shoulder. "Or you'd both be dead."

"And good morning to you too, Bud!" said Darlene.

Bud dismissed her comment away with the swipe of his hand and slowly made his way down the steps leading off the porch.

"The boy needs to get out there," he said, whistling once for Dolly to follow. "Needs to kill some of the Dead stuff. Needs to see the desperados we're dealing with too."

Dolly huffed, wearily picked her face up off the floor and trundled after her master.

"I'm sorry," Peter called.

"Sorry won't stop you gettin' killed."

Darlene squeezed Peter's arm and was about to say something else when his dad came out.

"Reckon I'll leave you two boys to sort it," she said, making her way inside. "Let me know if you need anything."

His dad's long johns were still completely sodden and dripping water all over the porch. He looked worryingly pale too. Peter picked the blanket up off the back of the rocking chair and draped it over his shoulders. His dad wiped more water from his stubble and leaned out over the railing. Peter tried to think of something to say other than sorry. But before he had a chance to come up with anything, his dad turned to him.

"Pete," he said softly. "Why did you need that old man to compliment you? Why did you need him to say you were good with an axe?"

Peter watched Bud's canoe set off across the lake and shrugged.

"Haven't I told you that myself?"

"I guess."

His dad slumped down into the rocking chair, rubbing his temple.

"Does your head hurt?" Peter asked.

"Just a little."

Peter pushed away from the railing. Headaches always came before or after one of his dad's fits, and he'd been through enough already this morning to trigger one.

"Did you fit this morning?"

"No, Pete, I'm fine."

"And what about now?"

"Pete, I'm good. Stop fussing."

Peter looked away. Dad didn't like being reminded of the one thing that could mark him out as being weak to the others, especially when they were in company.

His dad yanked his right leg up across his knee and started to massage his toes back to life.

"Look," he went on. "Haven't I told you that some people are better at some things than others, but it takes all sorts to make up a world?"

"Yes," said Peter.

"Well, I can't sew my own socks."

"I know."

"I can't do half the things you can."

"But—"

"But what?"

"But you're my dad. You're supposed to say nice things."

"What, so I'm humouring you now?"

Peter gazed out over the grey water.

"You don't need anyone's approval," said his dad, blowing hot air on to his feet. "Believe me. If I had an idiot son, you'd know about it, OK?"

Peter still said nothing.

His dad looked up. "OK?"

"Yes, OK," said Peter. "OK."

"But I want you to be safe. I dunno, maybe keeping you on the lake has been the best way to manage that up until now, but you're getting older and it's not entirely up to me any more. You know the rules. If we can't help keep everybody safe, we can't be here."

Peter nodded. "So what does that mean?"

"So the lake committee are gonna make a decision about you tonight at the watchtower during the First Fall festival."

Peter turned away and watched Bud's canoe disappear inside the snow. Over by the shore, something disturbed the pines. Snow tumbled from a bough and a pale hand withdrew round the back of a tree trunk. Peter opened his mouth to reassure his dad that he could take whatever the committee decided, but the words weren't there any more than the feeling was. When he looked back across the water at the tree, a woman-shaped thing was standing there.

Long black hair flanked a hollow face, all grey like driftwood now the skin had been bleached of blood. The denim dress hanging from its frame was just as faded too. But it showed no signs of coming undone at the seams any more than the figure's skin did. Neither had been spoiled by weather or time. This woman's body was only newly restless. His dad didn't even acknowledge the thing, their presence on the lake was so commonplace. He carried on rubbing life back into his toes, but Peter kept staring.

Her kind were the most unsettling of all – the ones that quietly appeared from nowhere. More like ghosts than monsters, they often found their way down to the lake and stood there, gazing out toward the islands' tiny homes as if to recall memories of such things. Or worse, if their eyes fixed on you, memories of having been human once too.

The Restless One stared at Darlene's chalet. Peter looked away. They had a habit of sticking around once they'd spotted you. He'd held eye contact with one of them once before while chopping wood at the foot of the island and when he came back outside the following morning, the darned thing was still standing there, waiting for him.

The screen door swung open. Darlene held up her arm

in a motionless wave. "Hey, girl!"

"Don't," said Peter.

"What?"

"You know what."

Darlene leaned over the railing and repeated the action.

"Wait for it," she said. "Just you wait for it."

The thing's head turned to gaze in Darlene's direction. Its dark eyes were lifeless but something inside it was able to process the new stimulus Darlene's wave had provided. Peter stepped away from the railing and the thing waved back.

"Jesus," said Peter's dad, slumping back into the rocking chair. "No matter how many times I see…"

Peter looked away. "I hate it when they do that."

"What?" said Darlene. "Look human?"

"Yeah."

"I know," she said, lowering her hand. "I'm sorry. That was in poor taste. I hate that more than anything too."

She took the rifle she kept propped up against the chalet wall.

"Too bad," she said, aiming the barrel at the Restless One's head and pulling the trigger. "I coulda had me a nice new outfit for tonight. Oh well. Call me if any eligible men turn up, won't you?"

The Restless One dropped face first into the water.

"But I've got you a nice man here," said Peter.

"Keep lookin', darlin'! Keep lookin'." Darlene took the rabbit carcass from the railing and strung it from the porch ready for gutting.

"Dad," said Peter after a little while.

"Yup."

"Does the word *snowflake* mean anything to you at all?"

His dad stopped massaging the cold from his toes and looked up. "Huh?"

"The river trader hurt me because I wasn't wearing the *snowflake*. What did he even mean by that?"

"You sure that's what he said?"

Peter nodded. His dad leaned forward in the rocking chair, staring at his son's bloody sweater with his brow all heavy like the wound was everything about this damned world he couldn't put right. But after a while he just shook his head.

"I dunno, Pete. Crazy times, crazy people."

"Except he knew what he was saying."

"Then I don't know. I'm sorry. Try and forget about it now, eh?"

"He wasn't a bad man."

His dad winced.

"But he wasn't."

His dad clenched his fists, locking eyes with Peter.

But it was Darlene who spoke next.

"No such thing as good or bad people no more, darlin'," she said. "Just people surviving the best they can."

Peter didn't know if he believed in that at all, but before he could say anything, Darlene changed the subject.

"Anyways, why don't you go down and thank Cooper?"

Peter's heart punched his chest. "What?"

Darlene nodded toward the far end of the porch, then disappeared back indoors. "He's been waiting there in his canoe for you this whole time!"

Peter ducked back from the railing so he couldn't be seen. "What does he want?"

"Probably just to see if you're OK," said his dad.

"He knows that already. By the end of tonight, everybody will know I'm only OK because of him."

"I thought you'd want to see him."

"No," said Peter. "Why would you think that?"

His dad cleared his throat. "You only chop wood so early in the morning because you know his canoe passes by around that time."

Peter narrowed his eyes. It was true though. He'd chopped enough wood to last them the next twenty winters. Not that it made much difference. Cooper didn't even know he existed. Peter tugged the bottom of his sweater down to straighten it and made his way to the far end of the porch. He'd got to the top step when a canoe broke out over the water and Cooper set off back across the lake.

"*See?*" he said.

Peter leaned into one of the porch's posts. He didn't know what the lake committee would have in store for him tonight, but the day was getting on and they should get back to their tree house to freshen up. He started to make his way down the steps to the water's edge.

"You coming, Dad?"

"Pete!"

"What?"

"I don't want you to worry that you'll never meet someone."

"OK. Well, I don't."

"Oh."

"Why, do you? Worry about me, I mean."

His dad scratched his stubble and shrugged. "A little."

"Why? Because there are more moose than men out here?"

"Yeah, something like that."

"Well, don't," said Peter. "Besides, you're not doing too well yourself."

His dad glanced over at Darlene's front door and smiled. But his smile faded from his face like sunlight behind a cloud. He turned toward the lake as people who were old enough to remember sometimes did, and looked to those places beyond its shores. Places in his head he'd never get to share with Peter.

"I just wish I could've shown you another world," he whispered.

Peter hung back on the steps. "It's OK."

"But it's not."

"But it's OK that it's not. It's not your fault."

His dad gripped the railing, quietly making his way toward Peter, and the snow drifted out over the lake.

5

It was good to get back to the tree house. The sun had come out too. Bundles of waxy pine needles at the windows, glistened in the thawing snow. Screeching blue jays took to the deck. And by late afternoon on these short October days, when the sun was just a ball of fire hanging low over the mountains, golden light streamed in broken beams through the front door, making the timber walls glow. But it always made everything look dustier than it really was.

Peter scooped his dad's patchwork quilt up off the floor. He stood at the open door to shake it and a thousand tiny dust particles exploded into the sunlight. He glared at the boxer shorts his dad had hurled over the deer antlers they should only use to hang their mugs from and sighed. Sure, this morning his dad might've had an excuse for making their home look like a bear had ransacked it, but the truth was Peter found tin cups, socks and other debris lying around the place like this every day. His dad liked to make out his son was 'particular' just because Peter made a point of sweeping the dust and pine needles out each morning and insisted on having all of the labels on their reused bottles facing forward for easy reference. But as far as Peter could make out, this was exactly the kind of thing messy people said to put the blame on someone else.

Peter wafted the quilt down over his dad's bed. He smoothed it out with the palm of his hand, pulling the corners down nice and tight on all four sides until the quilt was as taught as tarp stretched over a rack.

"There," he said, taking in both beds, happier now that the pair matched up. "That's real nice."

But his satisfaction didn't last long. A moment later, the dust fell. First it settled over the two beds, then the log burner in the corner of the cabin, the deer-hide rug and the rocking chair, until the whole cabin was buried in the stuff.

"Pointless," he said. "Thanks a bunch."

His dad came in off the deck with a towel wrapped round his waist, dripping water all over the place. He leaned against the door frame, scratching his armpit.

"What's up?"

"The place is a mess."

His dad raised an eyebrow. "Sorry, am I missing something?"

"Just look at it."

"Look at what?"

"All the dust."

"Doesn't look bad."

Peter huffed. "It looks like Pompeii."

"We don't live in a show home, Pete."

"You know I don't know what that is."

"Sure you do," said his dad, folding his arms. "You get me to tell you about them enough times."

"Yeah," said Peter. "Sounds like heaven."

His dad stretched out a big yawn and fell face down on to his bed making a mess of it again.

"Anyways," he said, "the water's still warm down there if you want to use the tub."

The water was probably filthy, but Peter made his way out all the same.

The timber roof jutted away from the front of the tree house enough for them to have a small bench with a plaid throw and some cushions by the door. One of the cushions toppled forward on to the deck and a racoon popped up its head.

"Yeah," said Peter. "I see you."

But the damned thing looked him square in the face with its button eyes and didn't budge. Typical. You'd come home to find one in front of the log burner with a book and a nice hot drink, given half the chance.

Peter huffed. "Trash panda!"

The racoon turned away, completely unfazed, and jumped down off the bench. A narrow rope bridge flanked with wooden planks linked the tree house to a shallow platform with a rope ladder. Peter followed the racoon all the way across the bridge until it scurried off into the overhanging boughs and clambered down to the ground.

His dad had done well to lug the rusty old pig trough in off the mainland and he'd recently completed the new wooden deck it stood on. It got chilly in its spot under the shadow of the tree house. But that kept the rain and pine cones out most of the time, and the tree house's wooden stilts made a handy place to nail the CD mirror and tuna tin he'd fashioned into a toiletries shelf.

Peter stripped off and folded his sweater and jeans into a neat pile on the deck.

"Catch!" his dad called down.

Peter caught the towel and hung it from one of the stilt's nails. He dipped his toe into the water. It was only lukewarm now, but he clambered into the tub, kneeling so that the bandage Bud had wrapped round his waist didn't get too wet.

A wedge of snow slipped from the roof, landing in a slushy pile beside the tub. The afternoon had been warmer, but they were in for a clear night. It wasn't long before the sun dipped behind the mountains, leaving a haze of dying light across the darkening sky behind them, and Peter felt the chill. He cupped his hands to pour water over his shoulders and looked out.

In the distance, past Darlene's island, at the heart of the lake stood the watchtower. In the spring and summer months, dozens of canoes could be seen on the water together, moored round its four vast timber stilts. A dizzying wooden staircase zigzagged all the way up the middle to the Sky Deck above. Swimmers dashed to the top and dive-bombed off it. Swishing fishing lines lassoed out from under the shadow of the overhanging roof to catch salmon. But after the First Fall supper tonight, all that would change.

After tonight, the sound of sizzling barbecues and chatter would no longer waft up into the starry night. The fiddles and guitars went back inside their cases. The crossbows and arrows came out of theirs. The wind chimes came down off their hooks. The brass toll bell went up. Then the rota was drawn up. Next came the watching and the waiting, first for the ice to form and then for the Restless Ones to come.

A shiver bristled down Peter's back. He pushed himself out of the water, quickly wrapping the towel beneath his armpits. He'd started to shiver violently now so he perched himself on the end of the tub and rubbed his legs. He couldn't understand why the old man hadn't destroyed his wife before she tried to kill him. How could he bear to see her that way?

A wolf cried out across the mountains somewhere and the word *snowflake* broke into his thoughts. But he didn't want it there so he shimmied the towel in between each toe and watched something bobbing toward the island, carried in by the current. Maybe it was a piece of driftwood or an item of clothing perhaps – the lake washed all sorts of flotsam and jetsam over to their place. In the summer, hardly a week went by when Peter hadn't returned somebody's lost bathing suit or towel that'd blown off the Sky Deck while hanging out to dry. But whatever it was had got wedged in between a couple of rocks near his dad's canoe. The light was too dim to make it out from this distance so Peter picked his underpants up off the pile and yanked his jeans and sweater back on. He hopped down off the decking and made his way to the shoreline.

He'd got as far as the canoe when he stopped. Peter lifted the paddle out with both hands and angled it down in between the rocks. The flat end of the paddle dipped under the water and Peter felt the weight of whatever it was on top. He heaved, stumbling backward, and a piece of cloth plopped in a sodden heap on to the nearest rock. He prodded the bundle with the paddle and flipped it over. It was the denim dress the Restless One had been wearing. Peter's stomach lurched. Someone should've fished the body out of the water by now. His eyes darted to the rocks. The thing might be standing there. But there was no one – no one he could see at any rate. He dropped the paddle inside the canoe, ready to make his way back to the tree house, when he felt the weight of someone watching him and swung round.

A canoe hung on the dark water as silently as a wolf in the woods.

Peter stumbled back. "Dad!"

"Aw hell," came a voice. "I didn't mean to startle ya."

A forest of tangled blond hair swished forward followed by a bloodied face.

Peter let out a deep sigh. "Cooper?"

Cooper tucked a strand of hair back behind his ears and shrugged. "I was just checking you was doin' OK is all."

"*Were*," said Peter.

Cooper cocked his head to one side like a confused dog. "Huh?"

"*Were* OK. Was is the wrong grammatical construction."

Cooper looked away and seemed to rummage around in his head for the right thing to say. And it should've felt good watching him struggle for a change. After all, it wasn't often that a chipmunk could outsmart a bobcat. Except it didn't feel good at all. It would've been easier to live with the fact that the only other boy around Peter's age happened to be the best Zee-wrangler the lake had ever seen if he was as mean as a westerly wind. But he wasn't. From the little Peter knew from watching Cooper out on the lake all these years, patrolling it or ferrying people back home late at night when they'd had too much to drink over at one of the neighbour's, he was more than useful. He was well liked.

It also didn't help that he had the bluest eyes either. Even now, with his face half caked in dried blood and dirt, like he'd just crawled out of some stinking geyser, they still blazed like the blue of a flame. Peter pulled down on his sweater and looked away. All he had were his dumb words. Cooper had everything.

"I should've come and found you to say thank you," said Peter at last. "Sorry."

Cooper scratched under his armpit and shrugged. "I din't come to chase you for no thank yous."

"Well, I should've."

There was another awkward silence so Peter filled it. "Did you bury the old man and that thing?"

"Yeah. Good and proper, out in the woods."

Peter turned to leave. "Well, that must've been hard work, so thank you."

"You going to First Fall soon?"

"I s'pose."

Cooper leaned forward and for some reason looked hopeful. "Me too."

"OK. Well, maybe see you there."

"Wanna lift?"

"What? No. I'm going with my dad."

"Oh, I know. But if you wanted to hitch a ride or somethin'?"

"No, it's OK."

Cooper dipped his paddle in the water and brought the canoe a little closer to the shore. "It's just that I sluiced out a bunch a deer guts from earlier and laid down a new hide on the seats and everything, so she's good to go if you wanted. If you wanted to travel with me, I mean."

Peter looked at Cooper's shirt. It was so bloodied you couldn't even make out the black and red plaid beneath it any more. Cooper must've noticed his hesitation and quickly glanced down to check himself.

"Oh," he said, wiping his muddy palms across his thighs. "I honk. Do I honk? I've not washed the guts off yet, but I got a clean tee back home. Well, kinda clean."

Peter narrowed his eyes. "I can make it across the lake without being killed most of the time, you know."

"Course. I din't mean that. I just wondered if you wanted to come with me is all. But it don't matter."

Doesn't matter, thought Peter. "Besides, I don't even know if I'm going to go yet."

Cooper furrowed his brow. "How come?"

"Well, your dad's gonna make sure Henry gets me out on the mainland for one thing."

Cooper looked out toward those dark places where only the pine trees dared stand still.

"They'll get off your back just as soon as you've killed one of the Dead," he said. "I can show you how things work. If you wanted, I mean. Besides, it ain't so bad out there."

"I don't see how it can be anything but."

"Well, I ain't saying it's not crazier than a dog chasing its own tail, but you can't see nothin' all cooped up on these islands."

"I can see plenty."

"No," said Cooper, "you can't. The view from where you're standing ain't wilderness, it's scenery."

Peter followed Cooper's line of sight, but he could only make out the black tips of the pines against the starry night. "Why, what can you see?"

Cooper struck the paddle down in the water like a post and rested his chin on the tip. "Oh, everythin'. The mountains, meadows, rivers roarin'. The way the stars aren't like a flat ceiling overhead at all, but a universe that wraps all the way around us deep beneath the planet."

Peter gazed up at the flat roof of stars you could see above the trees around the lake. He didn't even know what Cooper was talking about.

"There's something about open places that makes a man consider himself," said Cooper, as if his soul somehow belonged out there.

Peter watched Cooper's Adam's apple rise and fall in his throat when he couldn't even see his own in the mirror and marvelled at the ease he had in considering himself a man.

"Open places make you consider yourself?"

"Yeah," said Cooper. "Like the plains."

"And the stars?"

"Uh-huh. And the sea and the desert too, Pa says. But I dunno why that is."

Peter shrugged. "Perhaps it's because they make us feel small."

"No. They make me feel bigger, Peter."

Cooper sliced the paddle through the water and turned the canoe to leave.

"Well," he sighed, "as long as you's doing OK. I guess I'll see you around."

Peter felt a sudden tug in his stomach he didn't recognize. He took a step forward and went to delay him. But he stopped himself and a moment later the canoe slipped inside the darkness and Cooper was gone. Peter ran his fingers across his throat to feel for his Adam's apple and gazed up at the starry night. The tree house door creaked open behind him and light struck the shore.

"He carried you all the way up the steps to Darlene's from the canoe," called his dad. "Wouldn't a hurt you to say yes."

Peter felt the sharp tug in his tummy again. "Say yes to what?"

"Come on, Pete. Come inside, it's getting cold."

Peter held back, scanning the darkness for the canoe. But after a moment or two, the sound of the paddle cutting through the water had all but gone so he headed back toward the tree house. He'd clambered halfway up the rope ladder when the distant sound of music and laughter caught the air and he looked round. Across the lake, golden oil lamps glowed from the watchtower like fireflies round a tree. They circled the base where the canoes were already mooring and lined the staircase all the way up to the Sky Deck. The First Fall party had begun.

Peter sighed. They were good people. The Lake Landers had worked hard to build a community out here with what the military had given them when those who chose to stay behind in the towns and cities barricaded themselves into homes the Dead later turned into coffins. His mom and dad had done well to leave town, where

49

everything was so much worse, and trek the southern ranges when Peter was barely a toddler. His dad had done even better to stumble across this place when the region's largest refuge at Yellowstone was still several days north of here. He'd persuaded Henry and the others to welcome them on to the lake because of his valuable lumbering skills too. All Peter did was show up.

By the time he was old enough to lie on the island of Skipping Mouse watching the clouds roll by, a new life had already been achieved out here that made that kind of thing possible again. Now it was his turn to make sure he helped keep it that way. That's all. And about time too, he reminded himself, when a short while later, his dad dipped the paddle into the water and they set off toward the watchtower.

6

They crossed the lake in silence. The canoe cut a trail through a carpet of stars, making them quiver then re-form as the black water stilled behind them. The comfort of home slipped inside the darkness and Peter faced forward.

His dad had agreed to paddle so Peter could sit up back, sulking over the Hawaiian shorts with the pink blossoms Darlene had found for him. It was tradition to wear summer clothes to First Fall as a way of sticking the finger to the coming winter. Last year he'd made a garland out of plastic flowers for his dad to go with the grass hula skirt he'd decided to wear. But Dad had opted for a simple pair of board shorts and white vest tonight as if he knew the event was weighted by seriousness other years had been free from.

The nose of the canoe aligned with the watchtower like a compass finding due north, and they approached the great wooden structure.

His dad drove the paddle through the water and turned. "You OK back there?"

Peter looked up and watched a tiny spot of light darting across the stars – a satellite. It was still questing through space, none the wiser that there was no one left down below to even care what it was doing up there.

"Pete?"

Peter stayed with the satellite and felt sorry that its vigil over the planet was in vain. Poor thing, poor little thing. The satellite passed over the lake and disappeared further off into space.

"Pete!"

Just a little longer and he'd stop asking.

"Damn it, Pete, talk to me. I can practically hear you thinking back there."

Peter looked down, running his fingers through the icy water. He saw his dad's white face staring up at him from below the surface again and retracted his hand.

"Why did the old man stay with his wife?" he asked. "When he knew she was dead, I mean."

"Because he loved her," said his dad as a matter of fact.

"Yes. But why would he stay with her if she'd turned?"

"Because he loved her, Pete. Love makes you do stupid things. You'll see."

Peter looked up at him. Mom was still with them when they'd escaped town. Dad had never explained why she didn't make it out on to the shores of Lake Wranglestone. Only now it was as if he'd left a door ajar on the subject for the very first time and Peter didn't know whether to let himself in.

"Did love make *you* do stupid things, Dad?" Peter stared at the back of his dad's head and waited.

"When she was alive, yeah, all the damned time. I stationed my wagon outside her office to watch her leave work. I was out there so early most afternoons, her boss knocked on my window with a cup of coffee for me once and told me that—"

"You were killing Mom's feminism, but she'd see you at five. Yeah, Dad, I know. But after that?"

His dad lifted the paddle out of the water and let the canoe drift. "No, Pete."

"You don't sound so sure."

His dad slapped the paddle down across the width of the canoe and, with an impatience he hadn't given in to before, swung round.

"Well, I shoulda been. Because the thing that pulled you upside down by the ankle to take you into its mouth wasn't your mom any more. It was a monster."

His dad's eyes widened, locking on to Peter's. He held eye contact for longer than was comfortable, and the horror of the word monster danced in the air between them like wildfire. Peter's heart pounded. He never knew his mom would've hurt him if his dad hadn't stopped her. He never knew that.

The madness left his dad's face. His thoughts slowly shifted behind his eyes and eventually a strange calm fell between the two of them.

"Why didn't you do something in the canoe, Pete?"

Peter winced. His dad never let on when he was disappointed in him, never, even though he probably felt it half the time.

"I tried to," said Peter. "I tried real hard, but—"

"But what?"

"I hesitated."

"Damn it. Bud was right. I've done wrong keeping you cooped up so long."

His dad's brow fell all heavy with difficult thoughts and Peter knew it was one of those moments when he wished Mom was still around just so he could share the burden. He was more comfortable doing stuff to show he cared than he was making big statements, and tended to come out in hives whenever the need for a father-son talk presented itself. As far as Peter could see from life on the lake, this was the way of men more often than not. But he'd learned to accept it just as much as his dad had learned to accept him for being the other way round.

"You know this already," said his dad after a while.

"In the second it takes for you to mistake them for one of us, in the moment you think you see something in their eyes that reminds you of yourself, of being connected to another soul, of being human, they'll have taken you inside their mouth and devoured everything you ever were. They might look like someone you once knew, your neighbour, Darlene, your own wife even, but they're not, Pete. They're nothing. They're not even animals. They're as cold and lifeless as a Halloween pumpkin with its candle snuffed out. And they'll take everything you got inside you because they got nothing left inside them, nothing. They're not right, none of them. Learn that and you'll learn how to stay alive."

Peter looked down. It sounded like his dad was saying that for his own benefit more than Peter's, but he nodded all the same.

The canoe drifted under the watchtower and knocked into the other canoes moored there, making them clang into each other like wooden wind chimes. His dad stood, grabbing the mooring rope, and started to tie the canoe to the one next to them.

"I didn't mistake the monster for a woman," said Peter. "I didn't."

"I know, Pete."

"But I can see how the old man could've done. Because he loved her, I mean. I still don't know why he was angry

I wasn't wearing a snowflake though."

His dad's fist clenched the rope. But the talk was over. He slapped his hand down across his thigh as if to put an end to the matter. "Come on. They'll have cracked open the First Fall whisky and I'm not missing out."

Peter creased the corners of his mouth into a half-smile and stood. He straddled the width of the canoe to stop it from rocking and clambered across all the others moored there, to the base of the stairs.

The bottom step hovered about five feet above the line of the water to stop wolves and lynx from getting up the watchtower when the lake was frozen. But an extra wooden step had been fitted to the bottom one by a hinge that could be pulled down over the lake for easy access. Peter stepped up and turned back.

"Go on," said his dad, shooing him along. "I'll just finish tying this up."

Peter made the steep climb up through the middle of the watchtower. He'd gone a little way, where the cooler mountain air struck his face, when he paused to look out over the tops of the trees. To the south, far beyond the forest borders of Wranglestone, the Shark Tooth mountains sliced into the black sky. They'd beckoned many a wanderer's heart. Peter had never felt that call – he could see more than enough from here. But, for the first time, his sights were drawn toward their snowy peaks and he wondered why.

A canoe passed beneath the tower carried by the sad song of an old harmonica. Peter leaned into the handrail. Darlene said its music always spoke of lonesome nights and long-lost loves, but the revellers up top were in no mood for the sound of their sorry-assed lives. Not tonight. Not all the while the lake was still moving. Someone lobbed a bottle over the top of the watchtower. It plopped into the water, narrowly missing the canoe. This was followed by heavy booing and jeering. A fast country fiddle kicked in, drowning out the harmonica. Soon the whole watchtower boomed with feet thumping and hands clapping, and Peter pulled his own heavy feet further up the stairs.

He turned the corner and hung back just short of the Sky Deck. The lakes weren't the only area to offer protection from the Dead. Some people took to the mountains in the wake of the new world. But others had gone a step further. Half a mile east of the lake, a granite cliff face jutted up out of the forest. On a dark and moonless night like tonight, the only way you could tell where the Ridge ended and the sky began was the outline the stars made behind it. The Restless Ones roamed the higher ground in herds. But the sheer rock face belonged to trekkers and mountain climbers in their hanging tents, and the rock twinkled now with dozens of tiny lights as if the stars themselves had slipped from the sky.

"I saw Cooper save your sorry ass this morning," came a familiar voice from behind him.

Becky was perched on the handrail. Her legs swung to and fro so her flip-flops dangled from her toes. A bandana kept her tawny mane off her face. She was pretty much the same age as Peter, but her mom had passed away so she lived with the last of the old Morgan sisters, Essie, in her tree house over on Moose's Reach. Becky liked to make out she was better off alone, but old Essie could simultaneously skin a squirrel while brushing some sense into Becky's hair without the need to put her pipe down, and truth was Becky quite liked it that way.

She took a slug of beer from the bottle she was holding and held it out for Peter.

"No," he said. "I'm good."

Becky rolled her eyes and took another swig.

"Loser," said Peter.

"Peter," said Becky.

"Peter's my name already."

"Yeah, but it sounds just like loser."

Peter sighed. "Such a loser."

"Such a Peter."

Peter slumped over the handrail. "So you think they'll

all be waiting for me up there then?"

"Waiting?" said Becky, half spitting her beer back out. "They'll have the pitchforks out."

"S'pose I'd better go on up."

Becky shrugged. "Hang back here with me for a while if you want."

Another canoe passed beneath the watchtower.

More laughter came from above.

"How do you know if someone likes you?" asked Peter after a while.

"Oh, I dunno, Pete," said Becky. "Maybe they pretend to chop wood really badly down by the water's edge while fluffy pink hearts pop out of their undershorts."

Peter swiped the beer bottle from Becky's hand and took a swig. "No, not me. Cooper."

"Remind me what's wrong with you again?"

"I think he asked me out to First Fall earlier."

"Think? I watched his canoe circle your place about fifty times before he mustered up the courage to approach you. You're an idiot if you can't tell how much he likes you."

"You think?"

"What, that you're an idiot?"

"No, that he likes me!"

"Yes," said Becky. "You're an idiot *and* he likes you, so what you're doing sitting here, talking to this waste

59

of space, I've no idea."

Peter's heart pounded in his chest. "Why? Is he here already? On the Sky Deck, I mean?"

"Dunno."

Peter tugged his T-shirt neatly over his shorts. Why he'd agreed to wear these ridiculous things he had no idea. He huffed into his hand to check his breath and caught Becky looking at him.

"Jesus. You've made a wedding list already, haven't you?"

"No."

"You're so gonna choose curtains together."

"Don't poke fun at me. Besides, I don't even know why I'm thinking about that right now. Bud will have made sure Henry's come up with a plan for me over on the mainland."

"Well, you're screwed if they make you a wrangler."

"Wrangler? No. I couldn't possibly—"

Becky nodded. "Nope. You really couldn't. But on the plus side you'll be dead within the hour so you won't need to worry about it."

"You're a good friend," said Peter, passing back the bottle.

Becky nodded gravely and held the bottle aloft. "You too."

Peter smiled, but he simply didn't have the kind of

mettle someone like Cooper had. And Becky must've known she'd said too much. She broke eye contact and looked past Peter to where his dad was now standing.

"Er, hey, Mr Nordstrum," said Becky, jumping down off the handrail. "I didn't mean to worry Peter. I was just—"

"Becky," said his dad as if to draw a line under this conversation.

Peter felt his dad's hand against his back. But before he had a chance to ask if the committee could really see him working as a wrangler when they already had the best one in Cooper, someone clinked a glass to call for everybody's attention and the three of them made their way up.

The Sky Deck was fenced in on all sides and capped with an apex roof. Apart from the odd fishing rod left propped against the four timber support columns, it was usually free of any furniture or decoration throughout the summer and fall months until tonight, the biggest event in the lake's calendar. Moths fluttered round the rafters where golden oil lamps were hanging. A host of wooden wind chimes cling-clanged in the cold night air. Here and there, piñata snowflakes made out of papier mâché dangled from the wooden beams. And over in the corner, tucked up inside an empty beer barrel, was the poor soul who'd volunteered to play the spirit of First Fall this year, *One Who Follows*.

As ever, the barrel sat on its end. A single hole was cut in the top with soil sprinkled all around. Suspended from a piece of string above the barrel was a papier-mâché snowflake dripping berry juice for blood. Arnold Schmidt approached the barrel with his five-year-old daughter Emily hiding in between his legs.

"Now," he said, hoisting her up on to his shoulders. "Reach inside the hole and you might get a treat. Isn't that right, Peter?"

Peter scanned the crowd for Cooper.

Mr Schmidt cleared his throat. "Isn't that right, Peter?"

"Er, yes," said Peter. "Yeah, that's right."

Mr Schmidt lifted Emily up and leaned over so she could reach inside the barrel. She pulled down on her pigtails and suddenly came over all nervous. He gently squeezed her waist for her to go on and she gingerly hovered her hand over the hole. She waited. But she didn't have to reach inside.

A set of bony fingers, caked in white paint by the looks of it, wriggled through the hole like worms hungry for the light. Clenched between the forefinger and thumb was a wrapped sweet. Emily squealed. She snatched the sweet before she lost her nerve and turned back to show her dad, beaming with delight. A round of applause rippled round the deck, but the sound of a glass clinking called for attention again and everyone turned to the far end of the deck.

With his old fishing hat and eyebrows so bushy behind his reading spectacles that they looked like caterpillars trapped behind glass, Henry was the oldest member of the lake committee and the one responsible for organizing the winter watch rota. Overall, no one cared much about who you used to be in the old world any more than they cared about what the Restless Ones used to be before they weren't human any more. All that mattered was what this life had made you into and whether or not you were someone who could help or hinder the survival of others.

Henry was unusual in that what he used to be mattered a great deal. Newcomers to the lake looking to find a home there liked to think that their hunting and killing prowess was valuable enough to bag them a spot on the islands. The truth was that the new world had made hunter-gatherers of everyone. But Henry was a dying breed and that most prized of all vanishing treasures, a retired doctor. And as a former committee member of the prestigious Hamiltons golf club, he was a natural chairman, a position in all of the Lake Landers' lives that he humbly accepted.

Henry tapped his wedding ring against the side of his

glass once more and the chattering died down.

"And so, dear friends," he began, "another winter is upon us."

A murmur of resignation rippled across the Sky Deck.

Darlene looked back through the crowd and caught Peter's eye. She pointed at her chest and winked to highlight how camp it was of her to turn up in a polka-dot bikini.

You OK, darlin'? she mouthed.

Peter nodded even though it wasn't true and glanced round to see if Cooper had arrived yet.

"We've enjoyed a good summer," Henry went on. "And a safe one too. But it wouldn't be proper if we didn't start proceedings by saying goodbye to those we lost."

There was a collective murmur followed by silence. Peter clasped his hands together, bowing his head. He hadn't known Meredith Mathews too well, but she'd told him not to doubt himself once when he'd got into an argument with his dad for felling a tree right on top of her cabin and he'd never forgotten it.

As always, Henry judged the obituary well and gave just enough time for people to say their goodbyes in private, then moved things along again before he killed the party mood completely. A minute or two had passed when Henry looked up into the crowd for Mr Schmidt, as was the custom, in order to thank him for his continued efforts guiding infected Lake Landers off the islands to the extraction point in the woods by Wranglestone Falls.

"Our thanks as ever go to Arnold for his tireless efforts escorting our loved ones off the lake and, of course, to the military for continuing to take them, despite the fact we only have one officer in place inside the park now."

"That's right, Arnold," came a voice.

"Hear, hear."

"Now," said Henry, clapping his hands together once to mark the end of the serious stuff. "Moving on to gladder news, we only had one bear incident this year. I'd like to thank all you folks for continuing to keep your personal effects locked up in the bear boxes and remind you to keep any deodorants, toothpaste and other perfumed items you may have acquired locked away, and that colognes and scent are strictly forbidden. I'm sure Betsy and Don won't mind me saying that bears are attracted to any smell and will swim across the lake if they think something good's at the other end of it for them."

Everyone looked over toward the Carmichaels.

Henry gazed over the bridge of his glasses. "I think it's safe to say that you had a narrow escape, Don."

Don Carmichael wiped the back of his hand across his balding head and raised his tin cup as if to say,

Amen to that. When the committee had met to discuss the bear incident, he'd blamed himself for leaving his deodorant out in the sun, but everyone knew that Mrs Carmichael had bought a bottle of cheap perfume from one of the river traders and sprayed their island with it to get rid of the stench of dead flesh wafting in from the mainland.

"Now, lucky for us," Henry went on, "the bears will all be taking to their caves long before the big freeze. But the lake is still going to be susceptible to wolves and we, of course, have other visitors to contend with. So once again, after tonight, can I please remind you to take down your wind chimes and keep any outdoor noise to a minimum? I'm sure I don't need to remind you that animals are mostly attracted to smell, but the Restless Ones will always be drawn to our quarters by noise. So if I could kindly ask all you nice people with young ones to make sure that they play indoors just as soon as the ice begins to freeze, and remind anyone who's doing a run over to the mainland to make their way with quiet feet."

Becky nudged Peter. "Is he talking about us?"

Peter smiled. "Remember to take your toys inside, OK?"

"And when *will* the ice form?" came a voice from the crowd.

"Yes, Henry," came another. "When? We babysit Emily when Arnold's out. You try keeping a five-year-old cooped up indoors."

"The lake will always start to freeze," said Henry, raising his voice a little now, "like a scab around a wound, on the edges near the shore where the water's shallowest. So just as soon as that starts, I suppose."

"But when exactly?" said Drew Matthews.

"Well," said Henry, "we had the first snowfall this morning, so soon."

"But how soon?"

"Yeah. How soon, Henry?"

Henry took off his glasses and pinched the bridge of his nose. He said something else after that, but Peter couldn't make out what it was. Old Essie Morgan sidled up to Becky, her smoking pipe rooted to the corner of her mouth, and leaned in.

"I hear some of the hangin' bottles have come down from their strings in the westerly forest trail. I ain't doing no run until I know that's been seen to."

Then Becky chipped in. "I spoke to a couple of trackers up in the mountains, Henry, who said that they'd seen a herd of deadbeats out by Moose Creek. What if they find their way here?"

And so it went on. Soon the Sky Deck was brimming with the same nerves and anxiety the community experienced every year. Darlene looked back through the crowd, rolling her eyes. Peter smiled, but he didn't feel any different to the others. As the whole lake was about to go to sleep for the winter, the one thing that never slept was about to grow in strength and number.

Henry raised both palms to shush everyone and scanned the crowd for an ally.

"All right, folks," he pleaded. "There's no need to panic. All of your questions will be answered and all of your concerns addressed in good time."

But no one was listening any more.

"If a new herd is on the move," Henry went on, "then we'll need volunteers for a tracking party to see if they're coming this way and take action accordingly. Young Cooper can always herd them away if need be – we know that."

Henry fumbled to put his glasses back on and the din increased.

Peter glanced round for Cooper in case he'd arrived, then turned to his dad. "Help him out."

His dad put his two front fingers in his mouth ready to whistle. But before he got the chance, a single gunshot cracked over the watchtower and everyone was silenced.

Peter ducked.

The sound of the bullet ricocheted round the lake like a clap in a cave.

By the time he finally stood upright, everyone had turned to the back of the Sky Deck where Bud was standing.

Bud doffed his Stetson and leaned back against the railing at the top of the staircase.

"Busted-up fences and hungry bears are the least of you people's problems," he said, planting the rifle on the floor. "We got a weak link in our company."

Heads turned back in toward the gathering. Wicked whispers rippled round the Sky Deck as everyone tried to weed out the weak one hiding in plain sight. But one person wasn't scanning the crowd. Peter felt Henry's eyes on him from across the deck. He'd been told. Of course he'd been told. Henry furrowed his brow as if to say the whole thing was out of his control and quickly looked away to spare Peter the shame. But it was futile. A moment later, Bud did it for him.

"Why, oh why," said Bud, "are we not talking about the boy?"

"Yes, thank you, Bud," said Henry, cutting in. "I was coming to that, but I have a few other announcements to make first. So all in good time, my friend, all in good time."

Bud was having none of it. He brought the old tin can he was holding up to his lips, lugged on whatever it was he had inside and cocked his head.

"Now we can all listen to old *On Golden Pond* over

there until we're blue in the face, and I'm sure it's real nice to find out who won the fly fishing contest and which one of you nice people gave out the most hugs. But the truth is we had a breach in our security this morning and that trust was given away as freely as apple pie on the fourth of July."

Essie Morgan chewed on her pipe. "Is that true, Henry?"

"Who?" several voices asked all at once. "Who, Henry? Who?"

"Now, that's enough," said Peter's dad, stepping forward.

"That's right, Tom," said Bud, crunching the can in his fist. "And I reckon you of all people should've had enough more than most. I mean, you must be so exhausted stepping in and covering his weaknesses, it probably woulda been easier to shove a dress over him and make out you had a daughter."

Darlene folded her arms. "Aw, Bud baby, you're so right. Cos all us girls do all day is stay in waiting for our menfolk to come home."

Bud cleared his throat and looked Essie Morgan's way for moral support. But it was too late. Peter's dad was already elbowing his way through the crowd.

"I restored your goddamn house for you, you no-good son of a bitch," he said, seizing Bud by the collar.

"My son made the pillows you rest your thick head on every goddamn night."

Darlene wove her way through the crowd and Becky followed. The two of them grabbed Tom by the shoulders and yanked him back.

"He's not worth it, darlin'," said Darlene.

"Easy, fellas," said Becky, placing her hand on Bud's chest to pacify him. "Easy does it, boys."

But Bud was unmoved.

"Give your boy some of that there anger," he said, pulling down his Stetson to shield his face, "and we might survive the winter."

Peter's dad lunged forward in temper before Darlene could pacify him. But eventually his breathing steadied. He shrugged her hands off his shoulders and looked up.

"Come on, Pete," he said, wiping saliva off his chin with the back of his hand. "We're going home."

But Peter didn't move. "No, Dad," he said. "It's all right."

"No. It's not."

Peter stood firm. "All said and done, it doesn't really matter how he put it, does it?"

His dad shook his head and all eyes fell on Peter.

Bud looked up from under the brim of his Stetson and sized Peter and his dad up like one man does another when its undecided who's gonna back down first.

But after a moment or two, he cleared his throat and spoke.

"Thank you for making my pillows, Peter," he said under some duress. "I sure do appreciate it."

"You're very welcome," said Peter. "I'm grateful to you and Cooper for saving my life. Perhaps I can return the favour one day, if you'll show me the ropes that is."

Bud squinted. "Perhaps."

Peter let out a sigh and nodded. The crowd started to talk among themselves, even if it was just to spare Peter any further embarrassment, and Peter leaned in.

"Is Cooper here?"

Bud's silver moustache twitched. He was as surprised by the question as Peter was. It came out without him even thinking about it. But when Bud told him that Cooper wasn't coming, Peter's stomach ached and he realized he was disappointed.

"Why not?"

"Dunno," said Bud without much interest. "Said he weren't in no mood for it."

"But—"

"I reckon he's 'bout beat digging goddamn holes all afternoon, don't you?"

Peter glanced toward the top of the staircase when Henry clinked his glass to call for attention again and

Peter turned to face him.

"So what happens now?" he asked.

"Well," said Henry, removing his fishing hat, "if it's all settled, tradition dictates that a first-footer on to the mainland must shake hands with *One Who Follows*."

Peter nodded. "Then it's settled."

He looked round at the barrel and the pale fingers emerged through the hole once more like worms hungering for the light.

The oil lamps flickered.

The wind chimes stilled.

But before Peter had a chance to make his way over, there was a commotion at the back of the Sky Deck behind the stairwell and everyone turned.

"The stars are falling!"

It was Emily. She'd wandered off without her dad noticing, as was often the way, and was standing on tiptoes, leaning over the edge of the deck. The crowd parted to let Mr Schmidt through. He squeezed by everyone with his palms held aloft, saying *sorry* and *sorry* as he passed. He crouched down behind Emily and went to pick her up, but she yanked her shoulder away and pointed.

"Look!" she said. "The stars are falling from the sky."

Henry looked at Peter as if to say, *Sorry, this won't take a moment*, but Emily was insistent. Before he knew it, everyone was bundling down to the foot of the deck to see what all the fuss was about. Peter worked his way through the crowd and looked out into the darkness toward the Ridge.

"I don't see nothin'," said Bud, barging to the front.

"It's too darned bright, Henry," a voice called.

"Yeah," came another. "Turn the goddamn lamps down."

Hands reached up into the roof's beams and dimmed the oil lamps. Darkness fell over the Sky Deck. An eerie silence followed. Peter took a moment to let his eyes adjust. It was mostly just a black mass out there. But a moment later the silhouette of the forest emerged against the lighter grey rock of the Ridge behind it and he saw the climbers' tiny little lights in the distance, twinkling across the rock face. Peter narrowed his eyes to stop them smarting in the cool mountain air. There was a cluster of lights right up near the top of the rock where the largest group of climbers were camped.

Peter had started to count them when two of the lights broke free from the others and dropped clean out of the sky. There was a collective gasp. The lights bounced off a lower ledge and kept falling. Peter heard distant screams. They all did. But it was over in seconds. The lights disappeared behind the line of trees below and there was silence.

"Oh, sweet Jesus," said Darlene, turning away.

"Did you see that?" came another voice.

More followed. More tumbling lights followed by more screams.

"What's happening?" said Mrs Carmichael, leaning into her husband. "Why are they falling?"

There could be only one reason. Peter looked up toward the top of the cliff. A grey mass moved like sludge across the top of the Ridge and spilled right over the edge.

"Zees!" said Bud. "A goddamn herd of Rotters."

And the Dead just kept coming. There were hundreds of pale bodies tipping over the edge. One by one, each row of lumbering limbs tumbled forward and the next row followed. The bodies that didn't just plummet to the ground clipped the hanging tents as they fell, bringing the climbers crashing down with them. One oil lamp must've smashed into its tent before it fell, causing it to erupt into flames. It broke away from the rock face and a screaming fireball plummeted into the forest below.

Peter's dad took his shoulder and stood behind him.

"Something must've chased them over the edge," he said.

Bud shook his head. "Nope."

"Then what made them want to come this way?"

"Us."

Goosebumps bristled across the hairs on Peter's forearms.

"I knew we was making too much darned noise," said Bud. "And now they're coming for us."

Peter's dad turned. "Yeah. You're the damn idiot who fired the shot."

Activity broke out across the Sky Deck. Shoulders bumped into shoulders. Nervous whispers quickly changed into calls to action. Orders were barked to get home for safety or ammunition. Peter couldn't remember seeing so many Restless Ones in one go, but preparation for such an attack was well drilled for.

Bud pulled the brim of his Stetson down over his eyes and barged through the crowd.

"A few of 'em will snap in two on their way down, but the rest will be on us within the hour," he said, marching toward the top of the staircase with his trench coat swishing behind him. "We won't get rid of 'em once they're here. They'll just loiter on the shore until the ice forms. So get those goddamn wind chimes down and somebody snuff those lamps on the staircase out. Now!"

Bud stopped at the top of the steps. He drew himself up to his full height. The tails of his trench coat billowed in the wind and fell still.

"Boy," he said, without turning round. "It's time."

Peter's heart bucked like a rabbit in a trap and his dad's hand left his shoulder. He knew there was no way round it.

"But I don't know how to wrangle the Dead," he said.

"No," said Bud, turning his head into profile. "You're the bait."

7

There was no time for farewells. No time for Peter to change out of his First Fall outfit. Within five minutes, Bud had loaded the canoe with a crossbow and arrows and cut a quick course across the lake. The paddle sliced through the water. Left and right and left again.

Peter gripped on to the side of the canoe. His eyes smarted in the rushing air.

He swung round to catch a glimpse of his dad, but the last of the oil lamps went out across the watchtower, plunging the lake into darkness.

He folded his arms across his chest. He didn't care about the mess his dad made in the tree house any more. He didn't care that Dad rinsed a tin cup out with nothing other than a sock and spit. Towering pines lining the mainland rushed in and none of that seemed to matter.

Bud hoisted the paddle out of the water. He raised his hand to make sure they observed silence as they made their approach, and the canoe drifted toward the old wooden boathouse.

Peter had seen the boathouse from the islands. It sat directly on the water with a single arch cut out of the front like the mouth of a cave. Most of the red paint had peeled off it now leaving the wood grey. The roof sagged as heavily as an old nag's back. And yet it was the only safe way to come and go from the mainland. Not just because you could close the woods off behind you, but because the Dead didn't know how to use doors.

Peter gazed up at a human skull nailed to the top of the arch and they slipped inside.

The nose of the canoe struck something solid. Peter lurched forward and with a jolt they stopped. Bud tossed the crossbow overboard and leaped out on to the deck. Peter waited for further instruction while his heartbeat steadied and listened to the old boathouse creaking in the darkness.

Scythes and machetes clinked on their metal hooks.

A bird bolted from the beams and, screeching, took off over the lake.

There was another sound too. And as Bud strode back down to the canoe, his eyes ablaze behind the oil lamp he was now holding, Peter saw the horses. He smiled. According to Becky, most people took the brown one out on runs into the woods, but the white one with the freckles and tubby belly eating most of the straw right now was Cooper's.

"Is that Snowball?" Peter asked.

Bud squinted. "No time to play with the ponies," he said, beckoning him to his feet. "Up you get. The herd won't be far away and if they breach the boathouse because of you then I'll make damn sure this really is the worst day of your sorry-ass life."

Peter jumped off the nose of the canoe before it drifted backward and pulled down the bottom of his T-shirt.

"Now, grab yourself one of them there pelts over by the back door," said Bud. He swung the oil lamp round. The shadows shifted sharply, making the machetes and scythes lurch round the boathouse as if someone was cutting the air with them.

"Quickly does it. Any one will do. Now take a seat and get some food in your belly real quick. You're gonna need it before we go in."

Peter sat on the bench by the back door where Bud had tossed a small parcel. He pulled on the thin piece of string wrapped round the bundle and the cloth parted to reveal some slices of cured meat. Bud whipped the cloth from his lap and shoved a stone inside. He tied it off with a knot and tossed the rag into the water.

"Bears," he said, narrowing his eyes for maximum effect. "One a them gets the slightest sniff and I'll have more trouble on my hands than babysitting *you* for the night."

Peter took a deep breath and went to say something, but Bud held up his hand to silence him.

"Save it," he said, hanging the lamp on a hook. "You'll need all that hate you got bubbling away in your guts for later. Don't waste it on my account."

Peter ripped off a bit of meat between his back teeth. But he wasn't really hungry so he reached up for one of the silver wolf pelts with the animal's head attached for a hood and shoved the leftovers into one of the pockets.

"I've got a gilet back home I could wear," said Peter. "It's real toasty."

Bud raised an eyebrow. "Put it on. Jesus, boy, where do you even get a name like that from?"

Bud made his way back over to the water and took a leak while Peter struggled into the wolfskin coat. He poked the bear-tooth toggles through the hoops to fasten it.

"Were you always a trapper?" said Peter to drown out the splashing sound as much as anything.

"Nope," said Bud, shaking himself off. "I pumped gasoline and pointed tourists in the wrong direction for thirty goddamn years."

Peter looked away. "Why did you do that? Give people the wrong directions, I mean. Was it because you couldn't read?"

Bud's moustache twitched. "No. Because I found it kinda funny."

Peter offered a smile and turned back round.

"Those goddamn Rotters did everyone a favour," said Bud, walking back over. "Folks like me and Coop anyhow. The day one of them stumbled across the highway and into my station forecourt with its flesh all on fire like a ton of rib steaks all burned up on the rack was the day I got my life back. No dumb job. No bills or rent to keep me in that dumb job. Clean slate. Fresh start. Never looked back."

Bud slapped his hand firmly across the doorpost and patted it as if the boathouse was somehow everything his service station never was. His eyes glinted deeply beneath the brow of his Stetson.

"I can't read no words on no goddamn piece of paper," he said, "but I sure as hell can read the woods. Now, we must act quickly. They won't be far away. So follow my word and you might, just might, last the night."

Bud braced his hand across Peter's shoulder. He ran his other hand over his silver moustache and looked him in the eye, searching for his mettle. But the time had come. He turned away, twiddled the valve on the oil lamp to dim the light and quietly pushed open the door.

Snow fell silently over the doorway all bluish in the night. Bud leaned into the door frame, holding his hand out flat.

"The silence of snow," he sighed. "Not much else left quiet in this goddamn screaming hellhole of a world."

Peter watched snowflakes land then dissolve into the cracks of Bud's leathered palm and looked up. There was a clearing directly outside the door, lightly dusted with snow, illuminating the entrance to the forest. But a single footstep inside the trees was another matter. Beneath the draping pine was darkness. Spindly branches, too low to catch the light and grow, were withered arms jutting out at broken angles to scratch at anything passing by.

Peter peered into the darkness and others looked back. But it wasn't the Dead. The forest was watching. It was as if the blackened pillars of pine had stopped talking about him the second the door opened. His eyes darted from one tree to the next. He followed the forest back, further and further, but eventually the web of trees and branching limbs knitted together so closely they dissolved into the darkness within.

A twig cracked.

A lone owl hooted.

Peter clenched his fists and watched his white breath plume across the doorway.

"You think it's quiet now?" said Bud. "Just you wait. The forest will go completely still just before they come. Always does. It'll make you wish you'd never been born."

Peter took a step forward. His foot had just crossed the doorpost when Bud gripped him by the shoulder.

"Bah!"

Peter flinched, retracting his foot.

"Don't be brave," Bud tutted. "Be smart."

Peter looked down at the ground just beyond the door. He noticed that a mesh of criss-crossing twigs and branches had been deliberately placed there one on top of the other. He looked between two of the branches and saw the black hole beneath.

"A deadfall," said Bud. "A six-foot-deep pit to jump across if the Restless Ones should ever tail you, or a bear for that matter."

Peter ran his hand through his hair. "Sorry."

"Pah!" said Bud. "Sorry don't get you nowhere. Don't be sorry. Be safe. Now we're a little further south of the Ridge here so you won't be coming at the herd head-on, which is good news for you. I'll take as many of 'em down as I can. But this means you'll need to draw the others toward you so they don't make it as far as the lake."

Peter's lips parted to let his quickening breath escape. "But how?"

"You see them there tin cans hanging from that tree?"

Peter looked past the clearing to the pines and saw a pair of cans dangling from pieces of string.

"I see them."

"Well, that's your way in. There are plenty more behind. Pairs of tin cans, bottles, knives and all sorts stretching back into the woods just wide enough for you to walk through without making a noise. They make a hanging path so you don't lose your way, but they'll also ring the dinner bell if any unwanted visitors take up the path with you."

Peter fixed his sights on the two tin cans, but he still didn't see how he was supposed to draw the Restless Ones toward him.

"But…"

Bud pulled his Stetson down over his eyes and took a running jump.

"And remember," he said, clearing the deadfall, "when one of those things locks eyes with you and decides you're the one, you'll think of the bitch that held your daddy underwater and run. You'll be good at that. Running is what scared people do."

Pine needles crackled this way and that, but soon Bud's footfall disappeared inside the forest and he was gone. Peter drew back inside the boathouse and stared at the dangling tin cans.

"*Clock it. Kill it. Rid the world of it.*"

The trail was only twenty feet or so away from where he was standing, but the thought of running up to it was impossible. One of the horses whinnied.

"I know," he said, turning round. "I'm scared too. I guess Cooper makes you go out there when you don't really want to either, huh?"

Snowball looked up with his big brown eyes all wide as if to say, *Yep, that's exactly what he makes me do.* But a moment later there was a scream from out in the woods somewhere and Snowball buried his face back in the straw bag and left him to it. Peter swung round. The scream was faint, but it was constant. It was more than one person too. Perhaps climbers who'd survived the fall had to deal with what met them at the bottom. He didn't know.

Another scream ripped through the woods. Closer now. Violent. There was so much horror in the vocal cords, it sounded like someone had grabbed a fistful of fiddle strings and ripped them clean out. The sound was so disturbing, but before Peter had even decided what to do, his feet took a running jump and he leaped through the door.

8

Peter threw his back against a tree. He patted his hands across his chest to be sure of himself and took a moment. He'd gone some way inside the forest chamber now. He peered round to check that the boathouse was still there. The hanging trail of tin cans and bottles marked the way back, but it was as if the trees had played a trick and moved in to close the space behind him. The boathouse was nowhere to be seen.

Sound was different in the woods too. Peter wasn't even aware he could hear the lake lapping against the shore until it was gone. But the woods snuffed it out as quickly as fingertips over a flame. Ahead, the trail twisted on deeper inside the woods. Snowflakes started to settle on Peter's eyelashes so he drew the wolfskin's snout over his head and buried his back into a crook of the tree.

But he was stalling. He needed to do something. He needed to make a noise, create a scene, anything.

Bud had said he was going to be used as bait, and Peter hadn't doubted it. He started to wonder what would happen if he failed to do anything at all. Then he found out.

The alarm bell ripped through the forest quicker than a scream at night. Peter recoiled in horror. His eyes darted from one tree to another. But the sound was coming from him. He clawed at his pelt, patting it down furiously like he was putting out a fire. He pulled the alarm clock out of his pocket. The little metal hammer was pinging in between the two golden domes crazier than a woodpecker at a tree. He closed his fist round it and lobbed it into the woods. He fell back, relieved, and started to map his route through the hanging trail, ready to run back to the boathouse, when he froze.

The clock kept ringing. It started to tremor across the ground now. Peter shoved the head of the wolf back over his shoulders and cursed Bud for slipping it in his pocket. But he had no choice. He had to run further into the woods to stop it. He ducked in between two swinging wine bottles, broke cover from the hanging path and ran over to the clock. He drove the heel of his boot down on top of the damned thing. The clock cracked and fell silent. Peter clapped both hands across his lap and bent double, catching his breath. He stared at the bits of busted-up metal and broken glass at his feet, glad the thing was broken.

It was only now he noticed how quiet it was. He wiped drool off his mouth and slowly turned round. The silence was so thick it almost became an absent noise pressing against his face. He wiped a snowflake from his cheek and looked through the dense web of spindle branches deeper into the darkness.

A gap between two giant pines created a break in the forest canopy. Snow drifted freely here to form a veil. Peter edged forward and became aware of a black mass in between the two trees. He waited. He kept watching and the snow in front of the black mass spiralled as if caught by a sudden wind. Peter took a step back and the black mass broke out from behind the veil of snow and made its way toward him. Then he heard them. The crows. A ball of black wings hurtled through the woods followed by their appalling din.

Peter ducked down, throwing his hands over his head, and the cawing ripped right through him like a thousand screams.

The crows took flight over the lake and were gone. But they weren't the only ones abandoning this place. Peter staggered to his feet. A deer bolted out from the trees behind him, its eyes wide in terror. It leaped this way and that and in a bucking flash disappeared off into the woods.

Peter fell back against the tree and the snow bobbed gently over the woods once more. The world had never been so silent. He watched. He waited. He pushed away from the tree and went to make his way back toward the hanging trail when a twig cracked. He froze. The weight of a foot landed down heavily on the ground behind him, followed by the scraping sound of another being dragged to join it.

9

The corpse with the sunken face like a rotting peach was the first to arrive. Its naked body broke cover from the trees. It was a male. The area around its pelvis had rotted to the bone and its arms swung aimlessly by its side. The thing's milky eyeballs bulged in their dried-out sockets, rotating wildly like two boiled eggs swivelling in a bowl. Peter stepped away and his heel broke across a twig.

The Restless One's head quested for the stimulus the new sound gave it. It thrust its shoulder forward to swing its body back on course and made toward Peter.

Peter ran back in between the trail, tugged a wine bottle from its string and pinned his back to the tree. The thing used the sound to refocus its direction once more. Its jaws gnashed. Its fingers twitched at the prospect of flesh. A surge in strength entered the corpse's body, driving its arms upwards. It thrust its

91

shoulder forward once more, swung its body round and stumbled relentlessly on. Peter held the bottle by the neck like a club and hid behind the tree.

He realized his mistake at once. The deer that had bolted past him just moments ago was lying on the ground. Its legs were twitching in spasms like a dog dreaming. The whites of its eyes peeled back wide in terror. But it was powerless to move. The ashen figure bending over it withdrew its blackened hand from inside the animal's guts and moved directly over the deer's head to feed. Strings of black hair flanked the animal's face like rotting vines. There was a baying scream followed by a wet crunching sound. When the Restless One came up for air, blood erupted freely and the deer's face was gone.

Peter clapped his hand over his mouth, drawing back against the tree. The slightest sound and the thing would be on him. He turned his head toward the lake. His eyes darted from one tree to another, but he still couldn't see the boathouse. He waited. The snow shifted and the dim glow of the oil lamp twinkled ahead. Peter's heart pounded. If he ran back now and that thing followed, the deadfall would trap it. He clutched the bottle more tightly and mapped his route back toward the light. Blood surged through his fingertips and his feet readied to run, when he froze.

The male with the sunken face broke out from behind the tree. It turned to Peter. Its milky eyeballs roved wildly inside their hollow sockets, but they were so unseeing, it used its mouth as a third eye. The jaw sagged and its blackened tongue came probing out of the darkness.

Peter dashed the bottle against the tree, smashing the base. He held the neck up to his own nose so the jagged end jutted outwards, and the thing fell face forward into it. It was desperate to get to him. Its eyeballs swivelled back in their sockets. It drove its screaming mouth into the broken glass. Black gore pumped into the bottle, treacling down its neck. Peter winced. But it was over in seconds. The jagged base punctured the back of the thing's head, Peter ducked and the Restless One slumped forward into the tree.

He staggered away and the one on the ground stirred.

All that was left of it was shadow. Its blackened form had decayed so deeply it appeared to have been eaten away by the night. The shadow rose up. It lunged. Peter stumbled backward, reeling, then ran.

He abandoned the trail, bolting deeper into the woods. But his body was going quicker than his legs could carry him. He'd barely gone a few steps when he tripped over a root and fell face down on the ground. The stab wound stung his side. He scrambled to his knees, fumbling for the bandage to check that he wasn't bleeding, and glanced round.

The shadow moved silently through the trees toward him. And there were more.

Another figure stood inside the woods. Its silhouette was so indistinct against the darkness of the trees behind, you'd think you could swipe your hand right through it like smoke if it wasn't for the snow falling across its form. The figure gazed up toward the forest canopy and for a moment lost itself there. But the one who'd devoured the deer closed in on Peter and the other took up the trail and followed.

Peter panicked. His eyes darted this way and that. Then he saw it. The beat-up old car a little way off into the woods. There were signs it had veered off a road all those years ago. Its rusty hood was crumpled inside the tree. But its doors and windows were still intact. Peter glanced round. The shadows made their way through the trees. He set his sights on the car and ran for it.

He leaped over roots and darted between trees. He cleared a fallen log and hurtled into the side of the car. His fingers cupped the handle, the door swung open and he scrambled into the front, slamming the door behind him. He pressed down the plastic bobble to secure the lock and fell into the passenger seat. Cold sweat crept down Peter's neck so he shrugged off the wolfskin coat, stuffed it down the back of the seat and looked out of the window. But he'd made another mistake trapping himself there.

The shadows closed in. Peter pressed his nose to the glass and looked through the veil of snow. There weren't just the two of them any more. The forest was full.

Peter sank into the seat as low as the dashboard and stared down the length of the mangled hood toward the pines. There was brief comfort staring into the shadow of the draping boughs. If only he'd been the type to climb trees when he was younger. He scanned the crusted bark and something caught his eye. There were two pinpoints of light beneath the tree. They vanished, then returned. Vanished. Returned. It took Peter a moment to realize that one of the Dead was standing there, the crusted bark camouflaged its blackened body so well. But the wet glint on the surface of its dark eyes gave it away. It blinked and the glint returned. It was watching him.

Peter pressed as far back into the seat as he could and the thing peeled its body away from the tree. First a leg, then an arm, until a person-shaped nightmare broke cover from the overhanging boughs and lumbered toward him.

Peter glanced up into the rear-view mirror and gasped. Another one was standing directly behind the car. He ducked down even further. He opened the glovebox, furiously fumbling for something he could use as a weapon. But there was nothing. Just a pair of sunglasses and an old road map.

He quietly closed the glovebox and looked up. The one that had stepped away from the tree had gone. Peter slapped his hand over the bobble lock just in case and the one at the back started to make its way round. Its feet shuffled across the ground. Its joints crackled. It cleared the corner of the trunk and made its way down the side. Peter yanked out the wolfskin and started to lift it up over his head when the thing moved to the passenger door beside him and stopped.

It stood in profile against the window. Peter could only see its torso. He stared at the plaid shirt and waited for the figure to turn toward him. When it did, the check pattern was nowhere to be seen. Peter stared through the tattered hole where its stomach should have been and watched the two shadows behind it closing in on the car.

He scrambled over to the driver's seat, fumbling for the door handle. But it was too late. A hand smacked into the glass. Blackened fingers splayed out wide, desperate to get in. He looked across the hood. More stumbled out from the trees now. Within seconds, he had no way of knowing how many.

The light dimmed. The forest disappeared behind a cloak of hands and the car plunged into darkness. Peter shunted across the seat into the middle near the gear stick, gasping uncontrollably.

The car rocked.

Hands smacked into the glass.

Something moved across the back seat and grabbed Peter by the shoulder.

10

Peter flung the hand from his shoulder. He reached for the sunglasses in the glovebox, bent over the back of the passenger seat and jabbed the air wildly with them. But whatever had grabbed him was gone.

He gazed down. The back seats were missing. So was the chassis. The whole underside of the car had been cut out and beneath it was a hole. Looking up at him was a bloody face. An arm thrust up out of the hole and took him by the wrist. He resisted, but the hand squeezed him so tight he lost his grip on the glasses and they dropped into the hole. Peter pulled back and the hold loosened. But instead of letting him go, a thumb pressed his palm. It was soft, tender even.

"Easy now," said Cooper, gently stroking the heel of his hand. "Easy. Is OK now. S'all OK."

Peter couldn't hide his relief. His throat constricted, followed by the overwhelming urge to cry. But that wasn't going to happen in front of Cooper. He tried to pull his hand away and forced everything that was threatening to burst out of him back down again.

"Let go of me," he said.

"You go ahead n'cry if you need to, Peter," said Cooper. "Nobody's sayin' none of this ain't scary as all hell."

"I don't need to cry. And I don't need you to show up every time I'm in trouble."

Cooper spat a tendril of hair from his lips and maintained eye contact. It was clear from his expression that he knew Peter was lying, but for some reason he didn't say anything. He just kept quiet so as not to make it any harder for him than it already was. After a moment or two, he let go of Peter's wrist.

"I shouldn't have corrected your grammar," said Peter. He didn't know why he said that in this moment. "I'm sorry."

Cooper ducked back down the hole. "You might wanna follow me. They'll punch their way right through the glass if we give 'em long enough."

More blackened hands clawed at the windshield. Peter swiped his wolfskin up off the passenger seat and clambered through the gap above the gear stick.

"How far down is it?"

"In't far," said Cooper. "Five foot, I reckon. Maybe six."

Peter dropped the wolfskin into the hole first. It only

landed a little way down so he let go of the back of the seat and jumped.

There was complete darkness below. Peter couldn't tell how big the hole was, but when he got down on to his hands and knees, the heels of his boots grazed the wall behind him. The hole must've led off into a tunnel because he could hear Cooper crawling away. Peter felt around for a break in the wall. He moved his hands further along and suddenly lurched forward.

"Found it?" called Cooper in the distance.

"Yep. Found it."

Peter followed Cooper's voice into the darkness. It had to be dawn outside now because he'd barely crawled a few feet from the car when he saw Cooper sitting at the far end of the tunnel lit up by a rectangle of light breaking through the edges of a trapdoor overhead. Peter fell back against the tunnel wall opposite him. He flopped his legs out and listened to the sound of a hundred feet lumbering through the forest above.

"Will they find us down here?" he whispered.

"Not if we're real quiet."

"What happens now?"

"We wait. Pa knows to find me in the tunnel when I ain't come back. What we can't cull, I'll round up and herd out on to the plains with Snowball."

Cooper tucked his hair back behind his ears and

watched an ant run across the back of his hand and his easiness out here was at once so reassuring, it wasn't hard to see why he was the community's favourite son. It wasn't hard to see why at all. He put his hand down on the ground so the ant could find its way off and scratched beneath his armpit. He sniffed his fingertips, quickly glancing Peter's way.

"Dang it. I still honk."

"It doesn't matter."

"Yeah. It does. I'm real sorry, only I wasn't expectin' to see you tonight."

"Why would it matter anyways?"

Cooper shrugged and muttered, "*Cos,*" under his breath. But he didn't finish that thought.

The tunnel quaked and a clump of soil dropped on to Peter's lap.

"There are so many of them," he said, flicking dirt off his legs.

"Uh-huh."

"Sounds like a hundred, maybe more. I mean, I didn't get a chance to get a good look at them all coming toward the car or anything, but there must've been at least a hundred, I'm guessing. I mean, I am just guessing."

Cooper nodded and said nothing.

"But maybe more. I mean, I wouldn't be surprised if there were more. Say a hundred, hundred fifty or something.

I dunno, but there was a bunch of them out there, that's for sure."

Cooper still didn't say anything so Peter just kept talking and after a while he wondered if he'd ever stop. But as his calculations went up and up into increasingly more ridiculous numbers, his throat constricted again and this time he couldn't hold the tears back.

He clasped his hands over his eyes. "The deer's face was gone."

Cooper didn't speak. He just sat with Peter while he let it all out. He'd probably been out in the woods ever since he was knee high to a marmot. He'd probably seen far worse too. But he didn't say that. In fact, he didn't say anything. He didn't do anything. He just let Peter be, like everything about him was OK somehow.

A few minutes passed or maybe more, Peter wasn't really sure, when Cooper whispered, "Listen."

Peter wiped his face with the back of his hand and looked up. "What's wrong?"

"Nothin's wrong."

"The Restless Ones. Are they coming?"

"No, not them. Behind that."

Peter couldn't really make out anything above the general din of shuffling feet and cracking bones. He dusted more soil off his lap and leaned into the tunnel wall. He was wondering how much longer it would take for Bud to come for them when he heard it.

"Birdsong."

Cooper drew his knees up under his chin and leaned back. "Reckon the forest is waking."

Peter glanced at Cooper when he wasn't looking. There was that far-off look again. His eyes searched the tunnel roof, but somehow saw beyond it to the forest canopy and the clouds above that. Like his body was here, but his heart was somewhere out there where wild rivers ran free. Peter looked at Cooper's thick eyebrows, all blond from long days spent in the sun. He looked at the sharpness of his Adam's apple and his neck and the way blond stubble had already started to grow above his top lip and chin while he had none. He wasn't like Bud – he was more than that. He was beautiful.

Peter said sorry inside his own head. Sorry for mistaking him for Bud all that time, then sorry for not being enough for Cooper to want him. He looked down. He'd kill Darlene for making him wear these Hawaiian shorts. His legs were poking out the bottom of them like a pair of silver birch trees, they were so pale and skinny. Peter pulled the wolfskin across his shins and hoped Cooper hadn't noticed.

"Sometimes I sit down here and listen to the whole forest talking to itself," Cooper went on.

"Alone?"

"Yeah, 'lone."

"For how long?"

"Hours. Days sometimes."

Peter leaned his head back against the tunnel wall and listened to the trees creaking. The blue jays were up, caterwauling to each other from one bough to the next. Somewhere in the distance a woodpecker drilled. A wind stirred the trees and the whole forest rushed right over him.

Peter gasped. His heart was awake. It was as if the whole world had just awoken inside him. He looked up, pretending to concentrate on light breaking through the trapdoor above them. But he knew Cooper was looking at him. For a moment, he thought he was about to break the silence or change the subject even. But the silence wasn't awkward. It wasn't the look people hold when they're trying to strike up a conversation with you either. The butterflies in his stomach told him as much. No, it was like Cooper was trying to speak to him from a place beyond words.

Peter listened to the wind in the trees and thought back to last night. Cooper had come calling for him. He said it again inside his head and dared it to be true. It's just that it seemed so impossible that someone like Cooper would find anything he liked in Peter at all. But he could only pretend he was looking up at the trapdoor for so long. Peter swept loose hair from his face and made eye contact.

Cooper didn't look away. His blue eyes pierced through the tendrils of his hair like a wolf in the woods. He held Peter's gaze. He didn't smile, but Peter saw one all the same. He didn't speak and yet they were speaking now as if for the first time. There was friendship waiting to come in from the cold. But it was more than that. There was closeness. Unbound possibility. Peter unlocked the window behind his eyes and quietly let him in.

Cooper blinked once deeply and the feeling crossed the space between them like a kiss. Peter inclined his foot so his boot touched Cooper's hand and they both sat across the way from each other, and neither felt the need to say anything much at all.

A minute passed or maybe an hour, but after a while, Peter felt the mood shift somehow and Cooper spoke.

"Why din't you wanna be my friend?" he asked.

"But I do."

"No. Before."

Peter shrugged. "I didn't really understand why you'd want to be."

"But you should."

"I don't really know what you see in me."

"But *I* do."

Peter looked away. "Why didn't you come to First Fall?"

"Din't think you wanted me there."

"No. I wanted you there. I was just being—"

"Peter."

"Yes?"

Cooper just smiled and looked up as if he could somehow see the mountains from there.

"Nothin'. I just wanted to say your name is all. Peter."

Peter's heart leaped like a salmon up a river. His name had never sounded like that before. He'd never liked it. It was as if his dad hadn't even given him a fighting chance in this world by calling him something as meek as Peter. Only it suddenly sounded different. It's not that it sounded strong, that wouldn't be possible even if a bear had been trained to say it. But for the first time in his life it sounded precious.

Peter looked at Cooper, and Cooper looked back, and a secret understanding passed between them. They held contact for a little while longer until Peter suddenly became aware of other sounds in the wind and heard talking up above. He could make out a man's voice. It was distinguishable below the rushing sound of the trees. But Cooper clearly didn't think it was his dad or a search party because he held up his palm to warn Peter against giving away their whereabouts. Peter leaned back into the wall and listened.

There was a pause, then the man spoke again as if

answering a question. There must've been at least two of them out there, only Peter couldn't hear anybody else. The man kept chattering away, and Peter tried to see if he could pick up on another voice. But he couldn't and after a while it simply sounded like the man was talking to himself.

He looked at Cooper for further instruction. There wasn't another community for miles around, but it wasn't unheard of for trappers from beyond the borders of Wranglestone to travel great distances for the larger kills. The lake had come to blows on more than one occasion when it came down to who had first dibs on a herd's clothing and possessions.

The man's one-sided conversation went on for some time. Peter could tell by his tone that he was calm. A few minutes passed in this way. It seemed strange that the herd hadn't attacked him. That there weren't gunshots or signs of a kill. Peter leaned forward and was just about to ask Cooper why this was when the talking suddenly stopped, and something heavy landed on top of the tunnel.

Peter sat bolt upright. Cooper held his forefinger to his lips to silence him. Dirt was dislodged, dropping over their faces as the weight of the thing disturbed the earth. Peter drew his legs up under his chin. The light around the edges of the trapdoor dimmed as whatever it was up there moved into place directly above them. Something snuffled round the edges of the trapdoor, trying to find a way in.

Cooper scrambled to his knees. "We gotta make it back to the car. Now!"

Cooper pulled Peter toward him and crawled down the tunnel on his hands and knees. Only he didn't get very far.

Glass shattered. One of the Dead had smashed its way into the back of the car. Peter grabbed Cooper by the foot to stop him from going any further and bits of broken glass fell into the hole beneath. Then a body dropped.

Cooper scrambled backward, punching at the trapdoor. "Quick!"

But the trapdoor was pinned down by the weight of the thing above it. Peter gazed down the length of the tunnel. Whatever was down there responded to the stimulus the new noise gave it. He heard a hand claw at the earth followed by a wet scraping sound. It was dragging its body toward them. Cooper got up on to his knees, leaning his shoulder into the trapdoor and heaved upwards. Peter slapped both palms on to the wooden panel and did the same. But still the thing didn't budge and the body moved further along the tunnel.

Cooper collapsed to the ground. "It's no use," he panted.

Peter leaned his shoulder into the trapdoor and was

just about to give it another heavy push when light broke round its edges and whatever had been on top of it moved away.

Cooper took Peter by the shoulders. His eyes blazed from behind his forest of hair.

"There's a rope ladder hanging from a tree 'bout twenty feet from here," he said. "I'm gonna flip the trapdoor and you're gonna run. You're gonna run real fast and not look back."

Peter nodded. "But you're coming?"

"I'll be right behind you."

"But you're coming!"

"I ain't never gonna leave your side."

Rotting fingers probed their way out of the darkness. They burrowed into the earth and pulled. What followed was barely distinguishable from the tunnel walls it came from. The thing's putrid head and body had decomposed so badly, it was as if the worm-riddled soil had taken human form. It launched itself at their feet. But Peter barely had time to notice. In a flurry of light and snowfall, the trapdoor flew open. He clambered out of the hole, staggering forward.

Peter fell to his knees. He looked up. The rope ladder was dangling from one of the pine trees just ahead. He scrambled to his feet and ran. His body leaned so far over that his legs nearly gave way beneath him. He threw his body into the tree trunk, shovelling his foot on to the first rung, and climbed. But he still hadn't heard Cooper running behind him so he tightened his grip on the next rung and swung round.

The Dead had gone. The car was only ten feet or so behind the trapdoor, but it had been abandoned as if the herd had simply dissolved back inside the darkness.

Peter let go of the ladder with one hand. "Coop?"

Cooper leaped out of the trapdoor, kicking the dead thing's rotting fingers out from under his feet, and ran for the ladder. He very nearly made it too. But a dark mass broke out from behind a tree and something much larger than the Restless Ones bounded toward him.

11

The bear was on Cooper in seconds. A vast rug of shaggy fur rippled over rangy muscle and, in a bound, took him. It didn't rear up or bare its teeth. It just pinned him down like a dog with a chew toy. Cooper buried his face in the ground and played dead. But this only made the bear more curious. It pawed at his back. Sweat beaded across its black muzzle and dripped in globules on to Cooper's hair.

Eventually the bear got bored. It tilted its head, chewing down in between his shoulder blades, and tossed Cooper from side to side.

Peter jumped down from the ladder.

Cooper looked up from underneath the mass of brown fur.

Don't, his wide eyes told Peter. *There's nothing you can do.*

The bear stayed focused on its toy. But it wanted more

out of it so it let go. Cooper dropped to the ground. The bear pushed down on to his front paws for momentum and reared up on its hind legs.

The beast became a giant shadow bearing teeth. Peter was desperate to do something, but was pinned to the tree, frozen. The bear loomed over Cooper now. But at the moment gravity was about to draw its mighty chest and paws back down across Cooper's back, Bud broke from the cover of the trees followed by Peter's dad and Darlene.

One bullet struck the beast's belly. The other its head. Cooper twitched into action. He took his cue from the gunshots, rolling across the ground to get out of the way, and the mound of fur and muscle thundered into a heap next to him.

Bud raced forward, his trench coat swishing behind him. Cooper scrambled up into a kneeling position. Puncture holes in his shirt beaded blood. But the bear hadn't taken a chunk out of him. Peter started to shake uncontrollably when his dad rushed in. He dropped to his knees, throwing his arms round him. Darlene tossed her rifle to the ground and did the same with Cooper.

"Who in God's hell," said Bud, tossing his Stetson to the ground, "left goddamn food out for the wildlife?"

Peter dug his fist inside the wolfskin coat pockets. He felt the piece of cured meat he'd not finished back at the boathouse and nausea crashed into the pit of his stomach.

"Jesus, Bud," said Peter's dad. "Don't you ever ease off?"

Bud glared at Peter. "When are you gonna quit making excuses for him, Tom?"

"It's his first day."

"Don't get a second if you get yourself killed."

"You were supposed to be watching over him."

"Bah!"

"And if you pulled that damned alarm clock stunt on him—"

"You'll what?" said Bud, running his hand across his silver moustache. "Smother me in one of Peter's crocheted blankets?"

Peter's dad crossed the distance between them.

"No," said Darlene, wading in. "Enough!"

Bud took a deep breath and ran his finger round the barrel of his rifle. "Cooper," he said. "Coop?"

He squeezed more care into that last word than Peter had ever heard him exercise before. As much as it wasn't Bud's way to let on, the incident had clearly rattled him.

Cooper tucked a strand of hair back behind his ears and looked up. "I'm good, Pa." Then his eyes found Peter's. "Pete?"

Peter opened his mouth to speak, but Bud scooped his Stetson up off the floor and pointed it at him.

"No! Shut your mouth. You don't get to say nothin'.

You ain't got a goddamn scratch on you. All I want to hear is whose fault this all is. Tom? Any ideas?"

Darlene dug her hands into her back pockets and shook her head. "You're a damned bastard, Bud Donaghue."

Peter's dad held Bud's gaze. They could go on this way for as long as it took, especially where Peter was concerned. But the only thing that mattered right now was getting Cooper to one of the first-aid boxes at the boathouse.

Peter cleared his throat. He'd just have to suck up the consequences. He felt for the piece of meat in his pocket and was about to draw it out when Cooper stepped forward.

"It was mine."

Peter shook his head. But Cooper caught his eye to silence him.

"It was my fault, Pa. I left some meat in the tunnel when I was out here yesterday and I clean forgot to take it with me."

Bud squinted. "You's lying."

"No, Pa."

"You know better. Unlike some I could mention, I din't raise no idiot. I taught you better than that."

Cooper kept his eyes low. Peter couldn't tell if he was just in pain, but it was as if he was making himself smaller, like a dog that remembers what his master's punishment feels like. Rumours flew round the lake, but more than one person thought the story Bud stuck to, the one where his wife was killed by the Dead when Cooper was only little, was just a cover-up. Most suspected she'd simply walked her bruised and battered body out of his life.

Bud pointed the barrel of the rifle into Cooper's face.

"Bud!"

"Quit it, Darlene. What happens between me and my boy ain't none a your concern. Now you might wanna rethink your answer, son, cos this lake can't support no weak links or folks looking to cover up after them."

Bud closed one eye. His finger toyed with the trigger. Cooper stared down the barrel of the gun and neither one budged. But a moment later Bud lowered the barrel and turned his attention to Peter.

"Boy!"

Cooper staggered to his feet. "Leave him be, Pa."

"What you say?"

"I said leave him be."

A grim smile entered Bud's eyes. "I see. Like that, is it?"

"Yeah," said Cooper. "It is."

"Got yourself a friend, have you?"

Peter stepped forward, his heart pounding in his chest, and went to speak. But Bud nodded as if he'd got the situation sussed real good and sauntered off into the woods, leaving the word *friend* lingering behind him like dog dirt.

Peter rushed over to check that Cooper was OK, and Darlene's eyes widened. She glanced at his dad to see if he shared her excitement about them. But now wasn't the time. Something moved inside the woods, and everyone took that as their cue to leave.

12

None of the Ridge Dwellers survived the fall. According to Darlene, those who didn't break against the rock on their way down were taken out by the Dead at the bottom. Members of the herd not drawn away from the lake by the alarm bell made it down to the water's edge where Becky and a few of the others had stationed a fleet of canoes ready to take them out. Another group, who'd headed into the woods to assist Bud, had made it back safely. But not all.

By the time they reached the boathouse, a set of giant moose antlers nailed above the back door had been turned upside down. Peter entered the clearing and stopped. Snow fell gently over the boathouse and started to shelve the back of the antlers. Bud hadn't said anything about them before they'd headed out, but he could tell from the reactions of the others what this meant.

"Oh, sweet Jesus, no," said Darlene.

Peter's dad sighed. "But who?"

One by one, everyone made their way round the edge of the deadfall. As Peter's dad opened the back door, Peter could see Mr Schmidt sitting there, handcuffed to an iron hoop in the wall beside the coat hooks.

Darlene hung her machete on an empty hook and kneeled down before him.

"How, darlin'?" she said, resting her palm on Mr Schmidt's knee.

Sweat beaded across his brow, but Mr Schmidt didn't do or say anything. He just stared into the middle distance as if Darlene wasn't even there. She removed the black-rimmed glasses from his nose and folded them neatly on his lap. She leaned in a little closer as if to inspect him, then looked back to the group, quietly nodding. Peter saw it now. Blood curled across the whites of Mr Schmidt's eyes like red paint in water.

Darlene took his hand and looked back at Peter's dad. "Emily," she whispered.

Peter's dad scratched his beard and nodded. It was true. The lake would need to decide which household would take her in. Darlene turned back to Mr Schmidt and took a moment to compose her words.

"Arnold, where's Emily? Where is she now?"

"With Henry," he said vaguely. "At the watchtower."

Darlene closed her eyes and sighed deeply. "OK. And we'll take good care of her, you know that. We all will."

"I didn't think any more would fall," said Mr Schmidt as if somewhere far away. "I walked up to the Ridge and gazed right up the face of it to see if any more climbers were stuck up there, and one of the Restless Ones fell clean out of the sky. Couldn't get the darned thing off of me. So I came back on my own and handcuffed myself to the wall. I threw the key across the floor so I couldn't reach it. I've been sitting here waiting for someone to come for a while now, but you know what the stupid thing is?"

"What?" Darlene asked gently.

"The stupid thing is that no one's coming. I've got no one to walk me to the falls because I'm the lake's guide."

Mr Schmidt blinked and red tears trickled down his face. After a moment or two though, he held Darlene's gaze and focused his attention on the matter at hand.

"How long before I turn?"

"You know the drill, Arnold. Hours for some, much less for others. But just as soon as you can feel the forever sleep pulling you under."

Mr Schmidt nodded. "An hour at best then."

"You feel drowsy now?"

"Terribly. I need to get to the falls before the change."

"We'll issue the flare and get you on your way."

Darlene stood, placed her hand on Mr Schmidt's shoulder and turned to the group. Before she could ask for volunteers, Peter stepped forward.

"I'll walk with you, Mr Schmidt," he said.

"No, Pete," said his dad. "You need to get to bed. You'll be exhausted."

Bud grumbled. "None of us has had any sleep."

"He's right," said Peter.

He took one of the bearskin pelts from the rack, draped it over Mr Schmidt's shoulders and kneeled down in front of him.

"If you show me the way, I'll walk with you."

Mr Schmidt placed his glasses back on and shook his head. "It's a fair walk, Peter. And it'll be slow going."

"Then we'll have time to talk and you'll have time to tell me everything Emily likes and doesn't like."

"She doesn't like the mornings, Peter."

Peter glanced at his dad. "Dad's the same. Real grumpy."

"She's like a bear with a sore head."

"Best leave them be when they're like that."

"It's true." Mr Schmidt smiled. "It's a mystery to me. But she's like a wind-up toy once she gets going and she likes to help with the cooking as long as she doesn't dwell on the fluffy thing her dinner used to be. She does like plastic dinosaurs, but she doesn't like being chased up the stairs because it gives her the heebie-jeebies."

"Well, consider all that noted."

Peter picked the key up off the floor on the other side of the boathouse and unlocked the handcuffs. Mr Schmidt pressed down on to his lap to stand.

"Easy does it," said Peter, placing his arm across his shoulder to steady him.

Mr Schmidt leaned in to Peter. When Peter looked up, his dad's eyes were on him and it was clear he still didn't want him to go.

"Dad, let me. I want to help."

Peter's dad scratched the back of his neck the way he did when he was weighing one thing up against another.

"Tom," said Darlene with a degree of urgency. "If we're letting him go, they have to set off now."

"OK. OK."

He cupped the back of Peter's head and brought it into his chest. "I love you, Pete."

Peter's chest filled with emotion. He glanced up at Cooper but his eyes were already on him. In fact, they'd barely left him since they were in the tunnel together. They'd guarded him all the way back through the woods as closely as if his hand had been holding Peter's. Peter smiled and that only made Cooper's eyes burn deeper.

He was serious, so serious. But maybe that was the thing Peter liked best.

"Go home and rest," said Peter. "I'll drop by later if I can."

Cooper shook his head. "I'm comin' with you."

"No."

"I ain't lettin' you go out there by yourself."

"I have to do this. I want to, and besides, you need to get those bite marks checked out."

Cooper tucked his hair behind his ears and sat down on the bench beneath the pelts.

"Then I reckon I'll wait for you right here," he said. "It'll be late by the time you get back and anyways the horses need feeding. I'll take Snowball into the woods tomorrow. He gets depressed if I don't ride him and I need to herd any stragglers left out on to the plains. I can show you how it's done, if you like."

They held eye contact for a moment and Peter felt his closeness. But time was moving on. There were rushed hugs and goodbyes. Mr Schmidt handed over his staff with the Swiss army knife taped round the top in case of trouble. Then he guided Peter through the clearing to a different set of tin cans leading uphill through the forest in a south-easterly route from the lake. Briefly, they turned to watch the others' canoes leave the boathouse, then set off back inside the woods.

Mr Schmidt had been the lake's sole guide since the refuge was established. He told Peter of the privilege he felt sharing people's last walk with them. Not because he took any joy in it, but because of the way it allowed him to see what mattered most in this life from the things they chose to talk about in those closing footsteps. Love, he said simply. It didn't matter which life they chose to reflect on the most, the old one before the world turned upside down or the new, it all boiled down to love.

They journeyed deeper into the forest, the fresh snow creaking underfoot like leather belts flexing. They came to a shallow river where icy water bubbled over black stones. Mr Schmidt stepped across a particular combination that he'd clearly worked out was the best route over numerous trips and leaped on to the riverbank.

"So," he said, turning back while he waited for Peter to cross. "Don't waste any time wondering about all the things you might've seen or done if only you'd been old enough to live in the world before. The Restless Ones killed off a great many things, but all we ever needed is the one thing no one can get their hands on."

Peter threw his arms out either side to balance on a particularly wobbly stone and stopped.

"When I'm gone," said Mr Schmidt, "make sure Emily

knows that the love I feel for her is going nowhere."

Peter held his gaze for a moment. "I will."

They left the river behind them and the incline steepened through thick groves of tightly packed pines. They'd only gone a little way in when Mr Schmidt crouched down, burying his hand in the snow.

"Feel that, Peter."

Peter bent down, copying the action. The earth was rumbling like thunder. He looked up. The pines' towering spires disappeared inside a fine mist. Beads of water dripped from the boughs and melted the snow. As they walked on, the trees parted and the reason for this suddenly rushed in.

From the watchtower, Wranglestone Falls was just a silver thread hanging down the Ridge. But here, at its base, the white water boomed from its journey down the mountains, toppling and tumbling over the black rock face like an avalanche. Peter pulled the snout of his wolfskin over his head to shield his face from the spray and gazed up at the great white veil.

Mr Schmidt stayed inside the line of the trees and led the way along the foot of the falls toward a tall wooden signpost where a bench had been placed. The old sign creaked to and fro like an old porch swing and carried the words *Wrangle No More*. Mr Schmidt looked at peace with his thoughts as he sat there, gazing up at the falls. But he'd started to sweat hard in the last hour and his complexion had gone so white and waxy that he'd begun to look like a candle melting. Peter quietly made his way over and took a seat at Mr Schmidt's side.

"Do we wait?" he said, planting the staff in the ground.

"Yes," said Mr Schmidt. "But not long. The chaperone will be with us presently."

Peter gazed up at the vast wall of rock and wondered which direction the chaperone would come from. But then he found his head was taken over by many questions.

"Does he have to come far?"

"Not far. The Ridge behind the falls is a natural defence. So somewhere up there."

"And how many of the military team are left outside the park's borders now?"

"From what I understand, we lost most of them several years ago."

"Lost?"

"Killed trying to protect us from the Dead no doubt. It's why we have to govern our shores alone now."

"So there's only one left?"

Mr Schmidt wiped the mist from his lenses and sighed. "Yes," he said. "Just the one."

Peter glanced at him and leaned back against

the bench. "But why would he still do this for us if everyone else has gone?"

"Because he understands there are some things a civilian should never see."

"But—"

"Because his duty is all he knows, Peter."

"He must get lonely."

"Perhaps," said Mr Schmidt. "Or perhaps he prefers it that way."

Peter gazed up at the falls again. He couldn't see how anyone could be happy all on their own out here in the wild like that. He wondered if the chaperone had ever been invited on to the lake and if that was something they should do. He was about to suggest that it might be a nice thing to offer when he was overtaken by a stronger thought.

"Does the word snowflake mean anything to you?"

"I heard about that, Peter, but no."

"The chaperone comes from outside the lake. I just wondered if he knew what the old man meant."

"I have no idea."

Mr Schmidt turned to Peter. His glasses had completely misted over now so he removed them and took him gently by the hand.

"You think this role is something you can imagine yourself doing, Peter?"

Peter looked at his hand in Mr Schmidt's. It seemed morbid to say yes so quickly and without much thought. But the fact was that he could.

"It requires a delicate hand."

"Yes," said Peter quietly. "I'd take this position with pride."

Mr Schmidt blinked once deeply as if he took great comfort in that thought.

"Never take a walker's time up talking," Mr Schmidt went on. "It's their time to be heard or be silent."

Peter felt bad for asking so many questions now.

"And never let the person's loved ones join you. Farewells end at the lake."

Peter nodded. "I understand."

"But most importantly of all, whatever happens, never stay around for the change."

Peter shuffled in his seat.

"The chaperone is never late," Mr Schmidt went on, "but if one of the injured passes over before they arrive, you must secure them to the signpost and go before they turn. There's no more important a rule. No one should have to see a familiar face change into something they don't recognize any more. I wouldn't wish that on any of my successors, least of all you, Peter. The chaperone is the last surviving safeguard so let him do his job. Let him take care of that for us."

Mr Schmidt squeezed Peter's hand as if to emphasize the point. But something drew his attention back toward the falls, and when Peter turned, mist folded over the rocks and a figure was standing there.

It was just a shadow against the thundering water – the shadow of a great bear standing on its hind legs. A grizzly's bearskin, with the animal's head intact, cloaked the chaperone. Baubles of fine spray dripped from the beast's rugged fur. A set of clawed paws as large as paddle blades gloved the hands. For a moment, Peter thought the bear's nose made the mask because a black muzzle protruded from its face. But the mists of water churning up from the rocks shifted and he saw that the bear's face had been cut out. In its place was an old gas mask. The chaperone held up one paw in a motionless wave. But he didn't speak. He didn't come down from his place on the rock.

Mr Schmidt took his cue and stood up to leave. "Be well," he said, passing his glasses and pelt back to Peter.

"Farewell," said Peter. "And wrangle no more."

Mr Schmidt smiled a sad smile. "Don't trouble yourself with talk of snowflakes and strangers, Peter. Nobody's going to thank you for spending any more time thinking about those terrible people in the canoe. But if you wear this role well? You'll be the toast of next year's First Fall, I just know it."

Mr Schmidt made his way toward the falls. Peter placed the pelt and glasses down on the bench for a moment. He turned to wave one last goodbye, but both Mr Schmidt and the chaperone had gone and the old sign creaked to and fro, to and fro.

13

Cooper's canoe was still at the boathouse when Peter got back. It was bobbing gently on the water near the exit to the lake. It was getting dark, so he'd lit an oil lamp to tell whoever was on watch up at the Sky Deck that someone was still out on the mainland. Peter stubbed both boots against the doorframe to shake off the excess snow and propped the staff against the wall. He paused for a moment to say his final goodbyes to Mr Schmidt, but then he couldn't get inside quick enough. Cooper had waited for him.

"Cooper?"

Nobody answered. Peter bolted the back door to secure it and was about to call his name again when he heard straw rustling, followed by a soft snore. He hung up the wolfskin and turned round. Cooper was asleep on the floor next to Snowball. He rolled over on to his other side, his hair spilling across his face, and carried on snoring. Snowball looked at Peter for a moment as if to welcome him back from his travels, then lowered his head to nuzzle Cooper's neck.

Peter perched on the bench by the back door and watched them. They were inseparable. According to Becky, Cooper had saved Snowball when he was small. He'd found the foal curled up next to his mom out in the woods somewhere, completely unaware that wolves or the Dead had got to her. Snowball wouldn't budge. Nothing could get him to leave his mom's side so Cooper spent all night with him and the next morning the foal followed him all the way back to the lake.

Snowball moved away to graze on one of the two straw bags hanging overhead, and Cooper tucked his knees into a foetal position with his arms crossed tightly over his chest. He was cold. But he was something else Peter had never considered before. He was vulnerable. Peter made his way round to the stall and quietly kneeled down behind him. He reached for Cooper's head, but something kept his hand from touching him.

Snowball huffed and Peter glanced back toward the canoe. There were reddish-brown stains on the inside panels from the old woman's body. It was almost impossible to get blood out of the skin of a wood once it'd seeped in there. But Cooper had done a good job scrubbing the canoe clean. There was the deer hide set down across one of the seats, a couple of cushions too. One for himself and one for Peter. Blood flushed the surface of Peter's skin. He still didn't really know why he'd refused Cooper's invitation to First Fall.

He turned back, quietly got down on to the floor behind Cooper and lay there, staring at the back of his head. His head, his body, the whole perfect lot of him that he'd watched for so long from the bottom of the lake. Cooper was closer now than he'd ever been. But here, wrapped up inside his own dreams, he might just as well have been a million miles away.

Peter shuffled in a little closer and the scent of log smoke and musk drew up inside his nostrils. His kneecap tucked into the back of Cooper's leg, and Cooper took in a deep breath. Peter froze. But when Cooper exhaled, the weight of his body sank back into Peter's and their bodies clicked into place like lock and key.

"Spoons," said Cooper, half asleep still. "Two lil' spoons."

Peter sighed and snuggled in closer so he could smell the sweat on Cooper's skin.

"Pa says white collars never look twice at our kind."

"Don't say that," said Peter.

"It's true, ain't it?"

"But I did look at you."

"You did?"

132

"Yeah. All the time."

"I never saw you."

"I did nothing but look."

"But I never caught you lookin'."

"I was doing a good job chopping wood, that's all. But I was always looking."

"No you din't," said Cooper.

"Yeah I did. All the time."

"No. I mean you din't do a good job," Cooper said, stretching out a yawn. "Hell, you had that darned blade coming in at all kinds of wrong angles."

Peter put his arm round Cooper and squeezed him until it hurt.

"Still don't feel close enough," Cooper said.

"I know."

"But I can feel you there, Peter. All a you too."

Peter pulled away, suddenly embarrassed by how obvious it was that he wanted him. "Sorry."

But Cooper leaned back to reassure him. They locked into spoons again. Cooper gently pulled his T-shirt up and out of his jeans. He drew Peter's hand down further so his fingertips grazed the flat of his stomach.

There was a trail of hair running all the way down from his belly button to behind the belt buckle somewhere. The rest of him was so smooth that the thickness of the hair down there was shocking somehow. And yet it was so overwhelming, it almost would have been enough just to be shown that secret part of him.

Cooper eased Peter's hand down even lower. Peter trailed his fingers over the buckle of Cooper's cowboy belt and kept his hand there. He held his breath to see if he could stop his heart from bursting out of his chest. He felt Cooper waiting, but after a while Cooper turned himself over and his wolf blue eyes fell into Peter's.

"Reckon my heart's beatin' faster than a rabbit starin' down the barrel of a gun, Pete."

"Mine too."

Cooper creased the corner of his mouth into a sleepy half-smile. He lowered his gaze, and Peter felt his eyes searching the surface of his lips.

"Did you really carry me all the way up the stairs from the canoe yesterday morning?" whispered Peter.

"Uh-huh. But there was a time before that. When the water was all warm and the lake was purrin' with a thousand dragonfly wings and you lost your strength swimmin'. I carried you on my back through the water to the watchtower."

"You did? I don't remember that."

"Oh, it was a long time before," said Cooper. "When we was about twelve, I reckon. Everythin' I ever felt for you was long before."

Peter felt a surge in his heart like it had suddenly been granted more strength or heat somehow. He'd never known that feeling before, but he recognized what it was at once. It was the presence of someone else being there. Cooper cupped the back of Peter's head to draw him close and they kissed.

And when, some time later, a crescent moon hung over the water and the canoe cut a trail through the carpet of stars back to the islands, Peter watched the label on Cooper's T-shirt sticking up where he'd put it back on inside out. He smiled, happier than he'd ever thought possible, to see it that way.

14

Peter couldn't sleep that night. Something outside the tree house had woken him. Perhaps it was only a vivid dream, but he thought he'd heard someone calling his name. He propped himself against the headboard and listened to the wolves. Their cry was a lonely one, but then these were the lonely hours. He'd never known that before. He couldn't remember a night when he hadn't slept right through. But he knew it now, and Darlene was right: staying awake with your thoughts while the rest of the world slept was a nightmare in reverse. Like a monster hiding under the bed, dark thoughts that somehow managed to stay quiet during the day were suddenly let wild. And the night gave them time to breed. A minute was an hour and an hour was a day. And there was no escape.

Peter swung his legs over the side of the bed and sat up. Even home felt strange. Like animals in the night, somehow the tree house took on another life in the darkness while no one was watching. The mugs hanging from the antlers seemed odd and unfamiliar. The timber floorboards creaked as if to the footsteps of others.

Peter remembered Cooper's kiss. How his hand held the back of his head, his face, his chest and buttocks too. But for some reason the word *snowflake* broke across Peter's lips like a forbidden secret. He sat for a little while longer, but his head felt heavy. He slumped back into his pillow and felt the irresistible pull of sleep behind his eyes.

He was drifting off when he heard the front door creak open.

Peter sat bolt upright. He glanced at his dad, but nothing had disturbed him. He stared at the gap in the door and told himself it was just the wind. Nothing could get up to the tree house while the rope ladder was drawn up, nothing. Peter whipped the quilt aside and stood up to close the door. But it was too late. Something was already standing there.

15

A dark figure stood at the door. Peter could barely make it out against the black night behind it but somehow it was darker than the darkness, like a person-shaped hole had been cut out of the world. Peter closed his eyes in case he was dreaming. He opened them and the figure was inside the room. His throat tightened. He called to his dad inside his head, but the words didn't come out. Peter blinked and the figure had moved forward again. It hadn't made a sound. It was just closer.

The front door swung shut. The floorboards creaked and the thing came toward him.

Peter felt the mattress on the back of his knees and quietly lowered himself on to the bed. He edged back to the headboard, and the thing thrust its arms out. Its hands clawed at the darkness, but the thing didn't find anything there so it shuffled forward into the middle of the room and groped the darkness again. Its knees found Peter's bed first.

The thing fell on to the foot of the bed. Peter screamed inside his head, drawing his knees up under his chin. He took shallow breaths through his nostrils, but the thing still sensed the presence of life. Joints cracked in the darkness, and Peter listened to its fingers probing the surface of the bed. He held his breath. The quilt was tugged away from him. Then a cold hand found his foot.

"Dad! Dad!"

There were two gunshots. The first one missed and struck the wall. The second hit its target, and the thing tumbled backward on to the floor.

His dad's voice cried out across the darkness. "Pete!"

Peter stared into the black space in front of him and said nothing.

"Pete? You OK?"

"Yes," he panted. "I'm here."

He heard his dad fumble around in the dark. A moment later, light filled the room and he swung one of the oil lamps down over the body. His dad's eyes were wild. This was impossible. The Dead had never made their way up to the tree house before. But as the lamp started to tremble in his hand, it became clear that it wasn't the only reason.

His dad placed the rifle on the bed and crouched down before the body. "It's Arnold."

Peter peered over the side of the bed. "What?"

But it was true. He'd recognize Mr Schmidt's bald head anywhere. His dad shoved on his boots and hurried to the front door. He held up the lamp and stepped outside. Peter wrapped a blanket across his shoulders and stood at the door while his dad investigated. But it was only a matter of time before the question came.

His dad turned back. "How the hell did it cross the lake?"

Peter said nothing.

"And how the hell did it make it up the ladder?"

Peter watched his dad follow the footprints back across the bridge to the ladder. None of it made any sense. He kicked the wooden railing and looked out into the darkness.

It wasn't long before help came. Darlene was the first to respond to the gunshots, calling out across the water as she paddled. Her canoe rushed up on to the shingle and she hurried up the ladder.

She pushed the hood of her parka back off her face and stepped up to the door. "Jesus," she said, staring at the body.

"I saw the chaperone take Mr Schmidt away,"

said Peter.

Darlene cupped Peter's face with both hands to check he was all right. "Shh now."

"I was there when he arrived."

"It's OK, darlin'. Nobody's doubtin' that."

"I was right there."

Darlene placed her hand on Peter's shoulder and stepped inside.

"You're sure the chaperone came?" said Peter's dad, walking in behind her.

"Yes," said Peter.

Darlene shook her head. "But he didn't take care of Arnold properly."

"No," said his dad. "And someone will have to have words with him about that, but that really isn't the problem right now."

Darlene tucked her hair behind her ears and crouched down beside the body. She placed her hand on the back of Mr Schmidt's bald head as if to bless him somehow. After a moment or two, she looked up.

"The rest of the lake can't know about this."

Peter's dad shook his head. "You are kidding me, right?"

"Tom."

"No way."

"The ice is days away from forming. They're jittery

enough as it is at this time of year. Imagine the panic if we tell them that one of those damned things made it all the way across the lake and into one of our homes. There'll be hysteria."

"But that's exactly what has happened."

"Has it?"

Peter's dad narrowed his eyes. "Yes, Darlene. It has."

"Oh please. How? This thing has no more learned how to paddle a canoe and climb ladders than you boys have learned how to put the toilet seat down."

"But what if they've changed?" said Peter. "What about the ones that stand by the water's edge, watching us. What about the one that mimicked you waving yesterday? We think they've just stopped by the water because they can't go any further, but what if they're watching us come and go. What if they're learning?"

Darlene rolled her eyes. "See? This is how the madness starts?"

"But—"

"Darlene's right, Pete," said his dad. "It's nonsense."

Darlene nodded and Peter's dad sat down at the foot of the bed, burying his head in his hands.

Peter shrugged. "Then what?"

"A prank," came a voice behind them.

Peter turned round and Henry appeared in the doorway.

"You folks all right?" he said. "Darlene?"

"Yes, Henry," said Darlene. "They're fine."

Peter's dad looked up. "What were you saying about a prank?"

"Well," said Henry, "there's been a lot of tension in the run-up to Peter finding his feet on the mainland. Maybe somebody's making a point about things getting done properly."

Darlene looked up. "Bud!"

"It can't be," said Peter. "I saw the chaperone take Mr Schmidt away. I waited for him to come."

Peter's dad stood. "Yes, Henry, and it's the chaperone's responsibility to make sure the infected are taken care of properly."

"It is," said Henry. "And isn't it your job to manage him, Darlene? And to make sure the extraction zone is clear at all times?"

Henry held Darlene's gaze and an awkward silence passed between them. "But that still doesn't explain how it got up here," he said. "And as much as it pains me to think of the consequences for the culprit, a prank is the most likely explanation and it's for me to get to the bottom of things."

"A prank?" said Peter's dad.

"Yes. Most likely."

"Not even Bud would—"

Henry pressed his fingers into the rim of his glasses. "A dead thing can't evolve, Tom. That's all there is to it."

"No. But a dead thing shouldn't be doing anything. And yet here we are."

Henry took Peter's dad by the shoulder. "Let me deal with Bud if need be, but now isn't the time. We need to remove the body from the islands before anyone else responds to the gunshots."

They dragged the body out to the canoe ready to take it back to the mainland.

"I'll bury it," said Henry, jumping inside and taking the paddle.

"I'll help," said Peter.

Henry raised his hand and angled the canoe round. "Won't be necessary. Now, let's hear no more about this."

Peter's dad stepped forward. "But—"

"Bud says a storm is picking up over the mountains. It might just keep us all indoors for a few days if it's as bad as he predicts. Hopefully, this will all have blown over by the time all the white stuff has."

And that was the end of the matter. Henry paddled back inside the darkness, closely followed by Darlene, and Peter and his dad had no other option but to close the door behind them.

A little while later, the storm came. Peter propped his head up against the headboard, listening to the pine needles scratching at the windowpanes. But he wasn't the only one kept awake.

"The wolves are howling," he said. "They've come down to the lake."

"Uh-huh," mumbled his dad.

"Dad. Dad!"

"I hear them, Pete. Go back to sleep."

"Why are they here?"

"The ice probably. It's on its way. This is their time. They know they'll have the run of the whole forest just as soon as they can cross the lake."

"Dad, are you OK?"

"Yeah, I'm OK. Try not to worry."

"But how did that thing get up here? And how did it manage to open the door?"

"I don't know, Pete."

Peter stared at the ceiling and the wolves kept howling.

"I've never liked their cry," he said.

"No," said his dad. "It sounds like the end of the world has come."

"Don't say that."

"But maybe it has. Nothing is as it should be."

Peter tucked his quilt up under his chin and stared

at the door. But nothing else was going to make it through the blizzard to get to them tonight. No monsters. No wolves. No Cooper.

16

Wild winds brought the rest of winter crashing down around Wranglestone. Snow skittered against the windowpanes. Across the lake, the boathouse door whip-cracked on its hinges, making the horses buck and whinny. Peter pulled his sweatshirt sleeve down over his fist to wipe the misted glass and slumped against the tree-house window. The lake was barely visible behind the blizzard. It was as if the whole world was keeping him from seeing Cooper again.

Cooper had taken the canoe the long way round the lake before bringing him home that night. He'd wanted to hear all about the waiting bench and Mr Schmidt. He'd wanted to hear about a lot of things. Before that they'd kissed. They'd more than kissed. But three days had passed since then – that might just as well have been ten years ago. And so much had happened.

In the days that followed the incident with Mr

Schmidt, Peter's dad convinced himself that Bud was responsible for planting him outside the tree house and rued the storm for keeping them apart so he could have it out with Bud once and for all. Perhaps Cooper would stop Bud from testing him altogether if only he could tell Cooper about it. But then again maybe not. Perhaps Cooper had changed his mind about him now. Perhaps he hadn't even given him any thought at all. Peter clenched his fists and a wave of heat burned across his skin like the fever.

"You're missing him is all," came his dad's voice beneath the roar of the storm. "Never listen to the Missing Monster. He'll always feed you a pack of dirty lies when a loved one is far away."

Peter recalled the heat of Cooper's bare chest beneath his hands and said nothing.

"I'm sure he's thinking of you too, Pete."

The way Cooper kissed first his neck, his chest, his armpit and waist to tell each part of him that it was beautiful.

"I'm sure of it."

Peter turned away from the window, startled that his dad seemed to know about the things he was feeling.

"But it hurts," he said.

The cabin creaked beneath the strain of the storm.

A log on the burner popped.

His dad looked up from the piece of wood he was whittling and smiled. "Of course."

Peter turned back to the window and now more than ever willed winter to be over.

❄

By the time the storm had settled, and Cooper finally took Peter out on horseback to herd the rest of the Dead south some two days later, everything was just as it had been between them back at the boathouse and the world was buried beneath winter's glittering crust.

They set out in the dark. There was nothing but branches and boughs of plump pine scratching at their shoulders for the first few hours. Cooper had located the herd some distance south of the old car. Peter watched while he rounded them up by roping one of the Dead in something called a constrictor knot, then towing it through the woods on a leash. The others followed.

For a while, Peter couldn't stop himself from turning round in case a pale hand should reach out of the darkness behind them to take Snowball down by his tail. But Cooper kept pace so that the rope remained taut and it was the most the herd could do to keep up. Peter put his arms round Cooper's waist and watched one snowy pine tree after the other break out of the darkness ahead and draw back behind them.

They reached the plains by first light. Peter sat forward. He used to have an enormous pop-up book of the National Parks of North America when he was younger. He had to lay it flat out on the floor with his chin on the boards to tackle its pages it was so big. Forests of towering sequoia trees and sandstone arches sprang up above him with the turn of every page. But he remembered the middle of the book best. The flat centrefold of a snowy plain was so vast that the horizon at the edge of the page seemed a thousand miles away. Apart from one thing. On the right-hand side of the book, the flat page surged up into densely packed triangles of grey card capped with white. But even this hadn't prepared him.

Cooper pulled back on the reins to hold Snowball at the edge of the forest and softly whispered Peter's name. But he'd already spotted them.

The snowy plains yawned out in every direction as far as the eye could see. Apart from the occasional tuft of sagebrush, the vast terrain of pristine snow was unbroken, stretching out to the edge of the world or until it reached other worlds maybe: deserts, oceans. But to their right, the vast plateau buckled up sharply at the fringes, the rock clashing in frozen waves to form the Shark Tooth mountains. This land, this dizzying slab of white nothing rumbling up from the earth into a jagged spine of peaks to cut the clouds, was so vast and so unscalable that it forced you to see the world for what it really was – a planet.

Sunlight crested the back of the mountains, fanning through fissures in the rock in splintered shafts. Peter held his hand up to shield his face. The sun breached the summit. Light spilled down the mountainside out on to the plains and the land was flooded in dazzling light. Peter leaned into Cooper's back while he rode on, to be sure of him as much as anything else, and gazed out in wonder.

The snow was brilliant.

The doming sky, all big and blue, stretched right up over the top of them.

They might just as well have been the first people on Earth.

Cooper kept quiet most of the time, as was his way. But he was never absent. Mostly he looked directly out in front, holding the reins loosely in his left hand while patting the leash knotted round the saddle horn and two bucking rolls with the other. But just when Peter started to worry where Cooper's mind had wandered and if he was happy, Cooper turned his head just a little to doff his Stetson and said, "This is good, Peter. This is good."

Peter swept Cooper's hair from his neck to kiss him and watched a pack of wolves loping through banks of deep snowdrifts in the distance. Their bodies dipped and sprang, casting puffs of white powder up into the blue.

"The storm was bad," said Peter after a while. "I thought it would never pass. Course, I knew that it would eventually – no storm could go on like that forever. It just felt like forever."

Peter sat upright and waited for Cooper to answer. He wanted to know how Cooper had passed the time over the last few days. He wanted to know if he'd been on Cooper's mind. But Cooper pulled the brim of his Stetson down over his eyes to shield them from the low winter sun.

"We're together now," he said quietly and rode on.

They made it out to the middle of the plains, keeping a clear distance from a herd of bison to make sure the Dead weren't drawn toward them. Peter steadied himself on the cantle of the saddle and craned round to check they were still being followed.

When the herd had cleared the forest, boughs at the edge of the plains trembled as if shaken by a fist, followed by a wall of pale figures as the herd broke clear of them. A host of ghastly faces stared back at Peter now, their mottled skin translucent beneath the bleaching sun.

"They still following?" asked Cooper.

"Yeah. Will we be safe?"

"They ain't nothin' but a shadow on our tail. But you

can give 'em a whistle if some of 'em start wanderin' off toward the bison."

Peter put his thumb and forefinger inside the corners of his mouth just like he'd seen Bud do whenever Dolly wandered off. But while wolf-whistling and cracking bottles open with your teeth was probably the kind of thing Cooper had done in diapers, Peter didn't hold much hope of any noise coming out. So when the stragglers cleared the last of the trees and took up the trail with the rest, Peter let out a sigh of relief and swung back round.

"They're good."

Cooper clapped his thighs against Snowball's sides to spur him on. The snow was deep, deep enough that it had started to form in clumps like giant snowballs around some of the bison's beards, weighing them down. Some of them wouldn't make it to lower ground if it got any worse. Exhaustion would have them long before the wolves or the Dead had a chance. Snowball and Cooper, on the other hand, were completely untroubled. Cooper nudged the brim of his Stetson up off his face and leaned forward to rest his forearm across the saddle horn, as happy now on his perch as a bobcat on a branch.

"You ever seen a town?" Peter asked.

"One."

Peter sat upright. Cooper couldn't have sounded any less interested if he'd just given him the answer to what preceded the number two. But inside that little word was a whole world that Peter had only dreamed of.

"Which one?"

"West Wranglestone. The park's gateway town. But it's a two-day ride we don't bother with no more. Not since we took everything worth taking."

"What was it like?"

"It was like a town."

"Yeah, I know, but what's that like?"

"It was like a bunch of brick and wood that weren't trees no more."

Peter sighed. "Cooper."

"I dunno. There was Mainstreet with a general store and a movie theatre and a diner and, when you got to other end, which din't take none too long, the buildings just stopped and the road carried on back out into the wilds and din't never look back."

Peter looked out toward the foothills. "Was the movie theatre amazing?"

"If brown's amazing."

Peter sighed. Working in the place where people went to watch their dreams come to life must have been one of the best things in the whole world. He'd have made sure people got to their seats when the lights went out. He'd have been able to take good care of that kind of thing.

"You ever wish you'd been around before?" he asked.

"For what?"

"Before—"

"I know what yous meant. What for? TV? Nine to five? Money? Havin' to work nine to five just to stop you worryin' about money?"

"No. Not that."

"Then what?"

Peter looked down. "Oh, nothing."

"Tell me."

"No, just forget I said anything."

Cooper glanced back and smiled. "You mean before the world got all outdoorsy?"

Yes, that, Peter thought. But he knew better than to say it.

"Nope," said Cooper. "Pa says folks spent so much time messaging each other that they'd started to grow pale faces and ruddy fingers. I reckon the world got so pissed on account of folks not looking up no more that it sent the Restless Ones just to remind us death's round the corner while we still got the time to make the most of what's around us. Can't afford to look down now, not even to kick a tick off your shoe. But you don't miss nothin' no more. You don't miss a damn thing.

"Besides," he said, "if I had to ask you out to First Fall like that, by the time you was done correctin' my words, the whole damn thing woulda been over."

"You could've used predictive text."

"Huh?"

"You could've picture messaged me *snowflake*, *firework, smiley face.*"

Cooper scratched the back of his neck. "Jesus, Peter. You spend way too much time listening to Darlene."

Peter smiled. "Anyways, I would've messaged you back."

"But I came for you instead. I watched you fold your clothes down by the tub from out on the water that night, Peter. I saw you, all a you too, and then I came for you."

"I'm sorry I said no."

"I wanted you."

"I don't know what I was thinking."

"I wanted you so bad."

Cooper reached back so his fingertips grazed Peter's thigh. They were as rough as sandpaper. Peter smiled. But none of this made any sense. Cooper belonged here in the new world. *He* didn't.

"I wish I was born before."

Cooper swung his leg up and over Snowball's head and slipped down on to the ground. He checked that they were still a safe distance from the herd and stood there, looking up at Peter, with both boots planted down squarely in the snow.

"Do you, Peter Nordstrum?" he said. "Do you wish

you was born before?"

Peter shrugged. "I guess."

"Well, I don't. There's only one a you in the whole wide world, Peter. And there'll only ever be one a you. So what are the chances that you lived in this time? Not before, but right now and at exactly the same time as me. What are the chances of that? I'm grateful as all hell and you'll get no more worries from my pa or anyone else for that matter. Not now, not now you's with me. I'm glad you wasn't born before. I need you here. So I reckon this time suits you just fine, Peter. OK?"

Peter nodded and said nothing.

"OK?"

"Yes, OK." Then, "I missed you. I missed you these last few days."

Cooper looked at Peter's lips, then held eye contact in a way that now told Peter they were about to kiss. "I couldn't focus on nothing else during the storm. I couldn't sleep without your hand inside mine."

Cooper ran his fingers through the white needles of hair on Snowball's back and gazed out into the great white nothing.

"Ranchers could ride for a couple hundred miles from their door in any direction and still not leave home," he said. "It's just a bunch of sagebrush and rattlesnakes out there in the summer months, but I hope you'll like it."

Peter gazed up at the doming sky and smiled. Summer was at least six months away. He'd never been a part of anybody's future before.

Cooper took a toothpick from his jacket pocket and chewed on it. "But you see it, right?"

"What?' said Peter. "This place?"

"Yeah, but not just the snow and the sky and the mountains."

Peter gazed out. The stillness was somehow more immense than the size of the land that surrounded them. Only the land wasn't still at all. He and Cooper would sprout and wither so quickly but the land's violent life went unseen. The mountains were always moving, they were moving all around them even now, but they were moving silently and invisibly through time, shifting over millions of years.

A feeling welled up from the bottom of Peter's stomach. He looked off into the hundred-mile view and became aware of himself as something very small at the heart of something very big and didn't feel threatened by it.

"Yes," he said. "It's beautiful. But it's more than just the things I'm seeing."

Cooper turned round, squinting beneath the brow of his Stetson, and smiled as if Peter had finally made the journey and arrived somewhere he'd been waiting for him.

"It's the planet, Peter," he said quietly. "You feel the planet. The universe. You need never feel alone."

Cooper stepped up into the stirrup, hitting the saddle backward to face Peter, and they kissed.

❄

They rode on through the morning until they came to the woods on the other side of the plains. Cooper made his approach through the trees at a more easterly angle than he'd ever done before in order to avoid the bison. Soon Peter felt the forest's chilly grip across his shoulders, and the herd of the Dead followed them into the shadow of the trees. Cooper must have been satisfied that he'd led them far enough away from the lake. They hadn't gone very far inside the forest chamber when he stopped.

Snowball reared round to face the herd. Peter peered over Cooper's shoulder and saw the Dead moving through the woods toward them.

"Wait," he said. "Why are we turning to face them?"

The leash slackened and dropped to the ground. The Restless One in the noose approached.

"Coop. Why have we stopped?"

Peter watched the coil land across the snow and listened to his own heartbeat pounding wildly in his ears.

Snowball stomped his hoof in protest as the thing headed their way. But Cooper didn't wait for it to come any closer. He lifted the end of the rope from the saddle horn, placing it in the crook of his arm to take the slack, and brought Snowball up to a canter.

Peter threw his arms round Cooper's waist and Snowball gathered pace. Dry powder kicked up behind them. Just at the point they were about to collide with the thing at the other end of the rope, Cooper leaned out sideways from the saddle.

He drew his machete from its sheath and sliced the rope at the noose.

A set of gnashing teeth and raving eyes flashed before Peter. The Restless One lunged. But before he knew it, Snowball reared up and, with clashing hooves, changed direction away from the herd. Cooper whipped the end of the rope back across the saddle and they took off through the woods back toward the plains.

Peter lurched over the side of the saddle, catching a glimpse of Cooper's foot jiggling about in the stirrup. Any hopes that would stop him from noticing how tight the gap in between each tree trunk was were failing fast. He sat bolt upright, gasping. But there was another feeling, something other than fear and terror bubbling away inside him. He could barely feel his fingers and toes now, so much adrenaline was pumping through them.

He let out a crying laugh.

"We're gonna die!"

"Aw, not today we ain't."

Cooper's hair streamed behind him all gold in the dappled sunlight. "Peter!"

"What?"

"Nothin'! Just wanted to hear your name is all."

Peter leaned in to kiss Cooper's neck and watched the plains rushing toward them.

They were fast approaching the edge of the woods when Cooper suddenly stopped.

"Easy, boy. Easy does it."

"What's wrong?" asked Peter.

"There's smoke in the air."

"A campfire?"

"Maybe."

"Who else is out here?"

"No one. None of ours at any rate. Not this far out."

Peter held on to Cooper's waist and glanced around. Cooper sniffed the air to try and catch the direction of the fire.

"We can shake the dumb Dead off," he said, "but strangers in need of a home – well, that ain't so easy."

He dismounted, leading Snowball quietly back through the woods so as not to alert anyone of their whereabouts. After a while, the smell of smoke seemed to disappear behind them. But as Cooper picked up his pace, the trees parted and a log cabin came into view.

Cooper looked back. There was a nervousness in his eyes Peter hadn't seen before that told him Cooper didn't even know this cabin existed. But it was pointless trying to make their escape now. Someone was already standing at the open door.

17

The glint in the man's eyes caught the sunlight. But he held back inside the shadow of the cabin making it hard to see his features. A set of white teeth hovered in the darkness. His grin was unnaturally wide and fixed, like a smile long after the laughter had died. And it didn't falter. Snowball pinned his ears back, quietly whinnying, and something told Peter they should leave.

"Well, ain't this day as pretty as a snow globe," said the man without stepping forward.

Behind him, a chair scraped violently across the floorboards followed by the sound of clattering and hurried activity within. The man's eyes shifted. He broadened his smile. A moment later, the cabin fell silent and he disappeared inside, leaving the door ajar.

"Well, come on in!" he hollered. "We got soup on the stove if you boys need to take a break from your travels."

A string of smoke curled up from the crumbling chimney stack, but the roof was buried beneath a thick crust of snow. There were so many icicles lining the gutter, it was as if there wasn't any warmth coming from inside at all.

Cooper looked back. "Something ain't right. No one welcomes strangers into the homestead without holding a gun to their heads first."

"Maybe he's just glad of the company," Peter offered.

"Well, he shouldn't be. We could be anyone."

"But we're not anyone. We're just you and me."

Cooper pulled the brim of his Stetson down over his eyes and smiled. "You're too good for this world, Peter Nordstrum."

"Don't be catching your death," came the man's voice from within.

Peter looked across at the open door. "I'm starving."

"Same," said Cooper, tapping his gun holster. "But I ain't taking no chances. If they so much as move their hands beneath the table…"

Peter nodded, even though he didn't much like the idea of entering a home with a gun when someone was trying to make a guest of you. But Cooper knew the ways of the world better than he did so he clambered down off the saddle.

"Leave Snowball there," said Cooper, making his way

to the front door. "You won't wander, will you, boy?"

Snowball saw that there was nothing to graze on but snow and huffed. Peter patted him, then headed over to the cabin. He stamped excess snow off his toecaps on the stoop and stepped up to the doorway.

Inside was dark. Red gingham curtains at the windows were drawn, even though it was approaching noon. The only light came from a candle on the wooden dining table in the middle of the room. The timber walls ached beneath the weight of a hundred antlers. The flame flickered and their shadows roamed as if the cabin was alive with a herd of wild spirits. Peter glanced up at the beams where a mobile of feathers and eagle wings was hanging and watched the ceiling dance with the shadows of a dozen flying birds. The menagerie of bones and feathers was beautiful in its own way. But the room was cold.

Peter noticed his breath curl into the darkness and wondered why the fire had been allowed to die when the chimney breast was stacked full of firewood. He held back at the door. The kitchenette at the other end of the cabin was obscured by the glare of the candlelight, but as his sight adjusted, the wet glint of a pair of eyes caught the light and he realized someone was standing there.

"You can thank my brother for the soup," said the woman, setting two bowls down on the table where the man was now seated. "Can't say I care for unwanted visitors any more than you do."

Peter glanced at Cooper, unsure of what she meant by that. The woman brought two more bowls over and stood staring at the man with both hands on her hips. Her grey hair hung unbound about her face, masking her features, but she was quite a bit younger than the man whose gaunt cheeks were somehow at odds with the tight paunch at his belt buckle. He patted her arm lovingly as if to pacify her. But his eyes didn't leave Peter once.

"Boys," he said warmly, in a manner that belied his stiffness. "Mable's broth won't eat itself. Please, join us."

The woman huffed. "It ain't my broth."

Cooper gingerly made his way over to one of the bowls and looked at Peter to join him.

"Is it OK?" said Peter. "Us being here, I mean."

The old man's smile briefly left his face. "Sure," he said, slapping both hands down squarely on the table. "Well, as OK as a couple of old farts like us can be."

Peter smiled. "I'm sorry. I didn't mean it like that."

"No problem." His mouth smiled once again, but he forgot to tell his eyes. "Please take a seat. Don't let your broth go cold now."

Peter sat opposite Cooper, tucking his chair under the table. The woman sat at the far end. She'd forgotten to get herself a spoon, but she didn't bother getting up for one. She clasped both hands together in her lap and sat there, staring down the length of the table. The old man held her gaze and a silent understanding seemed to pass between them.

"So what brings you fine boys to these parts?" he said, dipping his spoon into the bowl.

"Wranglin' a hcrd of the Dead across the plains, mister," said Cooper.

"Yes," said Peter, encouraged by his upbeat tone. "Cooper's our wrangler."

"Is that so?" said the old man.

"Oh yes. He's the best we have."

"We?" said the old man.

"Yeah," said Cooper, clearing his throat. "Just the two of us and our horse Snowball."

Peter looked away. He shouldn't have been so careless as to mention there might be others. But the old man seemed happy enough with this answer and carried on as before.

"Terrible business, the Dead," he said. "It can only be a good thing that you both know how to protect yourself. And what is it that you do, er...?"

"Peter."

"Peter," said the old man, glancing at his sister.

Peter stared into his bowl. "Nothing really. I sew."

"No," said Cooper, wiping his mouth on the back of his hand. "You do much more than that. You take real good care of us is what you do."

Peter smiled. He'd never been an *us* before. He watched the way Cooper's hair spilled over the bowl like curtains while he continued to slurp his soup. He watched him for a while. He wished his dad's hair could do the same for all the mess he made eating.

"Me and Mable have always lived together," said the old man. "It's good to have a special someone in this crazy world."

He smiled again. But it was different this time, warmer. It was as if he'd hoped that making a connection with them would be enough. Peter smiled back and decided he liked him. The man nodded, brought a napkin up to his mouth even though he hadn't eaten any soup yet and looked at the woman.

"Eat your soup, sis."

The woman glared at the bowl, raking her fingernails across the length of her neck. She'd worked the skin so hard she'd drawn blood. Peter glanced at Cooper to see if he'd noticed, but he just looked away and continued eating.

The woman turned toward her brother. He stirred his soup, rotating the spoon clockwise round the bowl, round and round.

"Never seen this cabin before," said Cooper after a while.

The old man continued stirring his soup, but still hadn't lifted any to his mouth.

"No?" he said.

"Nope," said Cooper.

"And is it an important find?"

"I'm real grateful for the soup."

"Well, I'm glad about that. But is the soup all you came for?"

Cooper dropped his spoon. "Why, you think some redneck like me can't come here unless he's after somethin'?"

Peter looked up. "Cooper. Stop it."

The man kept stirring. A smile spread across his face again so wide now it looked like a gash running from one ear to another. But it was the woman who answered.

"We know where you're from," she said under her breath.

The spoon fell from the old man's hand. "Mable."

"If you mean us harm," she went on, "then just get on with it. We're tired and we've had our time in the sun. But leave the others alone."

Peter froze. "What others?"

The old man stared into his bowl, but the woman's gaze darted to the floorboards. She caught Peter looking at her and was quick to divert her eyes back to the table.

Peter leaned over the side of his chair. He looked down in between a crack in the floorboards and a pair of wide eyes looked back.

He sat upright. "Cooper!"

Cooper sprang to his feet. The chair tipped backward, clattering to the floor.

"Who's down there?" he said. "How many you got down there?"

"All that's left," said the old woman.

"All that's left of what?"

Cooper lifted his hand to his belt, drawing the gun from its holster.

"No, Cooper!" said Peter, standing. "We're not going to hurt you. Why would you even think that?"

The woman eased back in her chair. "Because he's pointing a gun at my head. Because that's what you people do at Wranglestone."

The name curled over her lips like frostbite. Cooper released the latch and took aim. But before he even had a chance to pull the trigger, the old man struck a match.

A ball of brilliant white light erupted across the table. The man held the match to a piece of cord strapped to the tabletop and the fuse sparked into life. It fizzed along the piece of cord to the lip of the table. A moment later, it disappeared over the edge.

The man held his sister's gaze. "At least we'll be rid of two of them."

"Yes." She smiled. "At least."

"Get out," said Cooper, flipping the table over. "Now, Peter!"

The soup bowls shattered into pieces. Peter scrambled over to the door, but his fingers could barely fumble for the latch. He just stood there, looking at the upturned table, transfixed by the dynamite strapped to its underside.

18

Peter pulled down sharply on the door handle.

"It's locked, Cooper," he said, falling back against the door. "Shoot the padlock!"

Cooper's eyes were wide. He dropped the gun down by his side. "It ain't loaded. It never was loaded."

The spark fizzled toward the dynamite. The woman brought herself up on to her feet and calmly walked over to the kitchen. But the man's eyes shifted and Peter saw a sudden change of heart.

"See?" said Peter, pointing at Cooper's gun. "You think we meant you harm, but we just thought the same about you."

The woman huffed. "He lies."

"No!" said Peter.

"He's lying and they know who we are."

"No. I don't. I don't even know what you're talking about."

"They know who we are," the woman insisted.

"Let us go and we promise we won't come back."

"Mable," said the man. "This is not the way."

The woman leaned over the sink. "But it's their way."

"Mable, please."

"They'll come back. They always come back."

The old man stared at the fuse and something resembling regret flickered across his face. Peter looked at Cooper across the upturned table. There was fear in his eyes. There was so much fear. But there was something else too, something his eyes were trying to tell him that his voice could not.

"Peter, I. Pete, I gotta tell you somethin'."

Before Cooper could say what it was, the woman crossed the cabin. She pulled the axe free from the woodpile next to the chimney breast and brought the blade down on the upturned table. The dynamite's cord spilt in two and the fuse went out.

"Satisfied?" she said, dropping the axe to her side.

The old man fumbled for the keys in his front pocket, nodding his agreement and thanking her.

"But this is on you, Martin."

"Mable, don't."

"When they come back, this is all on you!"

He stumbled over to the front door, quickly unlocking it. "Go!" he said. "Go, before we regret it."

Peter bolted out of the door before he could change his mind.

"Cooper!" he said, running toward Snowball. "Come on!"

He placed one hand on the saddle horn and turned back. Cooper fell forward into the doorframe, his hair spilling across his face. The man grabbed him by the collar to make sure he made it through the door this time and threw him on to the snow.

He brushed his palms together as if to rid their home of the pair of them and his sister took his side.

"We won't tell anyone you're here!" called Peter. "We promise."

Cooper scrambled to his feet, clutching at his neck and ran toward Snowball. "They struck me, Pete."

Peter shoved him up on to the saddle and briefly turned back. "We don't know who you are! Really we don't, but whoever you are, I'm sure it can't be that bad."

The brother and sister stepped away from the sunlight. Their eyes were four dark pools glinting in the shadows. They searched inside Peter to see whether there was any truth in his words. But neither of them spoke.

The door slammed shut. An icicle dropped from the gutter, shattering into a dozen pieces. A moment later, the shelf of snow on the roof followed. Snowball started at the sound, so Peter patted his side to quickly steady him and mounted. Cooper took the reins, clapping his heels against Snowball's sides to set off at a pace, but something made Peter turn back.

The symbol painted on the cabin roof hadn't been visible before. But the image of a white snowflake, its eight feathery points like quills on an arrow, was unmistakable now.

"Cooper."

Cooper clutched at his neck again and turned. "I see it."

"The snowflake."

"Yeah, I see it."

"The man who attacked me on the lake the other day was angry I wasn't wearing the snowflake. What do you suppose he even meant?"

"I dunno, Peter."

"The brother and sister were just scared about what we might do to them."

"All folks is scared," said Cooper. "There's all sorts out here meaning all sorts of harm."

Peter nodded and didn't take his eyes off the roof. "I'm glad the gun didn't have bullets, Cooper."

"I know."

"I'm so glad."

"Me too."

"But what's the snowflake for?"

Cooper had no answer. He just reached back and gently squeezed Peter's leg. "You done real good so far. You done more than Pa or anyone else expected of you, so don't be fillin' your head with other folk's worries."

"We won't tell anyone about them, will we?"

"No, Pete."

"And we won't come back."

"No, we won't come back."

"You think they believed us?"

But Cooper didn't have time to answer.

The explosion blew the cabin apart. A fireball full of snow and wood erupted over the tops of the trees until all that was left was flame.

Peter jumped down to the ground, staggering forward as bits of blazing wood fell clean out of the sky. But it was a while before he became aware of just how cold his shins were and realized he'd dropped to his knees in shock.

"Why?" he cried. "Why did they do that?"

Dark smoke funnelled up through the surrounding pines. The strangest silence hung inside the forest clearing. A moment had passed or maybe an hour, Peter wasn't too sure, when he felt Cooper at his side. He turned toward those wolf blue eyes and Cooper's hair spilled across his face until their foreheads touched.

"I love you, Peter," he whispered. "I can't not say it no more.

19

Betsy Carmichael made it all the way to the falls before Peter realized he hadn't been listening to her. When they'd returned from the plains, he'd found her handcuffed inside the boathouse, waiting for him. She'd flipped over one of the Restless Ones in the woods, thinking it had already been destroyed. She found out too late that it hadn't and the shock of being bitten came out in the form of a monologue about her days working in the local housing offices. But her voice, along with all of her recollections and memories, dissolved inside the sound of the thundering water. The only words Peter could hear were Cooper's. Three of them to be exact. Cooper had given him those words and by doing so had given himself. Peter hadn't said them back.

Mrs Carmichael took a lipstick and compact mirror from her purse and said something about needing to reapply her make-up in case the chaperone was the strapping military type. Peter sighed. How could it matter what she looked like when she'd just taken a seat on the bench nobody came back from? And yet her hand was trembling. Peter watched the lipstick falter as she struggled to drag a clean outline across the taut ridges of her lips and felt bad for thinking of her that way. She was terrified. She simply didn't want anyone to see that death had already taken her.

"Do you think?" came Mrs Carmichael's voice in the distance.

Why hadn't he told Cooper he loved him?

"Peter?"

What was wrong with him?

"Peter?"

Peter sat bolt upright. "Sorry. What?"

"Do you think he likes brunettes, Peter?" said Mrs Carmichael. "This chaperone guy. Come awn, you can tell old Betsy. You've seen him."

Peter withdrew his wolfskin hood to get a proper look at the perm Darlene had given her by heating a couple of old curling tongs over the fire.

"He wears a gas mask, Mrs Carmichael. It's real hard to tell."

"Betsy," she said, slapping him on the wrist. "Call me Betsy. Mrs Carmichael makes me sound like I'm old enough to be your ma."

Peter cleared his throat because the lake had her pegged as being at least seventy and held up the mirror for her while she did her mascara.

"Ta-da!" she said, holding the back of her hand underneath her chin just like they do in pictures. "Not bad for an ol' girl, huh?"

Peter smiled. "Not a day over forty-seven."

Mrs Carmichael's face dropped and for a moment Peter thought he'd made a terrible mistake by pitching her age too high. But she puckered her lips and leaned in.

"Aw, sweetie. How much did they pay you?"

She put her purse down beside her on the bench and looked out toward the falls.

Peter pulled his hood back over his head to shield it from the mist and felt the mood shift somehow. He glanced round. Mrs Carmichael's black mascara crawled down her face carried by a steady stream of tears. He brought her hand over on to his lap and clasped it there.

"I'm scared, Peter."

"I know."

"I don't know what to do with myself."

"I'm here."

"You must think me a foolish woman for even bringing my make-up here with me."

"I don't."

"It's just that I—"

She squeezed Peter's hand, as if by holding on to him she would hold on to everything else. But she didn't finish her sentence.

"Is there anything you want me to tell Mr Carmichael?"

"He loved me," she said. "He never said it too often, and God knows it wouldn't hurt him to have said it once in a while, but I never doubted it, Peter. He never let me doubt it. Not once in forty-five years. Tell him that."

Peter leaned forward. "How did you know you loved him? In the beginning, I mean?"

"Oh, in the beginning, everything other than being with him was just unbearable. Unbearable, Peter. A day was longer than a math class and a week was longer than a sleepless night. But in the end you know it's love because, well, your heart just stops searching."

"Stops searching for what?"

Peter felt Mrs Carmichael's hand tighten round his and the snow continued to fall.

"Anyone else."

Mrs Carmichael nodded as if to say, *That's what you tell him. You tell him that.* But no more words came out, and a short while later pillows of mist folded over the rocks and the silhouette of a great bear standing upright appeared at the falls. Peter stood and the chaperone raised his paw in a motionless wave. Peter drove his staff into the ground and took a step forward. He wanted to be sure Mrs Carmichael would be taken care of. That what had happened to Mr Schmidt couldn't happen again. But something stopped him, as if the thought of hurried talks and questions in these final moments would taint her peace somehow. Peter waved back and the chaperone nodded. But he didn't come down off his place on top of the rocks, so after a hug and one final, desperate kiss farewell, Peter let go of Mrs Carmichael's hand and she quietly made her way over to the foot of the falls.

The chaperone held back on the rock and Peter felt his invitation to leave. He quietly collected Mrs Carmichael's purse and earrings because she wanted Darlene to have them and slowly made his way down through the trees toward the shallow river.

He hadn't gone far when he felt breathless with worry and tucked himself behind a tree. She was in safe hands. He was being silly and she was going to be taken care of as best as possible. Peter unclipped the clasp on Mrs Carmichael's purse and stuffed her earrings down one of the inside pockets. But as he closed the purse and looked down into the woods, another thought presented itself. He'd follow them, just to be sure she was being safely taken away. Just to be sure what happened to Mr Schmidt didn't happen again. Peter counted out two minutes, saying 'bald eagle' in between each number to make sure he didn't count too fast. Eventually, he decided that he'd given them enough time to make a head start and peered round the side of the tree back up at the falls.

The chaperone stood motionless on the rock, watching him. Peter recoiled. Mrs Carmichael was nowhere to be seen, but *he* hadn't moved this whole time. Peter waved to make out that he only wanted to see them off. The chaperone's hand didn't move from his side. He just stood there, watching from behind the gas mask's two bulbous eye discs. Peter stared at the chaperone, but the chaperone stared back to hold his ground so Peter had no choice but to turn back toward the woods.

He made it as far as the shallow river, using the sequence of stepping stones Mr Schmidt had showed him to cross to the other side. He jumped on to the riverbank and was about to look back one last time when he saw something scrawled in the snow in front of him.

DON'T STOP
HE'S
FOLLOWING
YOU

Peter's stomach lurched. He looked up to see if he could spot who'd left the message and why. His eyes darted from one tree to another, but there was no one there. He quickly scuffed out the message with his staff and ran back into the woods toward the lake.

He dashed into the clearing just short of the boathouse, but tripped over something, falling face down on the ground.

A piece of wood jutted out of the snow. He was sure it hadn't been there when he'd set out with Mrs Carmichael. It was weathered and cracked like driftwood, except the grey wood had letters etched on it and one of them, the one catching the light, was painted in silver.

Peter crouched down and pulled on the old sign, but it didn't come loose in his hands. It was attached to a post with five other pieces of wood, each pointing in different directions. Peter heaved the sign up out of the snow and ran his fingertips across the silver snowflake that had been carved in place of the letter O.

CAMP WRANGLEST✳NE

One sign pointed toward something called the Wranglestone Registration Office. The others were for the Memory Garden, Medical Centre, Chapel and, finally, Camp Wranglestone Staff Quarters.

Peter lowered the sign, peering beneath the pines at the edge of the clearing into the woods within. The military were never stationed inside the refuge, not even when it was first built, and he'd never heard the lake being referred to as a camp before now. Peter ran his finger over the silver snowflake and glanced back at the trail.

"Hello?" he called.

No one answered.

"Hello?"

A twig cracked further off inside the woods. He scrambled to his feet and quickly made his way inside the boathouse.

20

Peter gasped as if breaking above water. He sat bolt upright in bed, tugging his sodden all-in-one away from his chest to release the heat. His eyes darted round the tree house, to the windows, the front door. But it was closed, and no one was lurking there. No Mr Schmidt and no Mrs Carmichael. No bear standing on its hind legs, watching.

The nightmare evaporated inside the darkness. His dad mumbled something in his sleep and rolled over. Peter swung his legs round, hovering his toes above the floorboards until they found his slippers. Except the timber was so cold, the chill radiating up from them struck the soles of his feet before they even touched it. The sweat on his chest turned icy. Peter glanced at the log burner. It had kept running through the night, but it hadn't been enough to keep the place warm, so he wrapped the quilt round his chest and parted the curtains to see why.

The bundles of pine needles at the window were a blur behind the frosted-up glass. The tree house was braced by a freeze. Peter shuffled over to the door and quietly made his way out on to the deck.

A haze of light broke round the fringes of the sky behind the pines, turning the night inky-blue. Dawn was upon them. Peter perched on the frosted bench by the front door and listened to a flock of snow geese pass overhead. But his eyes never left the water.

The lake was a white disc hovering in the darkness. The ice couldn't have been more than a few inches thick yet – a stone would probably crack the surface. It would need to be at least three inches deep before a single person could walk out on to it, fifteen before the ice could withstand the weight of the old pickup truck they pushed out on to the surface, showing everyone when it was safe to cross. And yet a crust had formed, joining the mainland to all the islands. It wouldn't be long now. Then you'd be able to step clean off Skipping Mouse and walk all the way over to the mainland. Anything could.

The back of Peter's skull throbbed and a thousand thoughts overtook him. It wasn't just the snowflake or Mr Schmidt or the explosion at the cabin, but Cooper. He'd said *I love you*. Peter played those three little words over and over in his head. Cooper's words were an invitation.

Peter hadn't invited him back. He didn't know why, but he'd left Cooper thinking his feelings were unwanted.

Peter drew the quilt up over his head and considered waking his dad. Perhaps he'd gone through the same thing with Mom if she'd said it first. Perhaps he hadn't said it straight back either and could explain how you knew when it was right to. Peter hugged one of the cushions for extra warmth, but the cover was stiff with frost. He went to stand, but his foot knocked into something. The bottle made a dull clink and rolled across the deck. Peter shuffled over to the railing, reaching forward, and tipped the bottle upside down to remove the piece of paper scrolled up inside.

We're gonna do so much together.
Meet me in the tunnle at midday.
Coop x

Peter ran his fingertips over the cross and turned back. The tree house was asleep, half buried beneath a crust of snow and draping pine. But everything was stirring. He clutched the note to his chest and listened to the island waking. The blue jays were up, squabbling for the morning's insects. A woodpecker drilled. Peter pressed into the front door when he felt a sudden burst of heat across his back. Light clipped the pines, fanning through the branches in broken beams across the tree house, and the frosted timber came tingling into the sun.

"Dad!" he said, dashing back inside.

His dad stirred, farted and fell back asleep. Peter stepped out of his slippers, tucking the bottle into one of them for safekeeping, and slid them under the bed.

"Dad, I'm going out for the day."

He pulled a pair of jeans and a sweater over his long johns and struggled into his boots. He couldn't tie the laces quick enough. He was opening the door when he had a change of heart about the choice of sweater he was wearing and dashed back for the chunky coffee-coloured one Darlene said filled him out a bit more. He was just about to pull the door to when his dad called out.

"I'm proud of you, Pete!"

Peter hovered in the doorway. His dad's hands poked out over the top of the quilt and stretched into a big yawn, followed by his creased-up face.

"I'm going to the mainland," said Peter. "I'll be with Cooper."

"Now?"

"Yeah. He left me a note overnight saying to meet him later, but—"

His dad's eyes smiled. "But you can't wait."

"No."

Peter turned to leave.

"You're doing good," said his dad. "You've more than proved yourself to the lake."

"I saw the chaperone take Mr Schmidt away. I swear."

"I know, Pete. I know. Bud and one of the others must've dumped him outside our door. I just can't prove it is all. But Mr Carmichael was very touched by your words when you came back from seeing Betsy off. You've more than proved yourself."

Peter shrugged. "It just feels right somehow."

"Something's troubling you though."

A sudden rush of blood surged through Peter's body. His dad lifted the top of the quilt up and peered inside.

"Jesus," he said, wafting it up and down. "I think something died down there."

He clambered out of bed, yanking the seat of his long johns out from in between his butt cheeks, and threw some logs on the burner.

"He's serious about you."

"Who?" Peter said. Then quietly, "Yes."

"And you can only keep them holding on for so long."

"Holding on for what?"

His dad chucked on another log. "Pete, nothing's made you put your clothes on over sweaty long johns before and it sure ain't money worries. So unless there's something else you're not telling me, he must've told you something big and now you're freaking out about it."

Peter narrowed his eyes. "Where's my dad? And what have you done with him?"

His dad winked. "Caveman read woman magazine."

"Anyway it's complicated."

"Is it?"

"Yeah."

"Is it though? Come on, Pete. What's holding you back?"

"Oh please, you can talk. What's holding you back with Darlene?"

His dad brushed bits of loose bark off his palms and stood. "I'm still in love with your mom."

He held Peter's gaze. Peter had never heard him say it before. But there wasn't any sadness in that statement, just a kind of burning pride that glowed deeply inside him, even after all these years.

"So," he said, tilting his head to one side. "I'll ask you again. What's holding you back?"

Peter still didn't have an answer, so his dad nodded. "Go get him!"

Peter released the ladder, pushed one of the canoes out on to the cracking water and made the journey to the boathouse.

He couldn't get there quick enough. Most of the way,

the nose of the canoe ploughed right through the thin crust of ice, fracturing it into dozens of tiny pieces. But the going was tough. More than once, Peter had to straddle the width of the canoe to plunge the blade of the paddle through the surface to crack it. Eventually though, he could hear Snowball whinnying across the water and the canoe slipped through the mouth of the boathouse.

Peter clambered out on to the deck, careful to duck beneath the hooks and machetes, and was making his way toward the back door when he stopped.

Cooper looked up from the bench where he was seated. He was somehow so small hiding there in among all the fur pelts that Peter almost didn't notice him at first. Cooper lifted his hand from his lap as if to say *hi*, but he didn't actually say the word. His other hand was chained to the wall.

"Pete."

Peter stared at the handcuff.

"Peter."

He didn't take his eyes off it.

"Peter, listen to me."

"No."

"Peter."

"I said no!"

Cooper looked down and his hair tumbled across his face. Peter felt him struggle to say the words he didn't want to hear, then how he said them anyway. How Cooper was ambushed while scouting the woods during the night. How one of the Restless Ones had fallen into the deadfall outside the door, but didn't break through all the branches because the snow was so thick. Finally, how it took a chunk out of his ankle. Only his voice was muffled inside Peter's head like a conversation taking place in another room. And in its place were pictures.

They were trekking out to West Wranglestone together, just the three of them. Just Cooper, Snowball and him so he could take a walk down Mainstreet and know what it was like to be seen out together. Next there was a tree house, only it wasn't the one he lived in with his dad. It was a tree house all of their own. Cooper had more stubble now, a blond beard even. His hair was as shiny as a blade of grass and long, tied down the length of his back. Their bedding was white and as plump as fresh snowfall. They were in each other's arms. Cooper's scent lingered in the air. His fingers played with the silver wedding band he'd placed on Peter's finger.

The whole world had seen that silver band. The whole world was witness to what they had and was glad for it. And Peter didn't even know he'd imagined all the things they were going to do together until the exact same moment he knew not to. It was as if someone had suddenly walked along their little path with a broomstick and quickly swept all their future memories away.

Peter noticed the sound of hooks clanking and water lapping against the boathouse, and slowly became aware of his surroundings again. He didn't know long he'd been standing there. When Cooper's voice finally came back in, Snowball was whinnying and a wild wind tumbled down off the mountains.

"Pete, we gotta move fast. We've gotta think about makin' a move now."

"No!"

"You can't be with me when it happens."

"I'm not leaving you."

"Say it."

Peter shook his head.

"Come on. *Clock it. Kill it*—"

"Don't!"

"You're doin' real good now. Don't make things hard for yourself."

Peter looked up and glared. "No. *You've* made it harder for me. *You* have!"

Cooper winced.

"Why weren't you more careful, Cooper? Why? Why would you tell me we were going to do stuff together if that was never going to be true?"

"Pete."

"I only did what your dad told me to because I wanted you to like me. Why did I even do that? I could've spent my whole life on the islands."

"No."

"I was fine before."

"No. You weren't."

"How could you leave me like this? Why did I even set foot off the lake and let you say all those things if this was what it was going to be like?"

"Because life's gotta happen, Peter."

Peter shook his head.

"Don't be goin' backward. You gotta promise me that."

Peter turned round. He saw the key to the handcuffs now, over by the crates where Cooper had thrown it in case he turned before he was found. He stared at the key. None of this was real if he didn't pick it up. He wouldn't be able to lead Cooper up to the falls if the key stayed exactly where it was. Perhaps it wasn't even there at all and he was about to wake up in bed but for real this time.

Snowball whinnied. The wind cracked the back of the boathouse and Peter cleared his throat.

"And Snowball?"

"He gets depressed if folks don't ride him," said Cooper. "And real fat too."

Peter nodded. But he was numb. He just stood there on

the off chance the key would disappear so nothing more had to happen. Only Cooper's skin was flushed with the fever and time was moving on.

"Pete."

Peter nodded.

"Peter."

Peter picked the key up off the floor, made his way over to Cooper and angled it inside the lock.

"I'll brush his mane if he'll let me."

Cooper nodded. "He'll take real good care of you too, if you let him."

The handcuff fell open and dangled from the metal hoop in the wall. Peter noticed that one of Cooper's bootlaces had come undone so he kneeled down in front of him.

"Don't want you tripping over these," he said, threading the lace through one of the eyelets. "There's a shallow river near the falls and the rocks get real slippy."

"Pa reckons another storm's on its way down from the mountains."

"Well then, all the more reason to be careful."

"He's just out back, sending the flare for the chaperone."

Peter nodded, pulled on both laces to tighten the boot, tied it off and sank back on to his heels. Cooper inclined his boot so it touched Peter's hand.

"I didn't even say it back," Peter whispered.

"Don't need to."

"I didn't tell you I—"

"Hush now."

"But I—"

"It don't matter."

Peter looked down, but Cooper leaned forward to cup the back of Peter's head and gently kissed his forehead.

A few moments passed in silence.

The back door flew open and Bud bundled in.

"It's gettin' wild out there," he said, falling back against the door.

Peter scrambled to his feet, but Bud swiped his hand to dismiss his worries.

"Oh, don't be gettin' all jittery on my account."

"I was just tying Cooper's laces."

Bud's silver moustache twitched. His eyes narrowed beneath the brim of his Stetson. "He tells me you've been a good friend."

Peter looked up. "He did?"

Bud nodded.

"Well, I don't know about that."

"Well, he sure as hell does. And I can't say I ever saw him check out his own appearance in the lake like it mattered before now. Even washed his undershorts and that's gotta be a first for a Donaghue."

Peter smiled. "Bud, I—"

"Nope," said Bud, pulling the brim of his Stetson down to shield his eyes. "Don't be gettin' all misty on me. Just reckon you made my boy happy is all I'm sayin'."

Peter nodded by way of saying thank you. He didn't utter the words, but he could tell Bud heard them all the same. Bud's eyes welled, but he was in no mood for soft sentiments. Bud held Cooper's gaze and Peter saw all the things that had been left undone and unsaid hover in the space between them. But even now they stayed just out of reach. As the wind whistled in through the wooden panels and the machetes started to jangle on their hooks, Bud pulled Cooper in for a quick hug, told him how proud his ma was before she passed, how proud they both were, and sent them on their way.

21

Cooper looked so small inside his dad's spare coat. Bud insisted that he wore his duster for the trek up to the falls to protect him from the sheeting snow. But it was so large, wrapping round Cooper's body twice over with its tail brushing the heel of his boots, that when Peter put his arm round him, the waxed cotton crumpled in his hands. It was as if Cooper was vanishing. And in a way he was.

They leaned into the stinging winds, pushing on higher up through the forest trail, and Peter wiped a strand of wet hair from Cooper's face. Cooper blinked dreamily as if to receive Peter's touch. But it wasn't enough to pull him back from wherever it was he'd started to drift off to. He didn't make eye contact or speak or hug back.

Peter drew his arm tighter round Cooper's waist, ready to cross the sequence of stones across the shallow river, then stopped. The night they'd spent together inside the boathouse felt so long ago now it almost belonged to somebody else's memory. Cooper's eyes roved round the stepping stones, but he didn't really see them. Peter's chest juddered. He didn't know how it was even possible to be with someone and yet be so completely without them.

They made it across the river into the grove of pines leading up to the falls. Cooper had become so small and withdrawn now, with the sweats wracking his body, that Peter was scared to squeeze him any tighter in case his arms crushed clean through thin air, leaving Bud's coat crumpled in the crook of his arm. He gently brought Cooper to the edge of the woods and finally they cleared the trees.

The wind churned the foot of the falls. Spray blasted up and over the rocks, hurtling boulders of pummelling mist into the woods. Peter held his hand up to shield his face and heard the old wooden sign careering back and forth.

"This way!" he cried.

The bench was half buried in snow so Peter dragged his forearm along the length of it, gently lowering Cooper down to take a seat. He turned back to face the falls.

"He'll appear on the rocks. The chaperone. He won't be long now."

Cooper gazed into the rushing water and said nothing. But an hour passed and no one came.

The storm didn't let up. Peter clapped both hands together to get rid of the balls of snow dangling from his woollen gloves and paced the foot of the falls. Cooper was hunched over the bench. His face was red-raw. Peter couldn't tell if it was from the sting of the spray or the fever, but the truth was he'd stopped feeling the cold some time ago.

"My flesh is all on fire, Pete."

Peter turned round and kneeled before Cooper. It was the first time he'd spoken since they left the boathouse. "Tell me what I can do."

"You should go."

"No! I didn't mean that. I meant—"

"I know what yous meant, but you can't be here."

"Don't say that."

"You can't be here when the time comes. I'm real tore up as it is. I ain't having you rememberin' me that way."

"I won't."

"It ain't safe."

"The chaperone must've been held up by the storm."

"*I* ain't safe."

"Don't say that."

"But I ain't."

"I'm not leaving you."

Peter glanced at a coil of rope tied round the base of the signpost.

"Yes," said Cooper, sitting forward. "Use it."

"No."

"You gotta."

"I won't."

"You gotta tie me to the post and leave."

"I said I won't."

Cooper sat forward, cupping Peter's face with both hands, and their noses touched.

"Pete," he said quietly. "My Peter."

Peter's throat tightened. There was his name again, sounding like something it wasn't. It would never sound that way again after this, not in his lifetime. But Cooper's eyes told him it was time to go.

Peter shook his head. "No."

"Let me go."

"But I don't know how."

"Let me go, Pete."

Peter went to stand when the hairs on his forearms prickled. The storm had passed. Snow hung in the air as if suspended by a thread and there was a sudden stillness, as if a window had simply been pulled to. But it was more than that. They were being watched. Peter pressed down on to his knees to stand, and faced the falls. Pillows of mist folded over the rocks and something stepped forward. But it wasn't the chaperone.

A pair of mighty antlers broke through the mist and a

moose entered the clearing. Peter dropped back on to the seat, but Cooper wasn't worried.

"Hey, moose," he said gently so as not to alarm it. "Pete don't need to be scared a you. You only eat twigs, don't ya?"

Peter's heart pounded at the sight of such an impossible creature. The body of a rugged bear was balanced on top of four stilt legs, and yet its head and gentle soul belonged to a horse. And its giant antlers were so strange; it was almost as if the forest had carved driftwood into a crown of praying palms. And yet here they were, on the border of each other's worlds, looking across the divide into another beast's heart and discovering there was beauty in another's strangeness.

"I ain't never been this close before," whispered Cooper.

"Me neither. It doesn't even look real."

"Maybe we're the ones who ain't real."

Cooper gazed up at the beast, his eyes blazing beneath the strands of his golden hair, and smiled. Peter took his hand and the pair of them just sat for a while, sharing a moment in this life, lost in the silent wonder of it all.

22

Cooper died at dusk. Peter had never felt a person's spirit leave them before, but he recognized it at once. One moment Cooper was right there with him. The next his story, his past, along with everything they ever were or ever would be, quietly left his body and, like a snowflake landing on water, he was gone. Peter stared at Cooper's limp hand cradled inside his. He was gone. *They* were gone and all that was left was a readiness inside Peter that had come too late and three little words without a home.

He placed his palm over Cooper's eyes to close them. "I love you. I love you so much."

And there it was. Those words hadn't existed behind his lips before now. Not ever. Not like this. He'd heard other people say them. People didn't stop saying those words in books and poems and songs, but he'd never understood why or how they got there until now. It was because they couldn't stop themselves. Those words weren't even words at all, not really, but a force that had been given a phrase for one simple reason. They were the only way to get everything that was now burning a hole right through Peter, out.

Peter kissed Cooper's forehead. He wished he'd accepted his invitation to First Fall. He wished a great many things. But the snow kept falling and the sun kept setting and time was moving on without them. He gently laid Cooper down on the bench, wound the rope across his body and tied it off round the back of the post. He held back at the foot of the bench and stroked Cooper's arms and legs and hair and face. Peter looked at his Adam's apple, now frozen in place at the centre of his neck. The blond stubble at his jaw. Leaving him alone like this and walking away would be a betrayal. But the change was coming. He should go and he should go now.

Peter pulled away, running back into the woods behind the bench. He crouched down under the cover of the trees. It was getting dark and he should go home. No one would expect him to stick around long enough to see Bud's coat start moving. No one. Besides, Bud would send a search party looking for him if he wasn't back before nightfall. But he wasn't going until he was sure the chaperone had come. Peter leaned against one of the pines and watched snow falling silently over the body. His throat tightened.

"It's OK," he whispered. "I'm still here."

Peter listened to squirrels scampering through the branches overhead. He gazed up and a flash of black fur darted from one bough to another. A branch sprang back, catapulting snow up through the air. Peter walked round the other side of the trunk before it landed on top of him and looked downhill through the grove of pines to where the shallow river ran.

Sunlight still dazzled over the bubbling water like starlight, making the woods glimmer. Peter squinted, leaning back into the tree to take a deep breath. The sun dipped back beneath the forest and the water dulled. Night was coming. He pushed away from the tree. But when he turned back to look at the bench, something was wrong. The rope was in a heap on the ground next to it. Cooper's body was gone.

23

Peter ran up to the foot of the falls, scanning the rocks for Cooper and the chaperone.

"Hello?" he cried. "But I'm still here. I haven't said goodbye yet."

He squeezed in between the rocks. He'd only had his back turned for a minute or two. The chaperone couldn't have taken Cooper already.

"Hello, sir?" he offered. "Hello?"

No one answered.

Peter looked down at the ground. There wasn't a set of footprints leading away from the falls. There'd be fresh ones if the chaperone had come. He ran back to the bench, scanning his own prints in order to disregard them. He saw the moose prints. But there was something else, a trail in the snow leading round the back of the bench and into the woods.

He ignored it for a moment because it looked more like

a bag being dragged through the snow than footprints. Then he realized why. Peter crouched down and saw the boot's toecap had left a continuous mark as the foot scuffed forward, but how there was no clear heel mark because the foot had never left the ground. He stood and faced the trees. His fingers patted the wolfskin pocket for his knife. He was about to draw it out when he stopped.

A veil of snow fell across the forest, all blue in the night. Further back, a strange green light travelled over the river and started to make its way toward him. It moved across the forest floor, turning the snow luminous green as it came. But it barely lasted a moment. The green light drew up inside the trees and, like breath striking the cold night air, pulsed and was gone.

Peter drew the head of his wolfskin back over his shoulders and gazed up. Ribbons of green light moved across the night sky as if by some strange calling. Few things were quieter than the silence of snow, but the aurora borealis was one of them.

The branches were free from prowling bobcats. The wolves were elsewhere. But Peter wasn't alone. He looked down through the trees and, like a ghost in the night, Cooper's eyes met his.

"Pete," he said, holding out his pale palms. "Why am I still here?"

24

Cooper was the same but not the same. He was so much paler than before that his skin was almost luminous inside the snow's night glow. The whites of his eyes, now darker, appeared to be all pupil. The darkness behind the wet surface glint was boundless. But there was another wildness. Over the years, some of the Lake Landers had headed up into the mountains in the winter months rather than take their chances on the frozen lake, only to return different people. Loneliness was the killer nobody much talked about. The person who went up wasn't always the one who came back down and Cooper's strangeness carried the weight of such a haunting. Only he shouldn't even be here at all.

Peter took a step backward, more out of instinct than anything, then felt guilty at once that he'd done so.

"Cooper?"

Cooper offered a smile as if his face had never tried

one before. Then his attention turned inwards. He patted his face. He held out his pale hands and turned them over, curling and flexing each fingertip in turn, terrified by the strangeness of finding himself back inside his body again. Peter watched his chest heave rapidly and as tears welled in the bottom of those two dark pools, his own throat constricted.

Cooper looked up. "Am I dead?"

Peter's lips parted, but the words didn't come out.

"Am I?"

"I don't think so."

"Am I?"

"No. You're here."

"How?"

"You came back."

"But how am I here?"

"I don't know, Cooper. I don't know."

"It's like I'm wearin' gloves. I don't feel nothin'."

"It's OK."

"I woke up back inside my body, but I don't feel nothin' at all."

"It's OK. You're just cold."

"I don't feel cold."

"You're probably just cold."

"I don't feel that."

"But you look it."

Cooper winced. "Do I? Why, how do I look? Tell me."

Peter's throat tightened again and he took a step closer.

"Don't," said Cooper, holding out both hands. "Don't come close."

"I want to."

"But don't!"

"I want to know you're real," said Peter. "I want to touch you."

"Do I look cold? Do I?"

Peter glanced at Cooper's pale fingers, almost indistinguishable from the snow.

"No," he said. Then, "Yes. Kind of."

"Kinda? But not just that?"

"Yes, you look cold."

"But somethin' else too."

"It's OK," said Peter.

"Then what?"

"Don't."

"Then what else do I look like?"

"Don't, Cooper."

"Tell me!"

"You look like a ghost."

Cooper turned away. His dark eyes flitted to the trees, to the bark, to the snow and the mist coming from the falls. He stared down at his hands. He turned those pale hands over and over. But finally his gaze found Peter's. And, as their story hovered in the space between them once more, Cooper's eyes lowered just a little and searched the surface of Peter's lips.

"Pete," he said. "My Peter."

Peter's heart leaped. "I'm here," he said, rushing forward. "And you're here too. But are you sure you were bitten?"

Cooper tucked his hair back over his ears, then stuck his leg out to show Peter the indentation the bite mark had made in his cowboy boot.

"Bit me clean on the ankle."

Peter turned the boot over in his hand, running his fingertips along the length of the bite mark. But it hadn't even punctured the leather.

"Are you sure you were bitten?" he said again.

Cooper didn't answer so Peter repeated the question.

"Cooper?"

"Yeah, I'm sure. I'm real sure."

"Anywhere else then? Any other injuries?"

"Dunno."

"Think."

"No. Well, just where the brother and sister in the cabin struck me."

"Show me."

"It don't matter."

"Cooper, show me."

Cooper shrugged off his dad's duster coat and yanked his shirt up over his head to expose the shoulder blades. Peter ran his fingers over the base of Cooper's neck. But it wasn't a bruise.

"There are teeth marks," said Peter. "That's where you were bitten."

"But that don't make no sense."

Saliva shivered across the walls of Peter's mouth.

"The man hung back in the doorway out of the light," he said. "They kept the cabin dark so we couldn't really see them properly. They were terrified of us being there."

Cooper gazed at Peter's hands. Then he looked down at his own pale fingers and quietly withdrew them.

"Ghosts don't come out at night to scare folks, Pete. They wait until it's dark enough to hide so they *don't* scare no one."

"There were scared of being found."

"Yeah. They kept the cabin cold so the smoke didn't give 'em up. They was as scared of bein' seen as I am by you right now."

Peter leaned forward. "Don't say that."

"But it's true. The brother and sister had come back from death too. But not like corpses. Like a curse."

"Cooper."

"I'm scared."

"I know."

"I'm real scared."

"Me too."

"What's wrong?"

"I don't know."

"What's happened to me?"

"I don't know, Coop. I don't know."

"I don't feel the cold."

"Shh."

"I don't feel *you*."

Peter looked at his fingers digging into Cooper's arms.

"I'm only holding you real lightly," he lied. "I'm right here."

"Promise," said Cooper.

"I promise."

Peter glanced back in the direction of the river. They needed help. He should go back to the lake for Bud. No, Dad. He turned back and was about to tell Cooper to go wait for him on the bench when a dark shadow passed beneath the falls.

The silhouette of a bear on its hind legs stepped out from inside the folding mist. The black muzzle of the gas mask angled down toward them and the chaperone raised his paw into a motionless wave.

Peter lurched forward. "Help us!" he called. "Please!"

The chaperone didn't move.

Peter squeezed Cooper's arm once for reassurance. "Stay here."

He ran back through the woods, falling across the boulder at the foot of the falls where the chaperone was standing. Peter gazed up. Beads of icy spray tumbled down the bear's rugged fur. They drizzled round the snout of the gas mask's rubber muzzle. But the chaperone didn't even look down to acknowledge Peter. He cupped his giant paw, beckoning Cooper forward.

"No," said Peter, tugging on the bottom of the pelt. "Please help us. There's been a mistake."

The chaperone's black muzzle tilted down to face Peter. But the gas mask's two bulbous eye discs were blank and unfeeling and a moment later he looked away.

The chaperone straddled the nearest rock, crossing it in a single stride, and started toward Cooper.

"No!" Peter cried. "There's been a terrible mistake. He's come back. He's still here."

He clambered back over the rocks to the bench where Cooper was now standing. But before he could reach him, the chaperone flung out his arm and pushed Peter to one side.

Peter fell back against the rocks. "But he's Cooper," he cried. "He's still Cooper!"

The chaperone stopped with his back to Peter, the great bear's head angled toward his shoulder so that the black muzzle was in profile. But he didn't turn round. He just stood there as if he was waiting for something. Peter stared at the beads of water coursing down the back of the bear's pelt, all the way down the length of the chaperone's arm to his paws. And that's when Peter saw it. The needle. Peter staggered backward. Only now could he feel the stinging sensation in the top of his right arm.

Peter felt woozy. His body lunged, like when you miss a step you didn't know was there, and he dropped to his knees. The chaperone withdrew his gaze, quietly made his way over to the bench and took a plastic object from his pocket. The head of a white chicken with a red crest, sat on a round base marked with numbers. The chaperone wound up the clockwork egg timer and it started ticking. He placed it on top of the bench and turned back to Peter. He pressed a giant bear paw against his chest and pushed him flat against the ground. But Peter only saw this happen. He could barely feel anything.

He watched the chaperone lift up his hand to make sure the injection had taken hold. He saw his own arm flop to the ground from inside the coffin of his own body. He screamed Cooper's name, but no sound came out. Nothing came out at all, just tears down either side of his face. The chaperone cocked his head. The mask's glassy discs were unmoved. He glanced back at the bench where he'd placed the plastic chicken. The timer ticked on, so he stood, stepping over Peter's body, and disappeared from sight.

"Pete!" Cooper cried. "Peter!"

Peter listened to his name crack inside Cooper's voice as he fought to get away. But the struggle didn't last long. His name came once more. It was soft, like someone leaning over you when calling you out of a deep sleep. Then it was gone. Peter felt the cold kiss of snowflakes on his face. Then nothing.

Another sound crept back in. He closed his eyes and listened to the relentless *tick-tock*, *tick-tock*, *tick-tock*. Three minutes later, the egg timer rang.

25

Peter heard the Dead coming before he could see them. The woods crackled down by the river and he heard one of them moving up through the trees toward him. He concentrated on his fingers, willing his hands back into action, but it was as pointless as instructing a rock to move. Another twig broke in a different part of the woods and he realized there were at least two of them.

Peter stared up at the dark night. His eyes darted from one tumbling snowflake to another and the Dead drew closer. Before long, it wasn't just twigs and crackling needles he could hear. The Restless Ones were so close he could hear their footfall.

There were at least three distinct patterns coming up through the woods. One of them lumbered and he heard the familiar motion of a foot thudding down, followed by the sound of the other one being dragged in to join it. Another shuffled through the snow without lifting its feet off the ground at all. But the third was different. Its footsteps were sure. They moved to a regular rhythm of one foot being set down after the other as steady as a beating drum. The egg timer rang on and the footsteps quickened. Only they didn't build into a run. They broke through the forest with all the confidence of a hunter that knew its kill was certain. But Peter didn't have time to consider just how many more of them were on their way.

One of the Dead broke from the trees. Peter closed his eyes and the stench of rotting flesh wormed its way up his nose. He gagged. He drew the cold night air in through his nostrils and inhaled it deeper. If he threw up now, at least he'd drown in his own puke before they got to him. But his body wouldn't even give him that release. Peter screamed inside his head. He willed his feet back to life. Willed his hands. Nothing.

A foot thudded. He waited and the Restless One scraped the other leg in to join it. It repeated the action and stopped just behind Peter's head, out of sight. Peter clenched his eyelids as if they were a hiding place and no one would find him if only he was quiet enough. But he was as exposed as a carcass beneath a sky of vultures.

The egg timer rang on. He waited for the foot to land, for bony fingers to claw at his skin, followed by the sound of his own guts being ripped out until his belly was as hollow as a Halloween pumpkin. But it didn't come.

The egg timer stopped ringing. For a moment, Peter thought that it must have just wound down of its own accord – it'd been going long enough. Then he heard the plastic object being set back down on the bench. Peter opened his eyes and a strange silence hung inside the rush of the falls.

Peter blinked to shift the snowflakes from his lashes and listened to the Restless One shuffle its feet. It was standing directly behind him now. Only it didn't attack. It just stayed right where it was.

Snowflakes fell across Peter's face and he felt their coldness. He parted his lips and let them gather on his tongue. He swallowed and their icy sting coiled down into his chest. Then his toes twitched back to life. But any relief he felt that he could make a run for it was short-lived. His torso and legs were heavy, like a boulder had been placed there. He gingerly lifted up his head, just enough so he could see down the length of his body, and froze. One of them was right on top of him.

A hooded figure straddled Peter's body, hunched over him in the darkness. But when the Restless One's pale fingers fumbled to unpick the toggles of his wolfskin coat, it succeeded. Peter dropped his head back on the ground and closed his eyes. Its limbs were completely coordinated.

The dead thing's knuckles clicked and clacked. Both sides of the wolfskin parted, falling across Peter's hands, and he knew now he could reach inside the pocket for the knife without being seen. He unpeeled his fingers from the frozen ground, then stopped.

The Restless One patted Peter down. But it wasn't looking for a concealed weapon. It wiped its hands down the length of Peter's legs and arms in turn as if it was smearing something across him. It repeated the action down either side of his face before finally swiping his forehead with the flat of its thumb.

"Aw," said the Restless One, "the little one's hurtin', but his body's still warm like a winter sun. He'll be just fine."

The southern drawl lingered in the air. It sang a song of whisky and long nights spent on hot porches and, when it spoke the word *warm*, it lingered on its lips like a long-lost memory. The One Who Talked fanned its fingers across Peter's stomach as if to catch the last of the dying fire, and the one behind Peter shuffled forward.

"S'OK, Bear," said the One Who Talked, even though nobody else had spoken. "I *am* bein' careful."

There was a crackle in the woods.

"Hush your noise now," he went on. "No, it ain't one of their traps and no, nobody's hiding behind the falls ready to ambush us."

Peter parted his lips to let his breath escape and listened to the One Who Talked mutter away to himself.

"Y'all stay back now, you hear me?" he went on. "He's not for you. Now, he's gonna be as scared as a newborn foal without his mama when he gets his movement back. He'll be buckin' about all over the place, his world has just changed so much, but he'll be all right."

Peter scrunched his fingers into a fist and pictured the knife inside his hand. He slid his arm beneath the cover of the wolfskin and was fumbling for the pocket when the One Who Talked's weight suddenly dropped down on top of him.

"Now, now, little one," he said, reaching inside the pocket for the knife before Peter could. "You gotta promise me you'll play nicely."

The One Who Talked tossed the knife across the snow.

"Y'all stop jabberin' at me, you hear?" he said to himself again. "I'm fine. He won't be able to reach that."

Peter's heart beat wildly.

The One Who Talked pinned his wrist to the ground. "Easy now," he said. "Easy does it. You calm your britches and I reckon you and me can have ourselves a little talk."

Peter took a deep breath and tried to steady his breathing. The grip loosened and the One Who Talked lurched forward.

"Boo!"

Peter flinched. There was a beardy mouth hiding inside the shadow of the hood, all cracked and full of tombstone teeth. His dark eyes were mad and raving.

"Didn't know the truth about the Dead, did ya?" said the One Who Talked. "Didn't know about the ones who come back to life with their heartbeat and souls still in place, I bet. Did ya? Did ya?"

Peter shook his head. "No. No. I didn't."

"Nope?"

"No, sir."

"No, SIR," said the One Who Talked, finding this amusing somehow. "No, siree."

"No, I didn't know that before."

"And why would ya? Too busy poppin' them off one by one to notice I bet."

"I, uh—"

"All look the same after a while, do we?"

Peter shook his head.

The stranger leaned closer. "So what *did* you know before?"

"I don't know."

"Sure you do."

"I said I don't know."

"Try again."

"I don't know. I knew what we were told."

The stranger cocked his head to one side like an

inquisitive dog. "And what *were* you told?"

"I—"

"Tell me."

"I—"

"Tell me now!"

"I knew that you were all monsters."

The word monster broke across the space between them. The stranger blinked deeply as if to absorb the horror of the word deep inside his bones. The madness left his eyes as if it'd only been a game and a seriousness entered his face. But his eyes didn't leave Peter's.

"And so, in turn," he said, tightening his grip, "that's what we become."

There was a face beneath the darkness of the hood, not a skull, or a half-sunken thing, but the pale face of a man. His brown beard was as thick as a grizzly's coat and as long as winter too. Two braids tied off with beads dangled down either side of his face. A necklace fell away from the hooded poncho he was wearing and sent its pendant spinning. Peter gazed at the silver snowflake and looked back up.

The stranger's eyes carried the imprint of death. Like Cooper, the whites were dark so they appeared to be all pupil. But everything he ever was, thought, loved or hated still swam inside those deep wells. Returning from death hadn't robbed him of his body, his heartbeat or his soul any more than it had Cooper. But he'd spent more time being this way. Time to adjust, time alone and time enough to learn to fear everybody else.

Peter closed his eyes. He had to find Cooper before the chaperone could hurt him. And, as he lost himself in that impossible thought, something shifted in the stranger's eyes, as if he saw the vast journey Peter had just taken inside his own mind, and he released his grip.

"I don't think you're a monster," whispered Peter.

The stranger's dark eyes narrowed. "Real kind of you to say so. But what about the others just like me?"

"What others? I didn't know about any of you until now."

"It must comfort you bein' able to pretend that's true."

Peter pushed against the stranger's grip. "What's that supposed to mean?"

"What about the old man in the canoe who was simply tryin' to protect his wife?" he said. "Was *he* a monster?"

Peter's eyes widened. "You saw?"

The stranger ran the tip of his tongue along his tombstone teeth and said nothing.

"No," said Peter. "Not that that kind of monster anyways. But his wife was."

"And you know that for a fact, do you?"

"Yes. She had my dad by the foot and was holding him underwater."

"Is that so?"

"Yes. It is."

"Cos sittin' calmly inside canoes, holdin' men underwater by the foot, is real typical of the Dead, ain't it? Don't ya think?"

The stranger sat back a little, scratching his thick beard. He was toying with him.

Peter pushed him back. "Get off me."

"Your daddy has epilepsy, don't he?"

Blood flushed the surface of Peter's skin. "What did you say?"

"Well, does he or don't he?"

Peter felt the stranger's dark eyes burn into his. The moment lingered longer than was comfortable, but when he didn't reply the stranger took his silence as a yes.

"I saw your dad fit and fall overboard as limp as a stunned fish," he said. "I saw the woman do her best to hold him up from drownin'. That's what I saw. But *you* tell me what you saw from your unconscious state, little one. Please, be my guest."

Tears welled in Peter's eyes.

"Tell me what you saw," said the stranger.

Peter looked away and said nothing.

"Tell me!"

"I saw one of the Dead drowning my dad."

"Even though you know that makes no sense."

"Get off me."

"Even though you know that makes no goddamn sense!"

"I said, get off me."

"And nothin' made you ask one single question, nothin' at all? Nothin' made you put one little piece together with another and start thinkin'?"

Peter stared at the silver snowflake dangling from the stranger's neck and pictured the brother and sister's cabin exploding. "No."

But the truth was he had noticed. He just hadn't pieced any of it together. Not until now. Not until Cooper.

"No," he said under his breath. Then, "I don't know."

Snow fell over the stranger. He ran his hand down the length of his beard as if to decide what to do with Peter next. But it seemed he was done. He pulled Peter's sweater down over his stomach and retreated back inside the darkness.

"Welcome to the other side, little one."

Peter rolled on to his side, gasping and coughing, when a figure shuffled out from behind him. Peter scrambled backward and the one the stranger had called Bear lumbered off into the woods. It was as bald as a boulder and its arms could crush logs. Drool poured from its parted lips down to its stained white vest. Its milky pupils roved. It was just one of the Dead, but somehow the stranger's presence restrained it from attacking Peter. Bear wandered off among the trees and a host of pale faces looked out. But they didn't advance.

"Y'all go along now," said the stranger. "And leave this poor boy in peace."

Peter brought his knees up under his chin and stared at him. He wondered how long a person had to be out here all alone in the woods before they made friends with the Dead. The stranger kept his back to Peter and started to collect bits of wood up off the forest floor while he waited for the Restless Ones to leave them. But he knew he was being watched.

"I know they can't understand me," he said, without turning.

Peter looked away. "It's OK."

"Please don't think me mad. I've been a lone star for so long I find it helps."

Peter clambered to his feet and stared at the egg timer. "Why didn't the Dead attack me?"

"Because I cloaked you in my scent."

"Why?"

The stranger shrugged. "My scent is their scent. I carry the same imprint of death they do. They can smell it in my bones. They don't want my flesh. Others do, mind. Others want us good n'dead, or worse than dead. But that's quite another matter."

"No. I meant why didn't you let them attack me."

"Because I didn't see you try to hide any disgust when you looked upon my skin. Because you haven't reached for your knife since I let you go."

Peter glanced at the knife in the snow and wrapped his arms round his body. "What's happening?"

The stranger dropped a pile of kindling beside the bench and lit a fire. Flames licked the cold night air, making the woods swim in the darkness. Shadows shifted and the pale faces meandered back off into the woods. After a while, the stranger sat cross-legged behind the fire and slowly withdrew the hood of his poncho. The wet glint on the surface of his dark eyes glimmered in the firelight, but there was so much sadness there that all the pain he held in his heart seemed to burn inside them.

"We're the Pale Ones the world never got to know about," he said as if somewhere far away. "In the early days, before the world went dark, our TV sets were full of public service announcements tellin' folks to kill the afflicted on sight. The internet was overrun with them. But that wasn't just to protect you from the monsters – it was to protect you from learnin' somethin' else, the thing folks in high places didn't want you to know. That not all of the Pale Ones became a walking nightmare.

"Some of us make it back, little one," he went on. "No one knows what caused half the population to close their eyes forever, only to get back up on to their feet to rip a hole right through this world. Some folks talked of a plague on our bodies; others whispered of a plague on our souls; but somehow some of those bitten by the Dead are returned to this world bearin' a resemblance to them, but not their darkness. Our hearts still beat like yours. We still dream and think and love just like you, but apparently that's to no avail. Because what good is a soul when it's trapped inside a shell the world knows only as a monster?"

Peter made his way over to the fire. "But why would anyone think that?"

The stranger creased the corner of his mouth into a kind of weary half-smile that made Peter feel he knew nothing of the world and started to stoke the fire with a stick.

"Because the same thing that made monsters of the Dead passed through us too," he said quietly. "What if the monster came out of us in time? What if we were just as bad as the rest of them? No, the world is at war with the Pale Ones and we're pale too. And no war is fought more fiercely than one fought without any doubts about who the enemy is. What if people did learn that some of us don't turn into monsters? Could a boy your age really go out there and take up the fight so freely if you weren't confident of who your enemy was?"

Peter looked away. "I don't know."

The stranger sighed. "And that kind of doubt is no use in a war, none whatsoever. So they took all that doubt away for you."

"They?" said Peter. "The government?"

"At first, yes."

"At first? Then who?"

The stranger didn't answer.

Peter sat down in front of the fire, drawing his knees up under his chin and stared into the flames. "We've been handing people over for execution."

"Yes," said the stranger. "In some cases."

"I only led Mr Schmidt here the other day. He might've been OK. He might've come back like you if we knew to wait and find out."

"Maybe. It's possible, yes."

But it was more than possible. What wasn't possible was for one of the Dead to make its way across the water, climb up the rope ladder and let itself in through the tree-house door. No, Mr Schmidt had returned just like Cooper had. Only he'd somehow managed to escape from the chaperone and come running back to the lake, looking for help. Peter's chest juddered. Vomit surged its way up through his guts, but he swallowed it back down before the stranger could notice and quickly dug his fist inside the snow. His fingers burned. They burned until they were numb.

"You awl right, lil one?" asked the stranger after a while.

"The one in the bearskin doesn't care," said Peter.

"No."

"He just takes them away."

"To keep you safe."

"But—"

"To keep you certain."

"But the lake would never have agreed to it."

"Don't be so sure. Nothin' keeps a monster alive in people's hearts more than their ability to see only that which is different."

"No," said Peter. "Not this. Surely if everyone knew the truth then things would never have gone this far."

"But people don't know the truth, do they? That information never got out."

"But why not?"

The stranger withdrew eye contact. He looked into the flames, his face all heavy with things left unspoken.

"Tell *me*!" said Peter. "Why didn't that information get out there?"

The stranger's eyes narrowed, but Peter didn't wait for an answer.

"I have to go," he said, scrambling to his feet. "I've wasted too much time already. I have to get Cooper back. I need him."

The stranger looked up from the flames. "Need?"

The word lingered on his lips as if memory of such a thing was somehow just out of reach.

"Yes," said Peter.

"Even if his skin is as pale as stone."

Peter's throat tightened. "You watched us leaving the boathouse? You saw—"

"Even if others will end up despisin' you for it?"

"Yes."

"No! You must be careful."

The stranger stood. His poncho billowed in the wind and he crossed the distance between them.

"You must be careful of strayin' down a path there's no way back from. Walkin' with the Pale Ones will place a bounty on your head that you'll never shake off."

"I don't care."

"But you should. You'll be an outcast."

"I need to be with him. I need to get to him before the Bearskin kills him."

The stranger stepped closer. Peter flinched, but the stranger fanned his fingers, placing his hand gently down upon Peter's chest.

"Your heart's beatin' like wild horses across sand," he said. "Why, it beats for the both of you."

Water pooled in Peter's eyes. He hadn't said *I love you*. Those three little words never left his lips. But the stranger's eyes twinkled deeply in the firelight.

"Why, you love him."

"Yes."

"And you still love him?"

"Yes. Of course."

The stranger's dark eyes marvelled as if the memory of those feelings was enough to save himself. He held out his own hand and swivelled a golden wedding band round his bony finger. He'd lost so much weight it was only being kept on by his knuckle.

"Then your boy and I are both as lucky as each other to have someone still. *She's* out there too."

"What's her name?"

"Josie. Or Josephine Thomasina Rider if we were havin' a fight on the porch, as was often the way when whisky was involved and the heat was madder than a frog in a sock."

Peter smiled. "Where is she?"

"Oh, across the mountains at Yellowstone. It's the nearest refuge. Me and the others were gonna inform all our loved ones we'd been relocated here when we were separated from them, but then, well, we never got the chance."

Peter narrowed his eyes. "Relocated here?"

"Yes."

"You mean Wranglestone?"

The stranger nodded.

"But *we're* here."

"You shouldn't be."

Peter flinched. "Why would you say that?" Then, "Why was the old man in the canoe angry I wasn't wearing a snowflake like yours?"

The stranger closed his fist round the silver snowflake pendant and said nothing.

"Why? And what others?"

The stranger reached under the neck of his poncho, twanging his braces back over his shoulder, and smiled even though his eyes didn't seem to have the heart to muster one. Peter watched him wrestle with all the pain he had churned up inside him and offered his hand.

"I'm Peter," he said. "Peter Nordstrum."

The stranger stared at Peter's hand and smiled as if he found the sound of his full name pleasing to his ears somehow.

"And you're a surprising prospect, Peter Nordstrum."

"Who, me?"

"Like a desert flower. Rare and most welcome."

"No. Not me."

"And I was right to watch you."

Peter's eyes widened. "You're the one I could hear talking to yourself when I was hiding in the tunnel that day. I couldn't understand why the Dead left us alone. But you did that. You led them away."

The stranger nodded.

"And you wrote the message in the snow yesterday to warn me."

"I did."

"Why were you helping me?"

"Because you can help *us*."

"But why me?"

"Because you mean no harm."

Peter's throat tightened. The stranger's big beardy face held his gaze. No one had ever said that about him like it was a strength before. Peter glanced at the silver snowflake dangling over the top of the poncho and the stranger braced his hand on Peter's shoulder.

"I'm Jonathan T. Rider," he said. "And I know where the Bearskin takes them."

Peter looked up. "Where?"

"We must go before it's too late, Peter!"

Peter swung round and faced the falls. He was crushed with a thousand questions now. "Where? Tell me. I have to find him."

"Listen," said Rider. "You miss him and it hurts like a damned twister has been let loose inside you, but you must listen to what I have to tell you about this place and you must listen carefully. You hold the key to changin' all this, but actin' rashly is not the way to save him."

"OK," said Peter, pulling away. Then, "No. I have to tell the others what's happened. Stay here. I'll bring help."

"No! Wait."

But Peter couldn't hold back any longer. He ran back among the trees toward the river and made for the lake.

26

The boathouse creaked quietly. Snowball looked up from the bale of dried grass he was chomping on and whinnied. Peter stomped excess snow from his boots and gently pulled the door to. He half expected someone to be waiting for him, his dad, Darlene even. But most of the coat hooks were empty and the gas lamp by the back door had been lit so perhaps a search party was out in the woods looking for him.

Peter pulled the hood of his wolfskin back over his shoulders and stared at the handcuffs hanging from the metal hoop above the bench. He wished he'd accepted Cooper's invitation to First Fall again. He wished it over and over as if the act of saying yes would have stopped all this from happening somehow.

He looked out toward the water. Someone would be on watch on the Sky Deck. Peter made his way over to the canoes, then stopped. A piece of paper was skewered to one of the old fishing hooks. Peter reached up and yanked down the note. His dad and Bud were in the woods looking for him. They told him to stay where he was to make sure they didn't miss each other. Peter scrunched up the piece of paper and tossed it across the boathouse. He didn't have time to wait around for them. He had to get back up there and start looking for Cooper before it was too late.

"Come on," he said, kicking the wall with the heel of his boot. "Hurry."

It was no use. He'd have to leave them a note saying he was out by the falls and hope they'd find him there. The paper ball was lying in a puddle of water beneath one of the old wooden packing crates. Peter glanced up at the ceiling to see if there was a leak in the roof but the dripping was coming from the crate itself. The lid wasn't flush because something was caught in it. Peter tried to stuff the material back in, squeezing excess water dripping from the rugged fur through his fists. The pelt was thick. It was greasy too. He ground his thumb and forefinger together and the oil slipped across his skin. But there was more than grease. There was blood.

Peter stood up and stared at the padlock. He had no idea where the key might be kept. He clocked one of the machetes, reached up on tiptoe to unhook it and before he'd made the decision to, stood over the crate. He brought the machete up over his shoulders, his heels left the floor and he swung the blade down.

The padlock clunked to the floor and Peter flipped the lid.

The gas mask wasn't even hidden. Its two bulbous eye discs stared back at him, as cold and unmoved by his discovery as they were by his plight earlier. Peter's chest juddered. The machete slipped through his fingers and clanked across the floor, causing Snowball to whinny. But the horse's distress was faint, not part of Peter's cares somehow. Much louder were the voices.

"Peter?"

Peter swung round. The voices approached the door and the footsteps grew louder. He hung the machete back up on the hook and heard Bud's voice at the door. But he wasn't alone – his dad was with him. Peter's throat tightened. He desperately wanted to let Dad know he was here, that he was safe, that his Pete was OK. Only he wasn't. Nobody was.

The latch to the boathouse door flipped and Peter dropped behind the crate to hide.

There was no military chaperone. There was no one else here at all. They were all alone on the lake and now so was he.

27

Bud strode through the door in a flurry of snow. He dashed the oil lamp with his fist, making the shadows of all the machetes and scythes seesaw round the walls.

"Dang it," he said, tossing his rifle on to the bench.

Peter drew back behind the crate, drawing his legs up under his chin.

"Go home, Bud," said Peter's dad, entering the boathouse behind him. "You've been through enough as it is already. You go home and get some rest. I need to get back out there."

Dolly's paws pattered across the floorboards. Peter scrunched himself up into a ball as if that would somehow make his scent disappear. But he needn't have worried. She trundled off toward the water, her sense for dinnertime keener than her sense of smell nowadays. Bud jumped into one of the canoes and a moment later the paddle struck the water.

"Come on, ol' girl," he mumbled. "It's just you and me now."

The boathouse went quiet, but Peter could hear his dad. His boots scuffed across the floorboards and he took a seat. Every minute that passed presented another opportunity for Peter to stand up and see the same face looking back at him that he'd always seen. But he had no idea who or how many of them wore the gas mask.

A moment later, he heard his dad stand up again.

"Pete?"

Peter froze. His listened to his dad pick the paper ball up off the floor and scrunch it in his fist.

"Pete?"

Peter held his breath. But his name wasn't called again. The door swung open and his dad took a running jump over the deadfall.

Peter gave it a few minutes, then scrambled to his feet. He ran back into the forest as fast as he could, taking the trail uphill through the pines toward the shallow river. He never looked back, and soon the sound of the falls came thundering through the forest, and cleared the trees just short of where Rider was standing.

Mist churned over the black rocks. Peter approached the waterfall and stopped, gazing up at the vast wall of water.

"It's behind the falls," he said darkly. "That's where we've been taking them, isn't it?"

Rider circled the fire.

His poncho billowed in the wind and fell still.

"Yes," he said without looking up. "But you won't like what else you'll find there."

"Will he be dead already?"

"Worse things can await the Pale Ones than death, little one."

Peter turned back. "What does that mean?"

"You'll find him at the Trading Post."

"Where?"

"Cooper's young. He's useful. The Trading Post is where the Bearskin will have taken him."

"What's the Trading Post?"

But Rider started to kick snow and dirt into the fire to smother it and Peter felt his invitation to go on.

Mist pummelled the moss-hewn boulders with beads of icy water. Peter yanked the snout of his wolfskin down over his eyes to shield his face and squeezed through, but the stinging water ravaged his lips and cheeks until his whole face was burning. He reached higher, running his fingertips along the ledge at the foot of the falls to get a purchase on the slippery rock and hoisted himself up.

Peter rolled on to his back. The force of the mountains

thundered right through him. So did the loneliness of facing such a task alone. But there was a voice.

"Go awn, little one!" called Rider from inside the booming waters. "I'll be right behind you."

Peter clambered to his feet and smiled. Perhaps he wasn't alone after all. He turned to face the great veil, drawing his fingertips together so they were as pointed as an arrowhead, and sliced his hand through the lashing water.

28

The cave was only dark for a moment. Peter barely had time to register just how smooth and even the rock was underfoot. Light spluttered and an old mining lamp illuminated the cavern wall beside him. A bat dropped from its hanging place. Its wings licked the air and it bolted back into the blackness beyond. But it wasn't in the dark for long. Further back, another lamp pulsed into action, followed by another, until a sequence of lights chased the bat all the way back into the distance, and Peter was left staring down the length of a long, narrow tunnel.

The lamps were activated by movement. The flat tunnel was man-made. It was as if an apple corer had been driven right through the black rock and drawn back out again in one swift move. Metal handrails had been fixed down either side. Peter shook the excess water from his wolfskin and moved away from the falls. Blood spotted the ground. Some of it was fresh, but not all. Peter looked up and the cold braced his shoulders. But it was more than just the icy falls behind him. There was a breeze on his face. There was a way through.

Peter carried on down the tunnel. Every now and then the string of lamps spluttered and he gripped the handrail while the tunnel went dark. But he kept moving and before too long the sound of the falls faded to a whisper behind him and he could see snow tumbling past the exit at the other end like a silent waterfall. He leaned into the handrail and held back at the lip of the cave.

The woods were silent. The piney boughs drooped wearily beneath the weight of the snow, their needles scratching the white pillows around each trunk, the snowfall was so deep. And it was blue. Moonshine on the forest floor cast long shadows, transforming night into eerie day. It was still, like the whole world had been buried inside winter's sleep. But there were signs of activity. Tiny potholes dotted a trail through the trees. A deer's tracks perhaps. And there was more. A trench of deep footprints led away from the tunnel all the way through the woods to a clearing.

Inside the ring of trees stood two branchless trunks. The canopies had been lopped off, the rough bark stripped down, turning them into posts. Tied up to each of them by thick coils of rope, with their back to Peter, was a naked body. Peter scanned the surrounding trees. There was no sign of movement, so he took his chances.

He stepped down out of the tunnel, ducking behind the nearest pine, and peered round. The body tied to the post on the left had slumped forward. Beneath it, a trail of black blood stained the snow all the way to the edge of the clearing. At the end of the trail was the head. Peter sank to his knees and Mrs Carmichael's frozen scream stared back at her own body from its grave amid the snow. He turned away. But unlike Cooper and Rider's dark eyes, Mrs Carmichael's were wide and milky. She had not returned.

"Sorry," Peter whispered, feeling some relief that any further pain had been spared her.

He leaned out further. The other body was still holding up its own weight. Its face was concealed behind tendrils of matted blond hair. Then Cooper moved.

Peter's body made the decision to run to Cooper before his mind had even caught up. He was stumbling away from the tree, when a hand clamped down over his mouth and yanked him backward.

Rider put his forefinger to his lips. His eyes said no. Peter wrestled to free himself, screaming into the fist still cupped over his mouth. Still Rider held his gaze. Peter relented and after a moment or two his breathing steadied.

Rider's eyes darted to the woods, and Peter heard someone coming. He peered round the trunk of the tree and hooves plunged inside the pillowing snow. A plume of hot breath broke from a black horse's muzzle and a lone rider emerged from the woods.

The traveller kept his Stetson pulled down low over his eyes to conceal himself. A red bandana covered his mouth. But he didn't scan the woods in fear of ambush and surprise at finding the posts didn't enter his body once. He'd been here before. The horse stepped into the clearing and the traveller weighed up the prospect Cooper's arrival presented to him.

"Boy," he said in a dull voice, younger than Peter had expected.

Cooper didn't respond.

"Look at me, boy."

The traveller rested the horse's reins over the saddle horn and placed his hand across his holster. "You can sulk or scream for ya mama all you want and wind up a flowerless stem like that ol' sow next to you, or you can do as I ask. And I am askin' you kindly."

Cooper didn't react so the traveller angled his head to one side as if he was searching for a way in. "Cooper, ain't it?"

Cooper clenched his hands behind the post.

"Least that's what it says on the sign around your

neck. Now, you're young and you look like the real athletic type. I have no doubt you'll be able to walk right on in to one of them towns crawlin' with deadbeats and bring medicines and liquor safely outta there for me. If you play your cards real nice, I'll clothe you and bathe you. I mean, I can see you've soiled yourself already. I'll give you a nice home in the outhouse round the back of my cabin, and you and me won't have a cross word.

"But then again," said the traveller, leaning on the saddle horn, "we might. Lucy, get down! There's a good girl."

Peter squinted. The bundle of rags slung over the back of the horse suddenly moved into action and a young woman with long red hair slipped to the ground. Her skin was as pale as Cooper's. Like Rider's, her dark eyes carried the journey to death and back inside them like a haunting. But she was wearing a clean white smock dress, and her cheeks and lips had been rouged red to colour them like a child playing with her mother's make-up box. The woman shuffled round the side of the horse and stood in between Cooper and the traveller. Her gaze never left the ground once.

"Now, show this nice young man how difficult it can be for your kind if you don't play nicely," said the traveller.

Cooper peered through the tendrils of his hair. The woman did as she was told and slipped the dress from her shoulders to reveal the blistering whip marks across her back. Peter held on to the tree. Rider breathed deeply beside him.

"Now," said the traveller, "I'll let her go. I don't need both a you. All you have to do is let her untie you, get yourself up on to the saddle here and we got ourselves a deal."

The traveller untied a parcel from the side of the saddle and held it up.

"What's that?" whispered Peter, leaning in to Rider.

"The trade with the Bearskin. Medicines for the lake, provisions and the like."

The traveller swung the parcel round to prove he had the trade in case he was being watched, then tossed it to the ground. Peter stared at the parcel in the snow. When he looked back up again, tears were falling across the young woman's rouged cheeks.

"Untie me, miss," Cooper said quietly.

The young woman shook her head. "No."

"S'all right."

"No, don't. Please."

"Everythin's gonna be OK," said Cooper calmly. "Just untie me, you hear me? And then you run."

The young woman hesitated. But the traveller wasn't worried. He eased back into the saddle. A moment later, she untied the rope and Cooper stumbled forward on to his knees.

"Any funny business," said the traveller, throwing down a blanket for him, "and the girl's dead."

Cooper did as he was told, threw the blanket over himself and scrambled up on to the back of the horse.

Peter leaned forward, but Rider took him by the arm.

"No," he whispered. "We wait. If the Bearskin is watchin' we'll all be dead."

Peter sank down to the base of the tree. But they'd been overheard.

The young woman's gaze held Rider's. Rider swept his hood from his face and nodded as if to say, *You're gonna be all right*, and a secret understanding passed between them. They'd never met before, but somehow they knew each other at once. They'd both faced death. They both knew what it was like to wake from it too.

The traveller turned his horse away to leave. Peter stood and the young woman's eyes fell on him. She smiled. It was hard to tell if she was happy to see another friendly face or happy to see the pair of them together, united despite the physical changes that marked them as different. But the smile didn't last long.

The traveller turned. Peter barely had time to notice him draw the revolver from his holster before he fired.

The bullet snuck in through the back of the young

woman's skull and broke freely through her forehead. All the pain and the loss and the briefest of smiles left her face at once and her body slumped forward into the snow.

"No!" Peter screamed.

He yanked his arm from Rider's grip and ran into the woods after them. The horse left the clearing and galloped off at speed into the distance. Peter cleared the last of the trees and ran past a burnt-out jeep. He skidded into the middle of what looked like a driveway and ducked behind another torched car where he bent over double, panting wildly as the horse's hooves pounded off down the icy road.

Peter looked up. They were nearly out of sight. But his eye was drawn higher. At the end of the drive was an entrance, like the gateway to an old cattle ranch. Two vast timber posts as grey as driftwood straddled the width of the drive with a beam crossing overhead. A wooden sign with a pair of deer antlers nailed to the top of it, creaked in the wind.

WELCOME TO CAMP WRANGLEST❄NE
SANCTUARY FOR THE RETURNED

29

Peter sank to his knees. The old wooden sign kept creaking above him, but his eyes returned to the horse. It disappeared behind a hill and came up the other side with its head down low, pushing on into the winter wind. It wasn't long before the traveller vanished back into the snow.

Peter felt Rider behind him. "The traveller lives in a cabin several miles east of here on the glacier trail," he said. "I know where all the scourges who do trade with your place hide. We won't lose 'em."

Peter scrambled to his feet and turned round. Rider's hood fell back over his shoulders so the snow flurried on to his braids and started to bank the length of his beard. His dark eyes blinked deeply, holding Peter's gaze. But somehow they looked right through him.

"Winter's tears," he said, wiping a snowflake from his cheek. "Nothing else left crying for us in this world."

"The lake was never meant for us, was it?" said Peter. "The snowflake you're wearing, and the one on the sign. The old man in the canoe was confused that I wasn't wearing one. What was this place?"

"A secret sanctuary for the Returned, to spare us from a world that wouldn't want us. And it was as silent as snow up here in the mountains too, little one. Not a single town or look of disgust for fifty miles in every direction."

Peter walked forward. "What happened?"

"It was a couple of weeks in, when the Dead had only just started swarmin' through whole towns like locusts through a corn crop, and folks were still holed up at home, glued to their TV sets, waitin' for news of a cure or containment that would never come. That's when I came back from the other side still talkin'."

Peter felt a sharp tug in his stomach. In his mind's eye, he saw Cooper's pale face looking back at him from inside the woods.

"What does it feel like?" he said. "Will Cooper be scared?"

Rider brushed the snow off his beard and watched it melt into his palm.

"No," he said. "Not scared. But aware."

"Aware of what?"

"Aware that our bodies are not who we are."

254

"How?"

"That flesh and bone are just the things that transport us through this life, but who we are is somethin' else entirely."

Peter nodded. But he wasn't sure he understood what Rider meant.

"So," Rider went on. "Josie was runnin' down the hospital corridor, screamin' for the doctors to assist us, when the figure sittin' at the other end of the row of chairs turned toward me. A silver snowflake hung from his neck, but it was his eyes I recall most. It wasn't just how dark they were so much as the fact that I was able to look upon them, a stranger's eyes, and at once know him. He'd woken from death too. His dark eyes searched mine and a secret understandin' somehow crossed the space between us. We'd never met, only we knew each other at once. But, more than that, he knew what I did not – that I'd never leave the hospital if I stayed.

"Josie was surrounded by doctors talkin' urgently into their phones. Men were comin'. There would be no time for goodbyes, the stranger told me. I was to travel north into the mountains to the crossroads at Moose Creek where another wearin' that symbol of frozen life, the snowflake, would come for me.

"And so I rode north, here into Wranglestone, where

a small band of my brothers and sisters had made a secret sanctuary for the Returned while folks in higher places tried to work out if us Pale Ones even had rights to such a thing. We ran tests and held talks. In time, we even established radio communication with an ally in the National Park Escape Program over at Yellowstone where our relatives were sent. The ally was gonna tell our loved ones about us, that we were here, that we were safe. We thought if they came here we could show the world it was possible. That we could live side by side in an integrated society. We'd prove that inside that one killer storm was a sea of souls and a people carryin' immunity to the plague and hope of a cure that could end all this. We prepared a statement to the government. But the world would sooner kill what it can't understand than see how much it has to offer. And soon the world found us."

Peter shook his head. "How?"

"I dunno, little one. People listenin' in on the airwaves. The ally over at Yellowstone perhaps."

Rider drew his hood back over his head and looked out into the flurrying snow. "The ally was about to tell Josie and the kids about our whereabouts when *they* came."

"They?" said Peter.

"Activists, if that's what you can call them. They

took Wranglestone down to bury the truth that not all of the Pale Ones were monsters before it became public knowledge. They wanted to keep fear and hate of the enemy simple. Their loathin' and weapons swept through this place like wildfire. Without us, or the question mark we posed, all that was left was black and white, people against the monsters, and the outside world simply destroyed itself. The planet went dark not long after.

"I doubt Josie ever even knew I was out here," Rider went on. "But the activists who decided to stay on at the lake had better reasons for keepin' the truth from the rest of you. They might despise Pale Ones, but they were quick to catch on to our uses. They've been keepin' your community in medicines and firearms by tradin' in your own Returnees for years now."

The old sign creaked in the wind and Peter looked back through the woods toward the tunnel. "Who started this?"

Rider shrugged. "I was out travellin' the backcountry in search of others we could help when they came. I guess I was lucky."

Peter nodded. But perhaps Mr Schmidt had found out who it was the night he came back.

"One of my neighbours tried to warn me," said Peter after a while. "The Bearskin took him after he was bitten, but he got away and snuck into my tree house to warn me. I thought he was one of the Dead. I screamed before he could get close enough. And then my dad…"

Rider closed his eyes. "Yes," he said, turning away and heading back into the woods toward the tunnel. "First the screams, always the thinkin' after."

Peter looked back at the trail the horse had left. Another unwanted thought let itself in. What if Mr Schmidt had crept over to his bed rather than knock because his dad had worn the bearskin? But the thought was unbearable, so Peter buried it deep enough so it wouldn't come back, and ran after Rider.

"Wait!" he called. "Where are you going?"

There was an old lodge house just beyond the entrance to the tunnel. Peter hadn't even noticed it before. It was bigger than the cabins on the lake – as long as the redwood trunks it was constructed from. A stone chimney stack gripped the side. The front door was wide open, but no light spilled out across the porch. It was clear nobody had lived there for quite some time. Snow banked the sides of the lodge, burying the windows. The roof carried a thick crust.

Rider crossed the deck and disappeared inside so Peter quickened his pace to catch him up. But, as he made his approach, it became obvious that the lodge wasn't a private residence at all. Picnic benches surrounded the building. Frosted-up noticeboards ran the length of the porch. Peter made his way up the front steps and passed beneath the wooden sign hanging above the entrance.

Camp Wranglestone Registration Office

He held back at the door, watching his breath break across the darkness within, then quietly made his way inside.

Three fat sofas bursting with plaid cushions framed the stone chimney breast. A coffee table littered with leaflets and a radio stood in the middle. Stuffed animal heads mounted on wooden plaques lined all four walls – elk, deer, grizzly, moose and bobcat. Beneath the moose was a large desk cluttered with picture frames and pens. But there were signs of disturbance.

Files and paperwork were strewn across the floor. A red Christmas-tree bauble dangling from the moose antlers had shattered. Shards of red glass littered the desk below. Peter got closer. It was only then that he saw the scratch marks scored across the width of the desk. Rider leaned over the desk to stand a lamp with a gingham shade upright and reached for the switch.

Peter squinted, startled by the sudden burst of light. "But—"

"Generator," said Rider. "Same as the lamps in the tunnel."

But his attention was elsewhere. Rider made his way over to the coffee table in front of the fireplace, tossed one of the cushions to the floor and kneeled down in front of the old radio.

"Wait," he said, flicking both braids over his shoulders. Then he started to fiddle with one of the dials. Peter took a seat behind the desk and stared into the brilliant light coming from the centre of the bulb. He blinked and a trail of white light flashed behind his eyelids.

"Will I go blind?" he asked.

"It's not the sun, Peter."

Peter leaned back in the chair while Rider played around with the radio to get rid of the sound of static. He noticed that one of the desk drawers was open. Most of the files were strewn all over the floor, but some of them were still alphabetized in carded slings inside. Peter glanced up at Rider, but he was still fiddling with the signal so he bent over and flicked through for the R's. He found the one titled J. T. Rider almost at once. He pulled it out on to his lap and stared at the snowflake symbol printed on the top of the file for a little while. Then he opened it.

Operation: Snowflake
Classification: Returnee Refugee Program
Candidate: Jonathan T. Rider
Nationality: American
Occupation Pre-Z: Barista/Kindergarten assistant
Infected Carrier: Positive
Status: Returnee. Approved for stay
Residence: Camp Wranglestone

Peter smiled to himself. It was hard to imagine who anyone used to be before the world turned upside down. But somehow the person he'd met muttering away to the dead with his beard full of snow wasn't at odds with a class full of five-year-olds at all. Peter was about to ask Rider what the T in his name stood for when the sound of static cleared and he heard a woman's voice.

"Easy," said Rider, turning the dial a little further. "Easy does it."

Peter sat forward and was about to speak, but Rider held his palm up to silence him. The voice became clearer.

"Pale Wanderers. If you're out there, issue a flare and we'll come."

Rider sank down on to his knees, playing absent-mindedly with one of his braids, and smiled at the radio.

"Pale Wanderers. If you're out there, issue a flare and we'll come."

"I come back here from time to time just to listen to her," he said. "It's only an automated message, I know, but I sure do appreciate the kindness in her voice, whoever she is."

"Yes," said Peter. "Of course."

"It must be Yellowstone."

"What makes you so sure?"

"It must be."

"OK," said Peter, nodding. "OK."

"They're the nearest refuge from here and it's on the same frequency they used when we were tryin' to arrange our loved ones' visits. It's like they left the light on for me. The mic on this darned thing is broken. If I could just get to the top of the watchtower to light the flare, they can let Josie and the kids know that I'm here. It's the only place high enough."

Peter stared at the radio and said nothing.

Rider looked up. "Please help me."

There was suddenly so much hope and pleading in those dark eyes it was almost a greater burden to witness than the hurt.

262

"If you promise to get me to the watchtower, I'll help you get Cooper back."

Peter shook his head. "I-I just don't know how I can get you up there without being seen."

Rider stared into the radio. As the message faded back into the static, the wind picked up outside, and snow came skittering in through the open doorway.

"He'll do more than make Cooper work for him," said Rider darkly.

Peter looked up. "What did you say?"

Rider pulled down on one of his braids and looked away. But Peter knew all too well what he was referring to. He pushed his chair back, dropping Rider's file on top of the desk.

"OK," he said, standing. "I'll help you. I'll help light the flare from the watchtower, I promise. Just take me to him."

Rider looked out of the window at the woods and quietly shook his head. But it was more at the madness of the world than anything else.

"I love her more than my heart can bear, Peter."

"Yes," said Peter. Then quietly, "I know."

Rider made his way outside. "If we leave now, we'll make the traveller's cabin by first light."

Peter leaned over the desk to turn off the lamp when he glanced back down at Rider's file.

Children: Billy aged 9. Deceased. Daisy aged 3. Deceased
Next of Kin: Wife, Josephine Rider
Next of Kin's Instructions: No further contact wanted

"You comin'?" Rider called from outside. "What's wrong?"

Peter wiped his eyes on the heel of his hands and stared at the page.

"Nothing," he said, closing the file. "Nothing at all."

30

They followed the trail east over the hills. However, it wasn't long before the tracks faded beneath fresh snowfall and Peter was left with nothing but hope that Rider would remember the way.

More snow came. They came across a deer carcass down by a shallow river. Most of the meat had been gutted from inside the chest cavity. The ribcage was stripped to the bone. Looking at the tracks, wolves working in a pack must have made the kill. But there were signs others had feasted. Black raven wings littered the ground. The talons of a vulture had punctured the snow. Coyotes had most likely fed too according to Rider when he eventually called back for Peter to keep moving.

Peter looked ahead. Moonlight clipped the pines where Rider was standing. Snow dust glittered the cones, his beard and eyelashes too, made white now just like an old man's by the frost. Rider blinked deeply to encourage them on. Peter glanced back at the carcass. Nature was beautiful and it was harsh. But it never lied.

Peter turned back toward Rider. He offered a smile, except he knew his heart was lying. Trust was as fragile as a scoop of water cradled in two hands. And yet here they were, willingly holding each other's. A pact. A bond. This man would bring him to Cooper, but all the while Rider's wife was never going to come back for him.

Peter felt Rider's eyes searching his face. "What is it, little one?"

"Nothing."

"You miss him."

"Yes," said Peter, relieved that he'd observed something else inside him.

"It's like bein' kept apart from the other half of you. When you're not together, there's just that big ol' force out there in the world, willin' you toward it. The missin' keeps you in the future. You just can't get outta the present quick enough because only then will you be together again."

Peter smiled. Rider turned round and carried on walking.

They trudged on through the night.

They crossed a ridge and watched a pack of wolves lope across the lower ground. They ran silently under the moonlight, their trails fanning out toward the horizon like tributaries in the snow.

A few hours in, they took a rest inside a small clearing. Rider bundled up the few bits of dry kindling and wood he could find and lit a fire. Next he made his way round the surrounding trees, wiping his scent into the bark and then Peter's skin again to shield him from the Dead.

"Darn it," he said, scratching his beard. "Your stomach must be going crazier than a raccoon tryin' to crack open a trash can, you won't have eaten in so long. I could try and hunt somethin' but, truth be told, I can't recall the last time I hosted."

Peter sat in front of the fire, clapping both hands together to warm them. "It's OK. I'm not real hungry right now."

"No? No. Course not. Stupid me. Your mind will be on other things."

"Yes."

"What about some water then?"

"I'm OK."

"Well, make sure you keep warm. We don't get so cold."

Peter looked up. "No?"

Rider squinted one eye into a *nah, not so much* kind of way. He started to fiddle with one of his braids and an awkwardness passed between them that hadn't existed before. Peter looked down into the dancing flames. The truth was there were probably lots of things he didn't know about the Returned or Rider and, now he thought about it, Cooper.

He drew his legs up under his chin and stared into the embers where the blackened wood burned molten-red. What if things had changed between him and Cooper? What if things were going to be different from now on and the difference couldn't be helped?

"We're still the same person," said Rider after a while.

Peter looked up, at once reassured and ashamed that Rider had read his mind so easily.

"Josie and I met in the coffee shop where I worked weekends," he said. "*Depresso!* You know the kind, so darn hipster they don't even do an Americano and the lattes comes in mason jars?"

Peter raked his teeth over his bottom lip and said nothing.

Rider pulled down on his braids. "No, of course you don't. Well, point is I worked there and I promised myself that by the time I'd stamped her loyalty card ten times I had to pluck up the courage to ask her out. However, when it came to that momentous day and she marched up to the counter with her card ready for me to stamp, before I could even say a thing, she told me that the tenth stamp had won me her phone number. But I wasn't to dilly-dally callin' her or nothin'. Oh no. Apparently, it'd taken us so long to get this far, if she had to wait any longer, she'd likely have to accept the offer of a dim, but very keen, Xerox-machine fixer from Bucktooth, Tennessee called Ron."

Peter smiled and said nothing.

"You don't know what a loyalty card is, do you?"

"It's OK."

"Or a Xerox."

"I get the point."

Rider leaned forward, flashing his tombstone teeth. "We had a bun in the oven by the fall."

Peter laughed. But his stomach was churning. He didn't want to keep the truth from him any longer. "Rider, there's something I—"

"So how'd you meet Cooper?" Rider asked.

Peter's heart bucked. It felt strange to hear his name said out loud. But it was reassuring. It made it sound like he still existed out there in the world. More than that, it made it sound like Cooper was his.

"We never met," said Peter. "Not really. I mean, I don't remember a time when I didn't know him. We grew up on the lake together."

"You're lucky to have been in each other's lives from the beginnin'."

269

"I guess. I didn't really speak to him properly until recently."

"How come?"

"I was scared."

The fire popped and golden sparks danced up into the darkness like stardust. Rider's eyes stayed with Peter. He ran his hands down his beard and smiled.

"Thank you for bein' my friend, Peter."

"But I—"

"Get some rest now, eh? I'll keep watch."

Peter stared at Rider's wedding ring, ashamed to have been awarded the title of friend. He lay down in front of the fire and stared into the darkness beyond. The only thing that would take that feeling away now was sleep.

Peter stirred. He didn't know long he'd been out for, but the cold had started to burrow its way into his bones now that the fire was too low to keep it away. He lifted his head up and looked through the last of the flames. It was still dark. But, more than that, Rider had gone. He scrambled to his feet and paced the circumference of the clearing that Rider had marked with his scent.

The glare coming from the flames made the surrounding woods seem darker than they were, so he leaned out further, careful to keep his toes well within the perimeter, and scanned the trees for any sign of movement. His chest heaved. But his fear that a pair of bony fingers might break out of the darkness to take him was replaced by an altogether different feeling. Peter took a step backward. He was being watched. He dug his fist inside his coat pocket and felt for the knife. Then he remembered. He'd left it on the ground in front of the falls where Rider had thrown it.

He gazed into the woods and became drawn to a spot between two trees. It was too black to make out an actual outline or shape, but something shifted as if the darkness itself was moving.

"Hey, bear," said Peter. "You're not going to be surprised now I've told you I'm here, so you can just move along."

Peter stared at the same spot. But whatever it was stayed right where it was. Surely all of the bears had taken to higher ground for the winter by now. Besides, they only ever attacked if you were on their patch or you had food on you. They nearly always ran along if you warned them. Not wolves though. No. Wolves were different. According to Rider, wolves would watch and bide their time.

Peter moved round the back of the fire. He kicked out a small log and gave it a moment to cool off. Then he lit one end and swung the blazing torch around.

The shadows of the trees lunged one in front of another as if the forest itself was moving. But the light didn't catch a muzzle or a pair of staring eyes. Peter lowered the torch and stared into the same spot. Something moved inside the darkness, but still it didn't give itself up. Finally, he swung the torch up into the air and lobbed it between the trees. The snow snuffed out the flame immediately and the woods went dark again.

Peter quickly collected more twigs and branches and was busy dropping them on to the fire to make sure he kept it going when something struck his back at force and he fell forward. He scrambled up on to his elbows, spitting out snow. He flipped himself over and stared at the burnt-out log by his feet. Someone had thrown it back to him. Peter gasped. He looked out into the darkness and two bulbous eye discs looked back at him. The silhouette of a bear standing on its hind legs stepped away from the tree. Peter froze. A twig snapped behind him and he swung round the other way. There was nothing there. When he turned back, the Bearskin had gone.

"We're not alone," said Rider, running up behind him.

Peter stumbled to his feet. "I know."

"I just found a third set of prints. Someone followed us out here and hasn't left our side once."

"It was him," said Peter. "It was the Bearskin. He was just there a moment ago."

Rider swept past him, kicking soil over the flames to put out the fire. Smoke billowed up into the sky. He quickly scanned the ground to make sure they'd not left anything behind, then turned.

"Y'all right?"

"Yeah."

Rider's eyes searched. "Did I frighten you?"

"No," Peter lied. "Course not."

"I didn't mean to startle you by leavin' you alone, little one."

"You didn't."

Rider gave a decisive nod and took Peter by the arm. "We must go."

Rider stepped out of the clearing, leading the way back through the woods. They'd gone a little further when he held up his hand and stopped.

"You hear that?"

"Yeah," whispered Peter. "A horse whinnying."

He ducked behind a tree for cover. Light was coming up through the woods. It was that strange time between one day and another when the night still hangs in the air, but there's a bright haze breaking out across the fringes of the world. A black horse was tethered to a tree. Beyond it stood a log cabin.

31

The cabin was as quiet as a box of secrets. The roof couldn't cope with another winter and sagged beneath the weight of the snow making the chimney stack stoop. An old wooden rocking chair leaned back on the porch as if frozen mid-tilt. But smoke wound up into the trees and candlelight coming from the side window cast a square of yellow light across the snow. Someone was home.

Peter ducked back behind the tree. "What now?" He watched the side window, but there was no movement behind the curtains. "The traveller's probably asleep. What are we going to do?"

Rider still didn't answer so Peter shoved his hood back over his shoulders and turned round. But he'd gone.

"Rider?"

The black horse wandered a little way away from the tree it was tethered to. But there was still no sign of Rider. Peter clenched his fists and a bead of sweat broke across his face. He gave it a moment to let the flush pass. When he turned back toward the cabin, Rider was standing on the steps up to the porch, looking at him.

Peter gripped on to the tree. *What the hell are you doing?* he mouthed.

Rider held his forefinger to his lips and patted the air for Peter to get down out of sight. Peter shook his head, but he had little choice. He squatted down behind the tree, and Rider turned to the front door. He knocked, then pinned his back to the wall next to the door hinges and waited.

A shadow passed behind the curtains.

The sound of footsteps crossed the cabin.

The front door flew open, swinging backward against the wall to mask Rider, and a boy with skin as pale as Cooper's stumbled out. Peter leaned forward. But it wasn't him. The boy stood shivering in nothing but his undershorts and it was hard to tell what he was more scared of – what awaited him outside or what had happened to him inside. The boy stumbled across the porch, his dark eyes wide with panic. A pistol cleared the doorway, pushing him forward. When nothing took a shot at him, the traveller must have realized that his homestead wasn't in any danger of ambush and staggered out.

The traveller was in his twenties. The red bandana that had covered his face back at the Trading Post hung loose about his neck now. Blond stubble hugged a clenched jaw. He hoisted the long johns hanging round his waist back up over his butt and tottered forward, waving the pistol all over the place.

"Go awn, take him!" he slurred. "He ain't nothin' special."

The traveller thrust out his shooting arm. His aim was shaky. He waggled it toward the woods, then swung it back round, pointing his pistol down the length of the porch. Then he remembered to check behind the door. He swung round and kicked it shut.

Rider had gone. Peter scanned the sides of the cabin and let out a deep sigh. But any sense of relief had been misplaced.

The barrel of a rifle pressed down in between Peter's shoulder blades and someone stepped up behind him.

"Tucker," came a woman's voice. "We got ourselves a live one!"

The traveller spun round, squinting to regain focus.

"Well, I'll be damned," he said, scratching the hair below his belly button with the end of his pistol. "He's just a boy."

"Is you alone?" whispered the woman behind him.

Peter scanned the four corners of the cabin for Rider and said nothing.

"Well, is you?"

"No," said Peter. "There's five of us. You're outnumbered."

"I only see two sets of footprints back here."

Peter's throat tightened and the one she called Tucker stumbled across the porch to get a better look.

"Well, take him out, girl!" he called. "What you waitin' for?"

Peter shook his head and the rifle pinched deeper into his shoulder blades.

"So where's the other one?" said the woman.

"I—"

"Tell me."

But Tucker was getting impatient and scooped an empty beer bottle up off the porch's railing.

"Now!" he said, lobbing it into the woods. "You pale-skinned witch!"

Peter turned his head. "Miss."

"Turn around."

But Peter ignored her. He held both hands up in the air and dared to hold her gaze.

Just like the others, the woman had returned. Only she wasn't really a woman at all. She was barely older than Peter. The cold winter sun coming up through the woods made flames of her long red hair. But it wasn't the paleness of her skin or the darkness of her eyes that haunted her. Peter's eyes fell to the girl's hand on the trigger and saw the bruises across her wrist and then her neck, her ankle, her face, her eye.

"Look away," she said, angling the rifle down.

"He did that to you?"

"So?"

"But he can't."

The girl's eyes narrowed. "You're funny."

"He shouldn't."

"It don't matter."

"Yes. It does."

"He takes care of us."

"How can you say that?'

"Real easy. Cos it's better than what came before. Or what might come after if people like you take over."

"No," said Peter. "We won't hurt you."

"You all say that."

"We won't."

"But you always do."

"The man I'm with is a Returnee."

The girl's lip curled. "What's that? A Pale Skin?"

Peter winced. "I guess. But yes, he's pale too and so is my friend Cooper. We're here to rescue him. We can free you too."

The word *free* took light in the girl's eyes. They grew wide as she dared to let the meaning of such a thing grow inside her. Tucker shouted something out. His feet left the porch and Peter heard his footsteps creaking through the snow toward him. But the girl seemed untroubled.

"Free," she said as if from somewhere far away.

"Yes," said Peter.

"Why would you do that for us?"

"Why wouldn't we?"

The girl's eyes widened further to take Peter in. But she was no longer counting on him to save her. She looked down at the rifle as if for the first time and smiled like she'd suddenly found herself in possession of all the answers she'd ever been looking for and wondered what had taken her so long to find them. She lifted the rifle.

The first shot took Tucker down. The second one made sure of it. She pulled on the forestock to release the cartridges, loaded another bullet and took aim to fire a third. But Peter placed his hand on the rifle's muzzle and lowered it.

"Enough!" he panted. "It's OK. It's over."

The girl's eyes welled. She nodded as if to say thank you. But the world had hardened her from feeling much relief.

"You's fightin' a losin' battle," she said.

Peter shook his head in disbelief that she should even think that way. But she didn't say anything further. She swept past Peter, hurrying toward the boy, when Rider ran out from behind the cabin.

"Hurry!" he said. "Peter!"

Peter nodded and stumbled down to the front of the cabin. He quietly stepped up to the porch and made his way to the front door.

Inside was dark. The traveller had snuffed out the one candle set on the table in the middle of the cabin. The room was sparsely furnished, but underneath the table was a good enough place as any to hide more trouble. Peter crossed the room to the window, calling out Cooper's name, and yanked the curtains aside.

A woman fell forward across the table. Her pale skin was stark in the shaft of cold light slashing the room. Her eyelids peeled back wide in fear that Peter's presence here might pose a greater risk than what had come before. But she was unable to move. A rope tied to a brass hoop in the middle of the table bound her wrists.

Peter raised both palms. "No, miss. I won't hurt you."

He rushed over to the table. He heard himself give the woman reassurance that he meant no harm. He kept saying it as he gently pulled the back of her dress down over her legs and untied her until she was able to stand upright again. But his thoughts never left Cooper.

The woman staggered backward, grabbed a bundle of clothes and blankets from the floor and stumbled out of the door into the other girl and boy's arms. A short while later, Peter heard the horse set off at pace. He dropped the rope on the floor and noticed a back door. He quietly swung it open and walked a little way away from the cabin.

The low winter sun blazed from inside the woods like a fallen star.

Spears of bare aspen creaked in the wind.

Peter leaned into a silver birch and somewhere in the distance a woodpecker drilled. He stayed with the sound for a little while. Eventually, the woodpecker must have disappeared further back inside the forest because the drilling faded, then was gone. But he wasn't alone. Peter turned and Cooper looked back from where he was sitting in a white tee and jeans with one hand chained to a bench.

He leaned forward, his hair spilling across his face. "You came?"

Peter took a step closer. But something stopped him from approaching. Suddenly a feeling of strangeness, or of being strangers even, passed between them and he felt frightened.

"Why didn't you call when you saw me?"

Cooper shrugged. "I was just takin' a moment to look at you. Scared I guess."

"Scared?"

"How'd you get here?"

"A friend helped me," said Peter. "You'll see."

"Pete—"

"Did he hurt you?"

"No."

"Did he?"

"No, Pete."

Peter looked away and nodded.

"And the others?" said Cooper. "Eddie and the girls."

"They got away."

Peter watched Cooper's Adam's apple rise and fall. His eyes fell to the top of his arms, his chest, and then finally his hands clasped between his legs and felt a sharp tug in his tummy. He wanted to touch him. He wanted nothing more than that, but he still couldn't move and he didn't know why.

"I got to thinkin'," said Cooper, scratching beneath his armpit.

"You did?"

"Yeah, that maybe you and me should take Snowball out for a ride down to West Wranglestone sometime to catch a movie."

Peter raised his eyebrows. "Oh yeah?"

"Yeah."

"But you hate towns."

"I never said that."

"You kinda did."

"They're just brown is all."

"Brown and what?"

"Bricky."

"Cooper."

"They got real architectural interest?"

Peter narrowed his eyes.

"Jeez," said Cooper. "Do you remember everythin' I said?"

"Yes."

"Good."

"Anyways. What are you going to take me to see?"

"Dunno," said Cooper, easing back into the bench and giving it some thought. "*Star Wars*?"

Peter shrugged. "OK. And what's that about?"

"It's about a brother and a sister and their evil pa who's up to no good, clenchin' his fist and rulin' the galaxy. And there's a space pirate who pretends not to care only he does really. And it's got robots and spaceships and aliens and sword fights, only they use glow sticks instead a swords cos it's spacey, except it weren't nothin' like sci-fi had ever been before because they spent money on goin' to real places and everything's dusty."

Peter smiled.

"Pa liked movies," said Cooper. "He's told me the whole classic trilogy a bunch a times, but I ain't doin' no spoilers until I know if you like the first one."

Peter nodded and said nothing. Cooper shrugged and scratched the back of his neck just like he always did when he was unsure of himself, and it still seemed so strange that someone as perfect as him could feel that way about him.

Cooper looked up with a hopeful look in his eye. "Or *The Sound of Music*?"

"I love you," said Peter. He said it before he realized he was going to. "I love you so much."

"I din't think it would come. Not now."

"It was always there. I just couldn't get it out."

"Peter?"

"What?"

"Nothin'," said Cooper, tucking his hair behind his ear. "I just wanted to hear your name is all."

Peter ran in, unhooking the key to the padlock by the back door to free Cooper and they embraced. Cooper held the back of Peter's head, the small of his back, his hands and finally his face and they kissed.

"You and me is in so much trouble," said Cooper, resting his forehead against Peter's.

"I know," said Peter. "But we'll fix it."

"How?"

"I don't know yet but we will."

Peter held Cooper's gaze and felt his closeness again. "And who is this friend?"

Peter told him about Rider and the Returnees, the camp and finally Rider's wishes to set the flare off over the lake for his family. But Cooper must have sensed that he was troubled by something and gently gripped his arms.

"There's somethin' else."

"No," said Peter. "It's just…"

"Just what?"

"It's just that Rider promised to help me find you if I helped him light the flare over the watchtower. But I found a file on him near the entrance to the old sanctuary. His children are both dead and his wife doesn't want any more contact with him. And I didn't tell him in case he changed his mind about helping me find you."

Cooper wiped his nose on his hand and looked in the direction of the back door. "Perhaps he knows she don't want him no more already."

"Why would you say that?"

"Perhaps he knew that and wants somethin' else."

"Like what?"

"His home," said Cooper. "Revenge."

Peter pulled away. "No."

"Hell, I wouldn't blame him even if he did."

"But I trust him."

"What," said Cooper, "like you trusted the old man in the canoe?"

Peter flinched. But Cooper realized his mistake at once.

"Hell!" he said. "Peter, I'm sorry."

Peter yanked his arm away.

"Your heart's so big," said Cooper. "It don't see what the rest of us see. It's what I love about you most, but—"

"But if we don't trust him…"

"Then what?" said Cooper. "What if we don't trust him?"

"Then nobody trusts *you*."

"Pete."

"And that's how all this got started."

Peter turned away. But the truth was he'd made mistakes before. He didn't know anything about Rider. He wasn't sure he knew anything any more.

Peter watched the sun flicker behind the creaking aspens and Cooper took his hand. A moment passed in silence, or maybe more, Peter wasn't sure, but eventually he heard footsteps cross the cabin floorboards and a big beardy face popped round the side of the door.

"You got a special one there, Cooper," said Rider.

Cooper turned. "Don't gotta tell me that."

Peter squeezed Cooper's hand just a little because he sounded hostile. But Rider stopped fiddling with his braid and held his gaze and a secret understanding passed between them.

"Come, brother," he said, turning back inside. "There's much to tell you."

Cooper didn't move. "I reckon I'm good, thanks."

"I'm sure you are. But plenty a folks won't know that about you and it's dangerous being different."

Cooper frowned, but he reluctantly made his way forward all the same. Rider stepped inside the cabin, but something caught his attention. His heel hovered above the floorboards and he suddenly turned back.

"What is it?" said Peter.

Rider held his forefinger to his lips and pointed at the front door. The floorboards creaked and someone stepped up to the porch outside. Peter stared at the iron handle and it twitched.

"Were there any other captors here?" Rider whispered.

"No," said Cooper. "Tucker operated alone."

Rider crossed the length of the table. "Both of you get behind me. Now!"

Cooper pulled Peter by the arm and dragged him inside the cabin, but in the second it took for Rider to swipe a set of keys off the table to lock the front door, it burst wide open.

Snow flurried across the floorboards. The gas mask hurtled in through the door. A rifle followed. Footsteps crossed the porch and a familiar face walked in.

32

Henry drew the bearskin hood back over his shoulders and staggered through the door. His white hair clung to his forehead, all matted in sweat. His round spectacles had steamed up so badly beneath the gas mask that they'd completely misted over. He pulled them from his face and leaned into the doorpost.

"I'm nothing but a rusty old man with an even rustier golf handicap," he said in a friendly way that belied the situation. "It should never have gone this way, Jonathan."

Peter glanced at Rider and watched history hover in the space between them.

"And what way might that be?" said Rider. "Gettin' rid of folks whose whereabouts was entrusted to you? Or havin' your secret discovered by the one person on the lake you underestimated the most?"

Henry put his glasses back on and looked across the cabin at Peter. Peter tried to hold on to his memories of the times they'd shared together – the storytelling, the fishing trips, the snowy days spent in front of the fire. But they were gone now. Like Santa Claus, Henry Foster was part of Peter's life one day, and the next he simply didn't exist any more.

"See what happens when you venture out into the world, Peter?" he said. "You find out that it's just full of grown-ups making stupid decisions."

Peter took Cooper's hand and stepped in front of Henry. "How do you two know each other?"

"Henry was one of the doctors over at Yellowstone," said Rider. "We had our own doctor on the lake. We didn't let anyone else in apart from other Returnees because we knew it was safer that way. But when ours became sick we radioed our allies over at Yellowstone who promised us that one of their own could be trusted."

Henry pressed his spectacles further up his nose and drew a match from the box on the table to light the candle.

"Yes," he said striking the match, "and my assistance seemed like a good idea at the time. There wasn't much left in the world that hadn't been labelled and defined by science, and I have to confess it appealed greatly to my vanity when you gave away your coordinates and invited me to Wranglestone. To think that there might be some new patient group that challenged my abilities or sought to somehow redefine them. In the history of humankind, no other plague has ripped a hole right through us, but left others seemingly immune. You were the hope the world was waiting for and I could've been the one to deliver it."

Henry shrugged the bearskin off his shoulders and placed it over the back of one of the chairs.

"May I?"

Rider sighed. "Be my guest."

"So what changed?" Peter asked.

"My heart," said Henry, collapsing into the chair. "Most saw the Dead as a warning of monsters, a last chance for humanity to take better care of itself. As something sent down by God – a common enemy that could finally free us all from our petty differences and unite us. The Dead ended wars and long-held animosities that existed between countries. For God's sake, I never saw so much harmony between all races and cultures as I did in Yellowstone following the outbreak. After so long in our history, one person could finally look another in the eye, regardless of their race or religion, and know that they could be trusted. The monster was finally outside, only ever outside of us, never one of us. Anything that interfered with such clarity would only ruin that. And who was I to stand in the way of such progress?"

Rider wiped his hand on the misted glass and watched the snow falling gently past the window.

"Progress?" he mumbled. "You did nothin' more than shift the focus on to another set of people and let us do what we've always done to each other."

"There were other considerations," said Henry.

"What considerations?" Peter asked.

"The National Parks were full, for pity's sake. The whole refuge program was at capacity and you'd taken one of them for yourselves. We were overrun with people in need of medical attention and sanctuary. Something had to give and we had to reprioritize."

"One human life over another?" asked Rider.

Henry drove his fist down on top of the table. "Goddamnit, Jonathan! Yes, life, not life after death. I'm a doctor. We spent time and diminishing resources trying to work out what made you immune while others perished, only for us to find nothing! You provided nothing of any use."

"And so you disregarded us."

"Yes. If you insist. Being here went against everything I'd ever known. My responsibility has been, and always will be, to put folks' lives first, to put real human life first."

Cooper stepped forward. "Real human?"

"No, no," said Henry, shaking his fist as if to cuss himself. "I didn't mean that."

"Then what did you mean?" asked Rider.

Henry swept his glasses from his face and pointed with them. "Listen to me, Jonathan. If you'd had it all your way, you'd have invited every Returnee out there to Wranglestone. God knows you tried. Then what? What if there were more of you than we could handle? What if there were more of you than us?"

Rider shoved a chair against the side of the table and looked at Cooper.

"And there we have it – them and us. And what, Henry? What if there were more of us? What did you think we'd do – turn against you?"

"No, no," said Henry. "Well, all right then, yes. And what if you did? What if you didn't feel protected? What if you felt sidelined up here in the mountains where no one even knew you existed, where no one would want to know you existed, and you grew in numbers until you were able to do something about it? Homo sapiens evolved to become distinct to the Neanderthal. And then they became dominant. We wiped out the Neanderthal because they were weaker. What if you did the same?"

Rider turned back toward the window and quietly shook his head.

"But they were another species, Henry," he said quietly. Then, "Sweet Jesus, you're talking about us like we're another species."

The snow kept falling.

The candlelight flickered.

Henry played with his glasses and said nothing.

"You intercepted the plan for our loved ones to join us," said Rider at last.

"Yes," said Henry. "We had to stop your allies before they had a chance to tell them you existed."

"But we coulda made it work."

"I'm sorry."

"How many residents over at Yellowstone did you persuade to take action?"

Henry bowed his head. "They didn't need any persuading."

Silence fell across the cabin. Henry played with his spectacles for a moment more, then set them down on the table. Rider furrowed his brow and motioned toward him. But before he could get close, Henry lifted his hand and held a knife to his own throat. Peter flinched. It hadn't been there a moment before.

"Don't become an old man, Peter," said Henry, angling the blade beneath his chin. "I'm not sure my fifteen-year-old self would even recognize who I am today."

"Give me the knife, Henry," said Rider, holding both palms up to appease him.

But Henry held his gaze and, with tears in his eyes, shook his head for him not to advance any further.

"I'm not here to cause you good people any more harm than I have done already. I'm here to atone for my mistakes. And I'm here to warn you."

"Warn us against what?" Cooper asked.

Henry lowered his chin and the tip of the knife dented his skin. "I don't know what it is you're hoping for, Jonathan, but it simply won't work."

"Warn us against what?"

"Not what," said Henry. "Who."

"Then who?" said Peter. "How many of the others know about this?"

Henry arched his eyebrows, almost pained that Peter had to carry the fear that everyone he knew might be involved. "Oh God, no. Is that what was worrying you?"

Peter glanced back at Cooper.

"No. It was just the two of us," said Henry as if the word *us* was somehow wretched and cursed. "Just two."

"Who?" said Peter, leaning over the table. "Who else?"

Henry's gaze went right through Peter to somewhere out of reach, the past perhaps, and his eyes seemed to question every choice he'd ever made and finally come to the realization that none of them were any good. He slid the blade further up under his chin. But he never got to answer Peter's question.

The bullet pierced through the window quicker than a winter wind. The hole barely fractured the glass. There was a moment of horror on Henry's face where he realized the fact his life was actually over. But his expression fell vacant in seconds. The knife dropped from his hand. Blood pumped from his chest and Henry's body dropped to the cabin floor.

Peter pushed past the table and made for the door. He leaped over Henry's body and ran out on to the porch.

"No!" said Rider, running out after him.

Peter jumped down. His eyes darted from one tree to another. A moment later, Rider sprang up behind him, pushing him face first into the snow.

"You'll get yourself shot," he said, pinning Peter down.

"Get off me."

"You'll get yourself killed and then all will be lost."

Peter lifted his face up off the ground, spitting out snow, and pushed him away. Rider fell over backward. Then, without hesitation, he clambered back to his feet and ran off into the woods.

"Get back inside and wait for me!" he called.

"No," cried Peter. "Stop!"

Rider disappeared among the trees. Peter scrambled to his feet and turned back toward the cabin.

"We should help him, Cooper," he said, running on to the porch. "Don't you think?"

Peter stood at the doorway, watching blood leak from Henry's chest down through the cracks in the floorboards. But there was no answer.

33

Peter crossed the cabin to the back door. "Cooper?"

He scanned the woods down to a shallow brook. Perhaps he'd gone that way in search of Henry's accomplice. But there was no sign of him. Peter crouched down on the doorstep and tried to work out if any of the footprints coming and going from the cabin might be his. But there were too many trails criss-crossing one another to tell.

He turned back inside and spotted Henry's rifle on the floor where he'd tossed it. He picked it up, cocking the barrel over his arm. He stared at the lone bullet. The recoil had blasted him backward to the ground the last time his dad had gone through this with him. The racoon that had got away was glad of it. And so was Peter. But he wouldn't be so happy about missing his shot today. Not if it came to it.

Peter looked at the back door. He should go. He was

about to make his way out when he heard footsteps crossing the porch. The hairs on his forearms bristled. The footsteps were slow. They were cautious and light so as not to make a sound. Peter took a step backward and spotted a wooden closet in the corner behind the front door. He crossed the cabin and quietly pulled the closet door open, squeezing in between the row of pelts hanging there. He pulled the door to, peering through a crack in the panel doors, and the footsteps approached the front door.

The barrel of a rifle pushed the door open and his dad stepped inside. Peter's heart thundered in his chest. His dad shoved the peak of his baseball cap off his face with the end of the rifle and unzipped his parka. He was almost close enough to reach out to, but he may as well have been on the moon. Peter opened his mouth to let his quickening breath escape. His dad crouched down beside Henry's body. He checked his neck for a pulse, then looked up and scanned the cabin. But shock or surprise didn't cross his face once.

Peter pictured his dad standing over him from behind the gas mask's empty gaze, then dragging Cooper back through the falls to the Trading Post. The thought was so outlandish that he leaned toward the closet door and went to open it. But he couldn't.

His dad was suddenly alien to him. He didn't know

who this man letting himself inside another person's home was any more than if a complete stranger had walked in. His memories of their life together were somehow someone else's. Peter wiped his eyes on the back of his hands and watched his dad leave by the back door. He let his breath out slowly again. But there was no relief. He pushed the closet door ajar and listened to his dad's footsteps crunching through the snow toward the brook.

Cooper.

Peter peered round the side of the back door. His dad was making his way down through the spears of aspen. He held back until he was out of sight, then ran out into the woods after him.

He got as far as the brook and stopped. It was red. Blood hung inside the stagnant water where another body was sprawled. Peter panicked. But the empty eyes staring up from beneath the surface of the water weren't Cooper's. Peter ran his palm across the boy's eyes to close them. He was only young, but whoever he was, the traveller had exhausted his use of him. Peter squeezed the boy gently by the shoulder and scrambled across the rocks to the other side of the brook.

He made his way up the bank and scoured the woods. He saw two distinct sets of footprints now. His dad's and what had to be Cooper's. Peter tucked the stock of the rifle into his shoulder, aimed the barrel out ahead of him and walked on.

The woods were quiet. There was no sign of movement up ahead, just the sound of aspens creaking in the wind like an old rope swing. Peter glanced up, watching the slender trees sway, then stepped over a fallen branch and followed the trail.

He'd gone a little further in when one set of prints changed. The gap between one step and another was wider. The snow was impacted deeply too. Whoever it was had broken into a run. Peter's eyes followed the trail back, but before he could tell if the prints were from someone running away or running toward someone, they stopped. Peter ducked behind a birch and watched his dad kneeling a little way off with his back to him. For a moment, he thought he was just tying his bootlaces. Then he saw the pair of legs on the ground jutting out away from him. Peter shoved the stock of the rifle back into his shoulder and fumbled with the trigger.

"Step away from him," he said, moving forward. "Now!"

His dad turned round. "Pete."

"I said now."

His dad's eyes flitted from Peter's face to the rifle barrel. Relief and fear changed places in the blink of an eye.

"Pete," said his dad, holding both palms up in the air. "It's just me."

"Don't."

"I've been looking everywhere for you."

"I said don't. Get away from Cooper. Now."

"I couldn't find you anywhere."

"I said get away or I'll shoot."

His dad shook his head. "Peter. Pete, please."

Peter closed his eye over the sight and cocked the flint. "I don't even know who you are any more."

"Pete, don't do this."

"Cooper?" Peter called out. "Cooper, talk to me."

There was no answer. His dad glanced down and said something about Cooper already being hurt when he found him. But Peter barely registered those words or gave himself time to figure out if they might be true.

Peter pulled the trigger. He fell backward into the snow, and the sound of the gunshot ricocheted around the woods. The stinging in his shoulder seared through his body like a branding rod. He rolled over on to his side, clutching his shoulder, but when he finally sat upright, his dad was lying on his back in the snow.

"Dad," he said, scrambling to his feet. "Cooper!"

Peter tripped over the rifle and staggered through the trees. He stopped just short of them and stared at the blood splatters in the snow.

"No," he said, rolling his dad off Cooper.

Peter bent double ready to be sick when a cold hand took his.

"It ain't him, Peter."

Peter scrambled up to Cooper's head, wiping a tendril of wet hair from his face.

"Cooper."

"I'm OK."

"But I thought—"

"I know," said Cooper. "I know. I ran outside to see if I could find who shot Henry and my legs got weak. They just gave way beneath me like a baby deer and I couldn't get up again. Then your dad found me."

Tears welled in Peter's eyes. He wiped them away and scrambled for his dad's hand. He pressed his forefinger to his wrist. But before he could feel for a pulse, his dad's body spluttered violently and, choking, coughed death right back out of him.

"Pete," he said.

"Dad, I'm sorry."

"Pete."

"I'm so sorry I shot you."

"Oh, Jesus," said his dad, clutching his stomach. "There's a damn sentence I never thought I'd hear. But we don't have time for this. We need to get this damn bullet outta my gut and cauterize it before I bleed to death."

Peter stared at the blood seeping from his dad's waist and said nothing.

"Pete."

Peter nodded.

"Peter," said Cooper, squeezing his hand. "The cabin. You need a knife, a candle to sear the wound with and some alcohol."

"Uh-huh."

Cooper lifted his head up off the ground. "Peter Nordstrum, I love you more than anythin', but you gotta go. Now!"

Peter leaped to his feet. "Yes."

Cooper laid his arm across Peter's dad's chest and held him. His dark eyes met Peter's for a moment. But there was no time, and before Peter knew it, he was careering back through the woods, splashing down through the brook.

He ran inside the cabin. There was cutlery in a drawer beneath the table. Peter fumbled around for a knife small enough or large enough – he suddenly realized he didn't know which. He wiped sweat off the back of his neck and stared at the options. He'd need something small to root the bullet out, then something large to cauterize the wound. He pushed the spoons and forks aside and rolled a dinner knife in his hand. He shoved it in his pocket, but he knew he'd need something larger.

Peter swung round to the kitchenette by the back door and rummaged through the drawers. But there was only an old hand towel and another matchbox inside them. He took the matchbox and stared at the work surface, panic pumping through his veins like venom. He had to get back out there. He didn't have time for this. Then he saw the knife block. It had been right there all along, the size of a log with seven large carving knives sticking out of it. Peter drew the largest one out by the handle and turned back toward the table to fetch the candle when he stopped.

Darlene was standing at the door. She glanced at Henry's body, then looked back down the barrel of the rifle she was pointing at Peter. Her expression took a moment to catch up with the scene she'd just walked in on, but as she stepped inside the cabin, Peter walked forward into the light and she lowered the rifle.

"Darlin'," she said quietly. "I didn't see you there."

Peter glanced at the rifle. "I'm OK."

"Oh, sweet baby Jesus, I've been looking everywhere for you."

"It's OK."

"Can I hug you?"

Peter took a step backward, and confusion flickered across Darlene's face that they were still standing on opposite sides of the table from each other rather than embracing.

"Have you seen your dad?" she offered. "He's worried sick. I came out here with him."

"You did?"

"Yes, of course I did. We've been looking for you all night together."

Peter stepped forward. "You have?"

"Yes, silly. Peter, what's going on?"

Darlene's eyes searched him. Peter could tell she sensed his hesitation. She leaned forward, gently setting the rifle down on top of the table, and offered a smile. Peter braced both hands across the table and sighed.

"I'm sorry," he said. "It's just – I'll have to explain later."

He should go. He was about to take the candle and head back outside when Darlene looked over at the open back door. Peter watched her eyes widen and water in horror, like a child staring under the bed and realizing something's hiding there. He turned round to see three figures clearing the woods outside. Peter's dad stumbled up from the riverbank with one arm across Cooper's shoulder. The other was around Rider.

"You look like you've seen a ghost," said Peter.

Darlene steadied herself against the wall and nodded. "Cooper. Sweet Jesus, what happened to him?"

Peter made his way round the back of the table behind her, picked up Henry and Darlene's rifles and emptied the cartridges on to the table.

"What the hell's going on?" whispered Darlene.

"You're trembling," said Peter setting the rifles down. "Why don't you sit?"

He leaned over the back of the chair and gently kissed the top of her head. Then he gazed out of the window through the snow toward the woods, the Trading Post and the falls, all the way back to the lake, and clenched his jaw.

"Here's how it's going to go."

34

The lake's founding members were to gather on Cabins Creak by sundown. No exceptions. That was Peter's invitation. And that's all they were told when he slipped a note beneath each door upon his return late last night.

Henry's house was the largest on the lake and the only one built on the ground on account of the island being steep enough to have its own natural defence without the need for stilts. Seventy-three wooden steps wound up the hill from the jetty through a densely packed grove of towering pines to the lodge. The Dead couldn't reach it, but the restless wind whistled beneath the front door now like a stranger biding their time before simply letting themselves in.

Peter wiped his fist on the misted glass and leaned into the window. Bundles of pine needles scratched at the glass. Snow hurtled past, banking the sides of the cabin.

It wouldn't be too long before it was buried inside winter's coffin just like the rest of the lake.

The ice had formed now, fusing all the islands to the mainland. The Lake Landers had already rolled the pickup truck out of the woods. Peter looked toward the middle of the lake to where the rusty-red hot rod was standing beneath the shadow of the watchtower. It would stay out there on the ice all winter now.

The timber creaked beneath the strain of the storm.

The candles flickered.

Peter was about to draw the curtains when a shaft of light broke from an open doorway over on Stone's Throw and someone made their way outside. The same happened on Moose's Reach until one by one a host of little lights set out, travelling through the islands' snowy chambers, down on to the ice.

"They're coming," said Peter quietly. "You sure this was a good idea?"

His dad looked up from the front door where he was standing guard and clicked the barrel of the rifle into place. "It was your idea, Pete."

Peter turned round and faced the room. They'd found the stash of cutlery and gingham napkins Henry used for the lake's Thanksgiving dinner in one of the drawers and dressed the long table by the window. Darlene was busy in the kitchen preparing fresh cuts of moose for everyone, while Rider took a few minutes to talk to Cooper in the bedroom. Thanksgiving wasn't too far off now, but it wasn't the magic of family gatherings that was hanging in the air tonight.

"Nobody's allowed in if they don't leave their weapons at the door," said his dad.

"I know," said Peter. "But what if Henry's accomplice doesn't give himself away? He's kept himself hidden till now."

His dad shrugged. "A person's face can only hide that amount of hate for so long."

"And what about the others? Do you think they'll accept Cooper and Rider?"

"I don't know, Pete."

"But do you think they will?"

His dad took a deep breath and watched snow strike the windowpanes. "It's a lot to take in. Not just the strangeness of it even, but the people we lost along the way. When they see Rider and Cooper, they'll need time."

Peter nudged a fork along the table so it was better aligned with the knife.

"And do you need time?" he asked after a little while. "Do you, Dad?"

"Yeah. I need a bit of time."

"Rider said that I never once looked at him like he

was any different."

"Then that's what we'll do, Pete. That's what we'll do. But what do you suppose they're talking about in there?"

Peter looked across the room to the bedroom door. "Things only they can understand, I guess."

"What kind of things?"

"Things that only Rider can help Cooper with."

"Well, can't it be said out here?"

"Dad."

"They're acting strangely."

"No. They're not."

"We don't know what they're doing."

"Dad, stop it."

"How well do you even know this Rider?"

"He used to work in a coffee shop and a kindergarten."

"But now. After he changed?"

"He still used to work in a coffee shop and a kindergarten, and he carried you back to the cabin and cauterized your wound."

His dad held his hand to his stomach and winced. Rider had done a good job carving that bullet out.

"Yeah," he said, pointing at Peter's waist. "Suppose you'll be wanting us to get matching tattoos next."

Peter turned round to face the window to draw a line under that conversation. A moment later, his dad cleared his throat.

"Pete."

"What?"

"That day on the lake. In the canoe with the dead woman."

Peter remembered what Rider had witnessed. "What about it?"

"I had a fit and fell overboard."

His dad scratched his stubble and shrugged. "I pushed it to the back of my mind because it just didn't make any sense at the time, but I fell overboard while you were unconscious and I think the woman was just doing her best to hold me up. I think she'd come back just like Rider. I should've said something sooner. I should've done something sooner."

Peter folded his arms across his stomach. "Don't."

"I'm sorry."

"Why didn't we ever notice?"

Peter's dad sighed. "We never let them get close enough. We just saw what we wanted to see."

"I love him, Dad."

"I know, Pete."

Peter's dad went to put his arm round his shoulder and give him a kiss on the forehead when there came a knock at the door.

"You ready?"

"Wait," said Peter. Then, "Cooper?"

The bedroom door opened and Cooper shuffled out, stuffing his black and red plaid shirt down the seat of his jeans.

"Came up real nice," he said. "How'd you manage that?"

"I washed it," said Peter.

"You did?"

"Yeah, with real water and everything."

Cooper looked up and smiled. "Sweet."

Peter made his way round the side of the table, and Rider walked out with his beard combed neatly and both braids sitting nicely across the breast of his poncho. He held both arms out in a *ta-da* kind of way, flashing his tombstone teeth in a broad smile.

"Reckon I smell sweeter than a tub of cotton candy at the Kentucky State Fair," he said. "Will I do?"

"You both look very handsome."

Rider smiled and the knocking came again. "I just want them to like me."

Peter nodded. "I know."

"I just want to let Josie and the others know it's safe to come."

Peter looked down. He still hadn't told Rider that he'd seen his file. But the door was knocked, more urgently this time, so he hurried them both back into the bedroom where they were to stay until everyone had arrived. His dad went to the door, and Peter briefly looked back. Cooper and Rider's pale faces carried so much hope and expectation, it was almost too much to bear. But he loved them both he decided now and he would marry Cooper someday.

"I'm proud to have you both in my life," he said. "Truly I am."

Peter held Cooper's gaze and felt his closeness again. Cooper stepped back inside the bedroom with Rider, his dad opened the front door and snow came skittering across the floorboards.

"Evenin', Tom," said Mr Carmichael, stomping both boots on the doorstep. "Peter. No Henry?"

Peter glanced at his dad. "Evening, Mr Carmichael."

"Nasty night out there."

"Sure is."

"And call me Don. You're a man now, Peter."

Peter gave a half-smile, steadying himself on the back of one of the dining chairs, and the enormity of the night ahead suddenly rushed in. His dad took Mr Carmichael's parka for him and hung it on a hook by the front door, but stopped him from coming any further.

"I need you to check your weapons in at the door, Don," said his dad.

Mr Carmichael laughed. "You're kidding me, right?"

"No."

"Now wait a second there, Tom. What is this?"

Mr Carmichael's eyes darted from Peter to his dad as he struggled to play catch-up. "I said what's going on, Tom? And where's Henry?"

It was Peter who answered.

"It'll become clear when everyone's arrived," he said. "I promise. Now, please leave your weapon by the door."

Mr Carmichael looked Peter up and down in a way that told him it was one thing for him to tell Peter he was a man now, but quite another for Peter to take it upon himself to become one. Peter held his gaze, extending his hand for the weapon. Mr Carmichael reluctantly drew a switchblade from his back pocket and dropped it into the bucket.

The fire curled over in a lick of wind and the door flew open. "It's wilder than a whorehouse on rodeo day," said Bud, bundling in with his trench coat flying.

He stomped across the floorboards, dumping snow all over the cabin, and made his way over to the fire. He steadied his hand on the mantelpiece and looked into the flames. But he knew he was being watched.

"I don't need your pity," he said.

Tom cleared his throat. "Bud, we need you to leave your weapon at—"

"Coop's gone and I reckon I've gotten enough hugs out of you people to make the Waltons feel queasy, so you can forget it if that's what this evenin's been called for."

Bud's silver moustache twitched as he chewed over his thoughts and his pain. For some reason, this only made Peter want to reach out to him. But he explained how the invitation was for something else entirely, and Bud reluctantly left his rifle by the door.

Soon the others arrived. Knives, guns, machetes and pistols were piled up high, glasses were poured and welcomes were made. Peter looked around at all the warm and familiar faces he'd grown up with gathered here now and remembered a simple truth – whether he liked it or not, the wolf was one of them.

"So you managed not to die then," came a familiar voice in the crowd. "Impressive."

Becky squeezed past Essie Morgan, whom she'd just arrived with, and held her bottle of beer aloft.

"I mean, nearly everyone else did these last few days," she went on, "but—"

"But what?"

Peter narrowed his eyes. You had to give Becky a second to walk in on herself. She normally saw the hole she'd dug and carried on digging an even bigger one, but for once she squeezed her eyes shut as if to cuss herself and quietly shook her head.

"I'm sorry, Pete," she said. "That was pretty shitty of me."

"Such a loser," said Peter.

"Such a Peter."

"What are you even doing here? It's only supposed to be—"

"I wanted to see you. When Essie showed me your invite, I made out she wouldn't make all the steps up here without me just so I could come too."

Peter smiled. Becky took a swig from the bottle and looked around the cabin where everyone else was milling. "God, First Fall feels like weeks ago. I can't believe it was only a few nights back."

"Hmm," said Peter, scanning the crowd.

He caught Darlene's eye. She mouthed, *You OK, darlin'?* and Peter nodded even though it wasn't true. He looked toward the front door where his dad had stationed himself. His dad looked back discreetly, shaking his head. Clearly, he was none the wiser as to who their culprit was either, but as Peter's eyes darted from one person to another, Becky took his arm and spoke with a seriousness he'd never heard from her before.

"You've changed, Pete."

"Cooper died, Becky. What part of that don't you understand?"

Becky flinched. "Peter, I—"

Peter clenched his fists. He didn't mean to snap, but perhaps he had changed. Perhaps it was time people started to acknowledge there was more to him than they assumed they could predict.

Peter watched Becky struggle to find a way to go off and talk to someone else without it looking like she wanted to, so she looked relieved when someone clinked two glasses together to call for attention before she got the chance.

"Why are we here?" said Mr Carmichael.

"Yeah, Peter," came Essie's voice. "Why? And where's Henry?"

"Let the boy speak and he'll tell us," said Darlene.

Old Essie Morgan tossed her grey braid over her shoulder and leaned into Bud. "Reckon he wouldn't even be in a position to call us all here in this godforsaken weather if Henry had a say in the matter."

Bud's moustache twitched. "Well, he ain't here, Essie. But this had better be worth it. Without Coop, I don't take too kindly to receiving notes I gotta get the neighbours to read out for me. I'm in no mood for festivities."

Mr Carmichael turned to Peter's dad. "We shouldn't even be out walking the lake at night, Tom. One of the Dead could hit the ice at any time."

Glasses clinked in agreement, followed by a series of *hear, hears*.

"Drew's on watch at the tower," said Peter's dad. "Same as any other Thursday."

The hubbub grew. Peter looked through the crowd. His dad quietly locked the front door, gave him the nod and Peter made his way to the back of the cabin. His fingers toyed with the doorknob to the bedroom for a moment. The lacquered wood was cold to the touch. He withdrew his fingers, but the weight of everybody's expectations bore heavily across his back, so he turned to face the gathering and gently opened it.

Cooper and Rider stood in the doorway, and silence crept into the corners of the cabin.

Peter stared at the others. And the others stared back. Their eyes were wild. No one spoke a word. The back of Peter's skull throbbed as if the bone itself would swell and crack, and in that moment something became clear in ways it never had before. Horror wasn't a child looking under the bed and seeing something looking back. Horror was the realization that all the stupid things you counted on as being safe in life, like order and security, were a lie.

A glass smashed across the floorboards.

Mr Carmichael staggered backward. "It can't be."

"Take a seat," said Peter.

"But—"

"It's OK, Mr Carmichael."

"But I—"

"You're in shock. Now, take a seat. All of you."

Mr Carmichael shook his head. And he wasn't the only one. Their eyes said *no* a thousand times over without ever saying a word. Mr Carmichael slumped into a chair and Bud stepped forward, his brow heavy with hurt and confusion, rage and fear. But he couldn't bring himself to look at Cooper.

"This great nation's already been destroyed once by monsters," he said, curling his fist over his Stetson. "Must we now save it from a plague of ghosts?"

"Not ghosts," said Peter. "Not the Dead."

Bud held Peter's gaze, his eyes glowering in the candlelight. With one look, he took all the good he'd only just started to see in Peter and snatched it right back again.

"Well, if they ain't ghosts," he said, "then what in hell are they?"

"Mimics!" said Essie, staring Cooper right in the eye. "Nature's full of 'em. They share the same characteristics as a harmless species and they sure as hell look just like 'em to avoid being spotted by their prey. But the ladybug spider that has a little red coat covered in black spots just like its harmless counterpart, in order to get closer to its prey, ain't no ladybug. It's a wolf in sheep's clothing and so are these two clever little devils."

The word devils ripped round the room. Feet shuffled across the floorboards and shoulders knocked into shoulders. Bud pushed through the crowd, lunging for his rifle.

"What the hell were you thinking, Tom," he said, shoving Peter's dad to one side. "Get the hell outta my way."

"Essie's right!" came a voice.

"Yes!" came another.

But as everyone started to bundle toward the door, Cooper stepped forward.

"Enough!"

They froze. Bud let go of Peter's dad, staring at Cooper like the ghost of a loved one had just reached out of the darkness and called him back. Cooper tucked his hair behind his ears and looked up, his dark eyes all at once hurt and raging.

"Pa, look at me," he said. "And shame on you, Essie Morgan. You bathed me and cleaned my diapers when Pa's fingers and thumbs was too constipated to know what to do. You brushed my hair and told me stories when I was young and made good our home when two dumb boys din't know a cushion from a pillow, and you dare look me in the eye right now like you never knew me?"

Water pooled in Essie's eyes. The crowd exchanged uneasy glances and Bud stepped away from the door.

"Boy," he said. "My boy."

Cooper's chest heaved. "Pa."

Bud gasped in shock at ever being called that again, and Peter took Cooper's hand.

"Some of the bitten return," said Peter, addressing the room. "Alive. They might look like the Restless Ones, but they're not. They're the same as they were before."

Confusion rippled round the cabin and Mr Carmichael looked up.

"Betsy," he whispered. "What about my Betsy?"

Peter glanced at his dad. He didn't want to have to be the one to tell Mr Carmichael. But his dad gently nodded for him to go on.

"Cooper was lucky. But, Mr Carmichael, I'm sorry. I'm afraid Mrs Carmichael didn't make it."

Mr Carmichael shuddered and tears broke across his face.

"I'm sorry," said Peter. "I'm so sorry."

The crowd looked down into their glasses to give dignity to Mr Carmichael's grief. But glances were exchanged, and jaws were clenched trying to hold back the flood of questions left unanswered, and time was moving on.

"Henry was the chaperone," Peter continued. "There are no military stationed here. There never were. It's always just been us, and Henry kept the truth that some of the bitten return hidden from us so we wouldn't question who the monsters were. To keep the enemy out there, but never in here. The ones he didn't kill outside the lake's borders he sold on in return for medicines and firearms that all of us have used. He sold Cooper – or his accomplice did – before they killed Henry for breaking cover."

Peter scanned the room to examine the look of shock flickering across everybody's eyes to see if he could single out the one who didn't seem fazed by the news. He looked over to the front door and saw his dad doing the same. But the culprit kept their allegiance to Henry secret.

The reasons for Peter's invite were finally made plain. Whispers whipped round the cabin now, quicker than the wind beneath the door. Suspicion turned away from Cooper, inward to each other. Which one of them had killed Henry? Who would lead them now? But something else: had Henry's accomplice been right to kill him if he no longer wanted to keep the wrong kind from their shores?

"And you with the ridiculous beard," said Essie, addressing Rider for the first time. "What about you?"

Rider stepped forward. "Evenin', Miss Essie," he said with his dark eyes glinting. "I get it. I'm a stranger to y'all and I'm strange. And wars have been waged for less. I'm also just some bearded dude who used to serve lattes in mason jars in fancy coffee shops when I wasn't teachin' kids that kindness to strangers was the one thing that should guide them through their life. So I doubt any of us woulda got along too nicely beforehand either. And yet I lived here long before any of you did, after I died and returned. All fifty-eight of the registered National Parks were reserved for the nation's escape program, for you to be safe in, but Wranglestone became a secret sanctuary just for us. This cabin we're standin' in right now belonged to my dear friend Selma. She was the first to find refuge here. While the rest of the nation was busy hidin' from monsters, we were hidin' from people. And your Henry proved we were right to do so."

Essie's eyes narrowed. "Is that so?"

Rider nodded. "Yes, ma'am."

"Got a lot to say for yourself, don't ya?"

"That I do."

"And what have you been doing out there all this time? Talking to trees?"

"No, just the Dead. I find they listen better than regular folks."

Essie chewed down on her pipe and Peter cleared his throat.

"Deadbeats don't take no notice of us, Essie," said Cooper, chipping in before Essie took offence.

"He's right," said Peter. "Their scent can be rubbed into our skin to disguise our own. It can be useful. It can help us."

"Hmm," Essie tutted. "I'll decide what's useful around here."

Peter stepped forward. "Since when did you get to decide anything?"

"Oh look," Essie went on. "You've been more nervous than a long-tailed cat in a room full of rocking chairs for years, but look at you now."

Peter clenched his jaw. Rider glanced sideways at him as if to tell him not to rise to the bait, so he turned back to the others.

Rider cleared his throat. "Any more questions?"

"Yeah," said Becky, raising her hand. "Where are you from?"

"Deep in the south where women rule the roost and sushi's still called bait."

"And what does it feel like? Returning, I mean."

Rider shrugged. "It feels like bein' funky enough to

make a maggot gag."

Becky took a swig on her beer. "OK, he can stay."

Peter smiled and caught Essie doing the same, but she refused to give in to her amusement.

"And what do you want?"

Rider took a deep breath and smiled to show he appreciated her candour. He looked round the room, at the fire, the dining table and the snow at the windows, and then finally back to Peter.

"I want to light a flare from the watchtower," he said quietly. "To tell my wife and children over at Yellowstone that I'm safe, and to prove it's possible to settle our differences and live side by side."

"And what are our differences?"

"Whatever you make them. Not much if you so choose."

Peter squeezed Cooper's hand and smiled.

"So what now?" said Mr Carmichael.

"Yeah, Pete," said Becky. "What now?"

But it was Darlene who spoke next. "We eat," she said, dashing through to the kitchen. "Please, sit. All a you. Come on now and let's get some of the good stuff down us. We can talk later."

Darlene squeezed Peter's arm as if to say, *You done good*, and left them to it. As everyone took their seats at the table, and the sound of cutlery clanking and drinks

327

being gulped down broke out across the cabin, Peter's dad sat at the far end of the table nearest the door with his rifle still in his hand and shrugged. The evening was somehow taking an unexpected turn.

"What are we supposed to do now?" said Peter, turning to Cooper. "People are starting to enjoy themselves."

Cooper didn't answer. Peter squeezed his knee to get his attention, but he was looking toward the middle of the table where Bud was staring into the candlelight.

"Give him time."

"He can't even bring himself to look me in the eye."

"He thought he'd lost you, Coop."

"He din't even come up to me."

"He daren't believe his wishes have come true. That's all."

Cooper looked down at his lap so his hair spilled across his face. "Did you really wash this for me?" he said, tugging on his shirt.

"Yeah," said Peter. "Water. I'll show you what it looks like when we get time."

"It never got more than spit and a grindstone before."

"But it smelled like you."

"It did?"

"Yeah," said Peter. "Part of me didn't want to wash it."

"Why, what do I smell like?"

"Log smoke. Sweat. You were embarrassed about it that day in the tunnel, but I could barely keep my hands off you."

Cooper smiled. "You used to have a grey T-shirt with Dolly Parton on it."

"Yeah. I used to pretend she was my mom when I was little. I loved that tee, but then I lost it."

"You din't lose it. You left it dryin' on a rock after you'd had a swim one mornin' two summers back, and I took it."

"You did?"

"I kept it locked in between my pillows for as long as I could."

"Why?"

"So it din't lose you."

Peter fanned his fingers, intertwining them with Cooper's so they were holding hands. "What happened to it? Where is it?"

"I'm wearin' it now, Peter."

Peter felt the tug in his tummy he now recognized as his body's way of telling him to say *I love you*, and the sound of people chattering away in the background washed over him. Cooper looked up, holding his gaze, and they both said the words without the need to say them at all, just so it was theirs and only theirs.

Peter glanced round the table and smiled. He never

dreamed it possible that everyone would get to see them together.

"So, what are we gonna see if *Star Wars* isn't showing?"

"Dunno," said Cooper. "*Jaws*?"

"OK. And what's that about?"

"It's about a monster shark who goes around killin' folk every time you hear the *der-dum*, *der-dum* music. The town don't wanna close the beaches in case they lose a bunch of money, but this cop warns them about capitalism and how the shark's a big'un. Besides, he's got a point to prove about bein' a man cos he wears glasses and he don't like the water."

"Sounds scary," said Peter.

"Nah. Not really. The shark's only made of rubber."

Peter laughed, leaning into Cooper, and someone cleared their throat.

"Get a room," said Darlene, squeezing in between the pair of them.

Cooper leaned back into Peter, smiling, and she set a plate of moose and wild mushrooms down for Becky and Mr Carmichael.

"Now, I'm sorry," said Darlene, throwing her hand towel back over her shoulder, "but I can't get all my plates out at the same time, so dig in darlin's or it'll get cold."

Those who had their food tucked in, and the others

continued to chat. Essie looked down to the head of the table where Rider was sitting.

"So," she said, planting both hands squarely down on the table. "You wanna light this flare from the tower tonight then or what?"

Rider looked up, his dark eyes glittering in the candlelight and silence fell across the room. "You're a surprisin' woman, Miss Essie."

"A woman don't get far in this world if she don't know how to disarm a man."

"Well, I thank you most sincerely. Truly I do."

Essie nodded. "Don't go getting all misty-eyed on me now. You haven't made it on to my Christmas card list just yet, but you got guts, I'll give you that much."

"No," said Rider, looking over at Peter's dad and Bud. "I got lucky. I got Peter. Your boys are a credit to you, sirs."

Peter's dad leaned back into his chair and smiled. "Thank you, Jonathan. He's the only thing I got right."

Bud looked up for the first time and nodded his thanks. "I hope you find her," he said. "Your wife."

"Thank you, sir," said Rider. "I thank you for your kind words."

Bud nodded as if to say, *You're welcome*, and, *You're OK by me*, and looked across the table at Cooper. "You're all right, boy."

Cooper gripped Peter's hand tightly, and Rider leaned forward.

"Miss Becky," he said. "I surely don't know why the Dead came back or why we returned, but I like to think the Restless Ones took to wanderin' the earth so we'd all be free to do the same. I'm just the one come back with a voice to remind y'all, because when death is comin' for you, you live."

Essie eased back in her chair and relit her pipe. "And ain't that the darned truth?"

"And so," said Rider, raising his glass, "I beg of you. Look up, let be and live."

Peter furrowed his brow and glanced back at his dad. Somehow it seemed so strange to commemorate the thing that had stolen so much from the world. And yet, he thought, glancing at his own hand inside Cooper's, he'd never be sitting here now without the Dead.

Peter looked across the table. Becky was watching him. She mouthed the words, *You love him,* and rolled her eyes. Peter pulled a face and Becky raised her glass.

"To second chances," she said.

Rider flashed his tombstone teeth into a big grin and winked. "Yes, Miss Becky. Indeed. To second chances."

Everyone raised their glasses and Peter felt his dad's eyes on him. He looked down the other end of the table, and his dad shook his head in a warm and bemused kind of way that said, *Perhaps they've changed their minds.* Peter smiled. Perhaps. Perhaps they had. He was about to lift his glass when a chair scraped violently across the floorboards. Peter turned round.

Sweat was crawling down Rider's face like rain across glass, making his skin grey and clammy. He was motionless. His dark eyes stared down at the dining table. Peter followed his line of sight to the dinner plate. Steam rose up from the pile of mushrooms, but the cuts of moose were cold. Blood seeped from the red flesh, pooling into the rim of the plate.

"Darlene," called Peter. "This meat's a bit rare."

Darlene moved quietly round the back of the table. But her eyes were indifferent to Peter's concerns. Rider gripped on to the arms of the chair with both hands to steady himself and shook violently. His eyes bulged wide. The blackness behind the surface glint became bottomless and unseeing. His lips peeled back to bare his teeth and gums like a dog just before it bites.

"Bet he didn't tell you how they react to raw meat now, did he?" Darlene said softly. "Course he didn't. Makes you wonder what else he might be hiding, don't ya think?"

Peter's throat constricted. He looked at the woman who'd been everything in his life and started to tremble. "Why?"

Darlene shrugged like she could no more explain all the hate that crawled across her face now any more than she could explain why she liked one colour and not another.

Peter shook his head. "Get the plate away from him!"

Panic ripped around the cabin. Everyone pushed their chairs aside to get away from Rider and bundled down the other end of the table.

"If they don't look right," said Darlene, "then chances are they ain't."

"I agree," said Essie. "Can they even be killed by normal means? Or are they immune to everything but damage to the head just like the Dead?"

Rider's teeth gnashed.

His raving eyes were unblinking.

"Good question," said Darlene, folding her arms. "Why don't you find out?"

Essie grabbed her knife and lunged across the table.

"No!' said Peter, standing.

Cooper scrambled up from his seat, pushing Essie back. He wrenched the knife from her grasp and dashed Rider's plate from the table. It flew into the wall, smashing to pieces across the floor. Peter pushed his chair from the table and went to stand, but Rider clapped both hands on top of his to stop him. He wasn't violent. He held Peter's gaze and an eerie calmness entered his eyes now as if all the pain he'd had to carry around with him had suddenly been taken away. But he was breathless. Unable to speak. Peter glanced down at the fork sticking out of Rider's chest and blood pumped across the tablecloth.

Becky fell back into her chair, staring at her reddened hands in horror. She turned them over and the blood seeped between her fingers. It was as if she didn't even recognize them as being her own. But it was her hand that had plunged the fork into Rider's chest. Her lips mumbled words no one could understand and she started to shake uncontrollably. Commotion surged round the table, but Rider's voice, as quiet as it was now, somehow drew Peter away from the chaos.

"Forgive me, little one," he whispered. "I didn't tell you about our reaction to raw meat because I didn't want you to be frightened of us."

Blood curled over the silver snowflake.

"Don't be afraid," Rider went on.

"But —"

"S'all right, I knew Josie was never comin'. I knew it all along. But I beg of you, Peter. Light the flare. This was about you. This was always about you two."

Peter looked into Rider's eyes. He smiled sweetly. Smiles like that kept friendships alive. Smiles like that kept lots of things alive. Then silently, and quite without warning, the glint in his dark eyes went out and his body slumped backward into the chair.

Peter's stomach burned. "No!"

He grabbed a knife from the table, tossing the chair to the floor, and stood in front of Cooper to shield him.

"Stay back," he said, jabbing the knife into the air.

Darlene sighed as if she was getting bored with Peter's hysterics and draped the hand towel she was still holding over the back of the chair.

"Darlin'," she said. "The reason any of us are even still here is because we never took any chances."

"Chances on what? People?"

"No. Not people."

"You don't know what you're talking about."

"And you've only been out there, what, five minutes?"

Peter shook his head. "You were able to find us at the cabin because you'd made trade with that man before. It was you who injected me and dragged Cooper away. Henry showed you how, but you did that. It was all you."

Darlene sighed again, like the day had been nothing more than a nuisance they should put behind them. She lifted the hand towel from the back of the chair and started to fold it neatly into triangles when there was a gunshot.

Peter stumbled backward, pinning Cooper to the

window. He looked around in horror. But Cooper was unharmed and his eyes directed him to back into the room.

Darlene dropped to her knees. She coughed up blood, and a mixture of rage and confusion ripped through her eyes. She briefly smiled, and Peter saw the woman he'd spent so many summers on the porch with, brushing her hair, talking about Cooper. Then the smile slipped from her face.

"Stupid boy," she said.

Darlene's body dropped to the ground. Peter's dad gently lowered the rifle, and silence filled the cabin. Becky slowly stood up from the table. Her eyes were red with tears. They spoke a thousand apologies for a pain a thousand words would never lessen. But Peter couldn't look at her.

Pine needles scratched at the glass. Peter gazed out of the window and watched the snow skittering past the cabin. The blizzard had worsened. He was barely aware of the winds breaking over the timber or the whistling through the cracks in the door. Everything was muffled. When Peter turned round, Becky was still looking at him, willing him to look back and recognize her as his friend once more. But when he returned her gaze, her eyes were wide with panic.

"Get out," she whispered.

Peter furrowed his brow and mouthed, *What?* Becky glanced at Essie and her expression ran cold.

"Get out," she said. "Run."

Peter felt round for Cooper's hand, more out of instinct than anything else, and Essie stepped forward.

"Becky," she said, without taking her eyes off Cooper, "why don't you clean that man's shit off your hands in the kitchen, there's a good girl. Mr Carmichael, lock Tom in the bedroom."

Peter's dad raised his rifle again, but Mr Carmichael and Bud rushed in to overpower him. Essie strode forward, her gaze fixed on Cooper.

"Come here, boy."

Cooper pulled the flare from his jeans pocket. "Pete!"

Peter looked around frantically for a means of escape. But there was no way out other than behind them. Then he clocked the chair at his feet. He lifted it up with both hands to bring it to the window and hurled it at the glass.

Sheeting snow ripped through the shattered window and whipped the length of the dining table.

"Cooper!" Peter cried into the rushing winds. "Go!"

Cooper clambered through the jagged hole. Peter followed, hurtling down the snowdrifts banked up against the side of the cabin and crashing into a tree. Cooper pulled him to his feet and together they freewheeled down the side of the hill.

They tumbled out on to the ice near the jetty, and gunshots cracked out across Cabins Creak. Peter gazed up. Bobbing lights broke from behind the towering pines and started to travel down the hill toward them.

"They're coming."

Cooper held out the flare. "What if nobody sees it?"

"What if they do? I mean, what are we dragging them into?"

But Cooper pulled him on.

The frozen waste yawned out in every direction. They cleared the end of the jetty and ran out on to open ice.

35

They made it to the watchtower. Boulders breaching the surface of the lake at its base were encrusted with ice like gums round a ragged tooth. Peter fell across one to catch his breath and turned back. Light struck the jetty at the foot of Cabins Creak. The others weren't far behind. Cooper ran on ahead to lower the hinged step down on to the ice, and Peter gazed up.

The watchtower's four giant stilts thrust up sharply above him, frost clenched across the timber beams making them as white as bone. He ran up to the foot of the stairwell and stopped.

"Pete," said Cooper, heading up the first flight. "Come on!"

"Did you know about the reaction to raw meat?"

Cooper turned back and nodded. "I did."

"Doesn't it worry you?"

"No. Why? Does it worry *you*?"

Peter looked away and didn't answer.

"Rider told me it's just residue from the plague. Like a scar remindin' us the monster's been."

"But that's all? Nothing worse than that?"

Cooper spat a strand of hair from his mouth and said nothing.

"But that's all?" Peter repeated.

"What's goin' on, Pete?"

"Nothing."

"Then why have you stopped?"

Peter shook his head and gazed at the canoe encrusted in ice at the base of the tower.

"I said why have you stopped?"

"I dunno."

"Sure you do."

"I'm just scared."

"Scared a what?"

"I don't know."

"Scared of what Rider looked like?"

"No," said Peter. Then, "Yes."

"Scared you might see me look like that one day?"

"Maybe."

"Or are you scared a me already?"

"No. I'm scared of doing the wrong thing again."

"Am I the wrong thing?" Cooper asked.

Peter looked up and said nothing.

Cooper turned away so Peter couldn't see his face and ran his fingers across the frosted railing. "Don't you love me no more?"

Peter's chest juddered. He started to shake his head, ready to say, *No, that's not it, that's not it at all.* But the words stayed inside him. He took a step forward, but Cooper held out his hand to stop him from coming any closer.

"Don't."

"Cooper."

"I said don't. Rider warned me about the way things are gonna be for me now. But I din't think he was right when he said I should prepare myself for you to look at me different."

Peter winced. He'd never seen love leave somebody's eyes before. But it left Cooper's now. It only took a second to undo everything. Cooper blinked and the word *Peter,* as something precious and beloved, abandoned him as if he'd never even existed.

Peter staggered forward. "No."

But it was too late. Cooper dropped the flare. It skittered out across the ice, stopping short of one of the stilts. Peter skidded across the ice to retrieve it. When he turned back, Cooper had gone.

36

The others were coming. Snow whipped round the base of the watchtower making visibility poor, but the wind was carrying their voices. They were out on the ice now and they were close.

Peter squinted into the driving snow and looked down toward the bottom of the lake. He could barely make out Skipping Mouse, but in his mind's eye he saw himself standing at the foot of the island as the stranger's canoe made its approach that morning. He wouldn't be standing here now if he hadn't been out chopping wood. He wouldn't have been stabbed, or sent on to the mainland, or watched Cooper die, or know anything he knew now. Everything would be the same as it always had been and nothing would have gone wrong. Nothing would have happened. Cooper wouldn't have happened.

Peter grabbed hold of one of the timber stilts and

leaned into the whipping wind. "Cooper!"

"*Peter!*"

Peter swung round. His name was faint, lost inside the winds somewhere, but he'd heard it all the same. He looked out toward Stone's Throw, then behind him toward Bear Island. He waited and it came again. Except more than one person was calling his name. Then came the gunshots. Peter ducked and a bullet struck the base of the tower, splintering the wood. The gunshot's echo ricocheted round the lake and Peter grabbed the flare.

He rushed to the bottom of the staircase and another gunshot cracked one of the beams ahead. He bolted up the watchtower, tumbling forward into each flight of steps in turn until he made it up on to the Sky Deck where Drew Matthews was leaning over the railing with the hood of his parka jacket pulled up over his face.

Drew turned. He held the rifle to his eye and stared across the deck at Peter.

"Peter?"

"What?"

"The gunshots. What's going on?"

"They're for me."

Drew let out a short laugh. "Why? Have your crocheted blankets started falling apart?"

Peter squinted. He didn't have time for this. He marched down the length of the deck. Drew edged backward, toying with the trigger. By the time he saw the flare gun and figured out there was a genuine threat of noise and light that might attract the Dead, Peter had pushed past him.

He craned over the edge of the railing on tiptoe, pointed the flare up into the sky and fired. A red ball of light travelled up into the clouds. It arched, then disappeared inside them. Peter sank back down on to his heels. He didn't know if it was enough. He dropped the flare gun on the deck and listened to footsteps break across the staircase behind him. He didn't even know if he cared any more.

"You're a traitor now, Peter," came a voice. "And a terrorist."

Peter turned round. Mr Carmichael stepped up on to the Sky Deck.

"Essie won't let you go," he said, pulling down the hood of his parka. "She's hell-bent."

Peter shrugged. "Won't she?"

"Peter, I—"

"You're still so sure that the thing I've betrayed is worth protecting."

Mr Carmichael looked away, and another set of footsteps made their way up the staircase behind him.

Slower than his, but deliberate.

"You know," said Peter, "Mrs Carmichael told me how much she adored you. I'm glad she didn't live to see you turn out this way."

Mr Carmichael looked up, his eyes all at once wide with doubt and fears. He was about to say something when a hand patted him gently on the forearm and Essie stepped forward.

"You used to be as useless as a trapdoor in a canoe, Peter," she said, shaking the snow from her shawl. "It's a shame you made yourself useful to the wrong cause."

"Where's my dad?"

"Where's Cooper?"

Peter clenched his jaw and said nothing.

"Yellowstone can come for you," she said quietly, "or the Dead. Reckon you can take your chances on whichever comes sooner. But you ain't wearin' no coat so if it drops real low tonight, and it will drop real low, chances are the ice will get to you first. Make you cough blood it will. Then it'll riddle your guts and freeze your lungs. By the time you start cryin' out for us to come get you, your lungs will burst and this will all be over."

Peter held Essie's gaze.

"Tie him to the base of the tower, Don," she said. "Everyone inside and lights out."

Essie gripped the railing and headed over to the stairwell, but held back at the top of the steps.

"I ain't none too sure what your dad told you," she said quietly, "but the world din't fall apart because of the Dead. Hell, the world was already being ripped apart by terrible people doin' terrible things and God knows that shoulda been good enough trainin' for all this. But no, it fell apart because by the time the Dead came along we were livin' in a world where people like you made people like us look like we were wrong to mistrust others. The world got soft, Peter. Well, not any more. Not on Darlene's watch and not on mine."

Essie continued down the steps and Peter called out after her.

"People that only ever encounter themselves know nothing and will die knowing nothing."

Essie looked up at the sky as if to acknowledge the flare and walked on. "We'll see about that. We'll see."

Mr Carmichael left Drew on watch and dragged Peter off the Sky Deck back down on to the ice. He tied him up against one of the stilts, then broke into a run to catch up with Essie and the others, eventually disappearing inside the blizzard. Peter threw his head back against the post. Barely a few moments passed when the air suddenly stilled.

Peter could see the whole of the lake now the storm

had passed. He gazed out across the vast white disc of ice, past the pine-peaked islands to the dark border of the forest beyond. His white breath plumed in the air. That was the only movement though. There was no wind. There was no snow. It was as if time itself had stopped.

But he wasn't alone. There was a presence out on the lake. Only it wasn't anything he could see. He could feel it. Peter gazed out across the ice and something boomed over by Stone's Throw. He pinned his back to the post, and the boom rumbled across the surface of the ice toward him, reverberating through his boots. He glanced up at the sky. But it wasn't coming from above. It was coming from beneath the lake.

He waited and it came again. Another boom erupted, this time right underneath the islands, followed by a low rumble like distant thunder. As before, the rumble travelled beneath the surface of the lake, and a moment later made it all the way over to Peter and into his boots again. He fixed his gaze on the spot of ice near Stone's Throw and waited for the next one. But the source of the disturbance had shifted.

An almighty clack struck the underside of the ice right in front of him. Peter gasped, and high crackling sounds like the electricity inside a clap of thunder rippled out in waves across the lake. Peter looked down at his boots and a huge mass passed beneath him. It rolled out from underneath the watchtower toward the other islands, making the ice surge then bow beneath his feet. Peter gasped and the lake fell still again. He sank back into the post, panting. He'd never heard the ice growing before. Cooper probably had. He probably came out here and chased ice thunder across the lake every winter. It was probably something they'd have done together.

Peter's throat tightened. He suddenly became aware of just how cold it was. He gazed up at the sky and more snow came twisting out of the darkness, all blue in the night. Peter shivered. His eyes scanned the shoreline, darting from one pine tree to another, then further back behind the line of trees into the woods for any sign of help. What if the flare hadn't worked? What if no one was coming?

His body was starting to twitch now, shaking in uncontrollable spasms, when he saw someone out on the ice. They were too far away to make out anything more than the outline, but they were slowly making their way across the ice down the bottom end of the lake near Boulder. Peter kept watching. They disappeared round the back of the Whistles. He waited and a few minutes later the figure broke out from behind the trees round the other side of the island. It was making its way toward him. "Cooper," he murmured. But it wasn't him. Its bare feet were as blue as the ice it walked on.

Peter froze and the Restless One kept coming.

He strained forward. "No."

He leaned out from the post, pressing his weight down to try and loosen the rope. He snapped back, breathless. It was too tight. He looked up and the Restless One walked on toward the watchtower.

The frosted figure used to be a woman. But its face wasn't contorted into a silent scream as was often the way when one of them laid its eyes on you. It was calm, as if lost in a dream somehow, and it was gliding so gracefully across the ice that it came more like a ghost than a monster, sent down from the mountains to quietly take him away. Peter felt the cold kiss of snowflakes on his face. His eyelids drooped.

"Mom," he whispered.

He blinked to regain focus and the figure moved silently through the snow. It was getting closer. Its white arms were outstretched now. But he wasn't frightened. No, *her* arms were outstretched as if to welcome him in. *Come, my darling*, they seemed to say. *Come.* Peter's eyelids drooped again. He opened them and she was closer still. Her fingertips were searching. They wanted him. They wanted to welcome her love, her darling boy, in from the cold. But she wasn't alone.

Peter's head lolled forward and another one broke

out from inside the forest borders. A moment later, a grey mass moved from behind Stone's Throw on to the open ice. Peter smiled and the group started to make their way toward him. It wouldn't be long now. It wouldn't be too long at all.

Peter's head fell back against the post. He supposed the cold had burrowed its way into his bones by now. Then he'd stop breathing. But he didn't feel any pain. He just felt the need to sleep. Mom would make it over to him soon and then he could sleep forever.

Ten pale fingers broke through the veil of snow. Peter didn't know what his mom looked like. Dad didn't shove any family photos and keepsakes into their backpack the day the three of them fled for the mountains. He wasn't to know she would never complete the journey. But this bedraggled wretch with her eyelids frosted wide open to take her boy in, would do.

The dead woman was mostly bald. What was left of her hair looked like bits of long black string pulled out of the top of a swimming cap. Her milky eyeballs roved around Peter's face. They were searching for him. Somehow that connection to another person was still important to her, and Peter felt something about the Restless Ones he'd never felt before. That she was lost. She was simply lost inside herself, drawn to another soul not because she wanted to destroy it, but because she recognized it as being something she'd once had too. Perhaps *that's* why they came. Perhaps that's why they were so restless.

The dead woman's jaw fell open.

Peter's eyes watered. "It's OK, Mom," he said.

She staggered forward to take him inside her mouth. Peter closed his eyes. He was ready to receive her. But she didn't come any further.

A gunshot ricocheted round the lake. Peter jerked upright. The Restless One dropped on to the ice at his feet and Mr Carmichael ran up to him.

"Please," said Peter woozily.

Mr Carmichael turned to face Peter. His eyes were wild beneath the hood of his parka.

"Cabins Creak is surrounded," he panted. "We couldn't make it back."

"Where are the others?" said Peter.

"They're on the ice too."

"My dad?"

"Locked in the bedroom still."

Peter pushed forward against the rope. "Untie me."

Mr Carmichael nodded, but he didn't come any closer. He glanced back toward Stone's Throw. The grey mass was now an ashen horde of jangling limbs behind the veil of snow. He turned to face Peter and Peter smiled hopefully. But Mr Carmichael pulled the hood further down over his eyes and ran past him toward the stairwell. Peter screamed inside his head. He pushed forward, but the rope burned into his sides, and still the Dead travelled out across the ice.

There were more gunshots now. One. Two. The group that had gathered round the base of Stone's Throw turned in the direction of this new stimulus and moved en masse in its direction. But not all of them. Two of the Dead making their way up from the bottom of the lake were drawn by the shot fired by Mr Carmichael and moved slowly on toward the watchtower. Mr Carmichael's footsteps took to the first flight of stairs.

"Mr Carmichael, please!" said Peter. "Please, Don."

The footsteps stopped.

Peter angled his head to the right. "Thank you," he said. "Thank you."

But he didn't come back. Peter heard the rifle drop to the ground followed by a wet crunching sound. Then he heard Mr Carmichael topple down the stairs, screaming.

"Mr Carmichael?" Peter whispered. "Mr Carmichael?"

Peter froze and something moved round the back of the post. He held his breath and prayed the post would hide him. Except the Restless One sensed his flesh. It moved silently across the ice. Peter turned his head sideways, and the thing fell forward into the wood. But it never reached him.

A pair of calloused hands took hold of the rope and started to tussle with the knot.

"Cooper?"

"Quit your wrigglin' or I can't cut you loose."

"Cooper!"

"Shh."

"I'm sorry."

"Shh now."

"I'm so sorry I doubted you."

Peter felt the flat of a knife angle up under the rope. Copper slashed it once and the rope fell away. Peter swung round and Cooper's hair spilled into his face with his dark eyes all deep and lonely.

"You're mad at me," said Peter.

"You lit the flare, din't you?"

"Yes. But you can still be mad at me."

"We don't got time for this."

"But—"

"No," said Cooper. "I had all them years on the lake without you, I ain't havin' no more of it."

Peter wiped a strand of hair from Cooper's face. "I won't let you make a mess of our home."

"Sweet," said Cooper, kissing him. "I won't let you make a mess of us."

Cooper took Peter by the hand and started to pull him back toward the staircase, but more of the Dead broke out

354

from behind the tower, toppling over Mr Carmichael's body like wolves feeding on a carcass.

"The other way," said Peter.

"But where?"

Peter swung round, scanning the islands for a safer route. The Dead were coming from every angle now.

"Cover me with your scent," he said. "Then we can make it past them to the boathouse."

Cooper quickly ran his hands down the length of Peter's arms and chest, then cupped his face. He held Peter's gaze for a moment and told him he loved him without saying the words. Peter did the same. But they had to reach the boathouse. He grabbed Cooper by the hand and they ran out on to the ice.

Peter threw his free arm forward, forcing his body on, but his feet kept slip-sliding from underneath him. Gunshots sounded just ahead of them, but nothing came their way. Peter squinted through the flurrying snow to see if anyone else was trapped out on the ice, fixed his gaze in the direction of the boathouse and ran on.

They made it as far as the hot rod. Peter stopped just short of the vehicle. Snow fell over the truck's rusty hood and shelved the back of the cargo bed. One of the Dead lay decapitated at its side. A little way away from the truck was another body.

Bud's limbs jutted out at broken angles from his torso. Blackened blood around his neck had already started to crust over the jagged bite mark. His Stetson sat further across the ice gathering snow. It looked odd, lonely somehow, parted from its lifelong companion. Bud hadn't made it to safety in time. But others had.

Peter looked toward the driver's seat and Essie looked back. At her side was Becky. Again, he could barely bring himself to look at her. Essie pushed down the lock and eased into the seat, wiping blood from the machete laid out across the dashboard. She stuffed the sodden rag into the glovebox so the herd wouldn't be drawn by the blood and looked past Peter at the grey mass coming up behind him. She knew he was trapped.

Cooper stared at the Stetson and nothing else came out of him.

"Coop," said Peter quietly.

"He's dead, Pete."

"Yes. But you're going to have to grieve for him later."

"Pa never even came up to me."

"The herd are coming, Cooper."

"Pa never even—"

"Cooper, now!"

Cooper turned back. "Pete."

"They're coming. And there's no time."

"Essie killed him to save her own neck."

"No. One of the Dead got him."

"He ain't that stupid. He'd never let that happen."

"Coop."

"She pushed him. I know it."

Peter looked back at the truck and caught Becky's gaze. She sat forward, glancing first at Essie and then at the machete, and nodded to communicate that Bud's death was Essie's doing. This wasn't about Essie's loyalty to the lake any more, only her own survival.

Becky's eyes were wide. They begged Peter to forgive her unforgivable mistake. She glanced at the door handle at her side, as if escape from Essie was within touching distance if only she'd reach out and give herself permission to take it. Peter clenched his jaw. Becky could rot for all he cared. But the lake had made a graveyard of enough friends and loved ones. He swung round to check on the Dead.

Stragglers that had broken out from behind the islands at the foot of the lake had gathered with the Restless Ones at the watchtower. They formed a mass, spilling out from underneath the tower. But it was no longer possible to make out any one hollow face or lumbering limb, only a vast shadow crawling silently across the ice toward them.

Peter turned back, frantically mouthing the words, *Do it.* Becky shook her head in case he didn't mean it. But Peter inched forward, urging her to make the break and make it now. "Do it!"

Essie didn't see Becky wrapping her fist round the door handle. She was too busy watching the Dead approaching behind Peter to notice.

The truck door swung open and Becky's foot struck the ice.

She swiped the machete from the dashboard and tumbled out of the truck, slamming the door behind her. She spat at the glass and stepped away.

Essie briefly looked at her girl, her dear, sweet child. But whatever they'd shared before this day was done with. She leaned across the driver's seat, pushing down the bobble to secure the lock again, and eased back into her seat, her pipe clenched at the corner of her mouth.

Becky jostled the machete in her hand to gain a better purchase on the handle and stood across the ice from Peter.

"We weren't just friends," she said, "we were the best of friends."

"Yes," said Peter, "but she—"

"I wasn't talking about *her.*"

Peter flinched. "Becky."

"You could've come to me when Cooper returned."

"I know."

"You should've come to me. I didn't have time to process any of this. Rider's teeth. His eyes went dead, Peter. I was scared."

Peter looked away. But whatever was left to sort out between them would have to wait.

"The Restless Ones are almost here," she said.

"Cooper can't camouflage both of us," said Peter. "His scent alone won't hold that many of them back."

"And you don't have a weapon." Becky looked across the expanse of ice toward the top of the lake. "And you know your dad's still locked inside Henry's bedroom."

"But—"

"I can get us back there with my machete."

Peter nodded. They should take their chances and go. Only there was something he needed to do.

"You go," he said. "But Essie needs to see she was wrong."

"You sure?"

"Yes."

"You'd better make sure the herd comes this way."

Peter nodded. "I promise."

Becky ran back across the ice with her tangled hair trailing behind her. Some way ahead, light from Henry's cabin twinkled from inside the island's piney chamber. But hidden right up there in among the pines it might as well have been a million miles away. Peter swung round.

What had been a grey shadow moving silently across the surface of the lake, was now a living wall of teeth.

"They're here."

Cooper, who'd stood silently watching over Bud's Stetson until now, suddenly turned. His hand reached for the sheath at his belt, then drew back when he found it was empty. He grabbed Peter's hand.

"What if my scent don't hold?"

"It will."

"But what if it don't? We ain't never tried it on anythin' this big before."

"Just hold me."

"Pete—"

"We got this."

Peter pulled Cooper up to the truck, standing directly in front of the hood. He drew Cooper's arms round his waist like a rope and pressed his back into Cooper's chest. He squeezed him once to tell him everything was going to be OK, even though he could only trust that was true, and held Essie's gaze.

He clenched his fist, striking the hood – once, hard – just to be sure the Restless Ones came their way. All of them. Essie sat back in her seat, hate curling across her lips. But she wasn't scared. She presumed that the truck's windows would hold if she kept quiet enough. Her eyes glowered and they came.

A hundred rotting souls lumbered past Peter. The herd broke across Cooper's back like rapids round a boulder, pushing him forward into the drag. Peter couldn't withstand the momentum behind him and toppled forward over the truck. He planted both hands squarely on top of the hood to brace himself and looked up.

The truck buckled beneath the weight of the surge. Glass shattered. Rotting fingers thrust through the passenger window. They rooted for Essie's neck. Got tangled in her hair. She winced and yet, in that moment, Peter saw her eyes land on Cooper. She watched how his arms gripped lovingly round Peter. How his face buried into the crook of Peter's neck to shield him so perfectly from harm. All the while, she had no one. And a greater horror rolled across her eyes than what was about to crash in and take her: a realization that her life would be defined by this, her final thought. She had been wrong. And in her decision, she was alone.

The grey mass enveloped Essie, then her scream, swallowing the truck whole.

Cooper drew Peter back into the herd, and the Restless Ones spilled across the hood. The weight of the Dead bundling in behind Cooper caused some resistance, but Peter pushed backward into Cooper and the Dead squeezed past to close up the space in front no sooner had they stepped out of it.

Finally Peter felt the weight behind them shift. They toppled back and the last of the Dead stumbled out ahead of them. Peter pulled Cooper to his feet and they scrambled back across the frozen lake until they reached a safe enough distance from the herd.

They collapsed on to the ice beneath the shadow of the watchtower and Cooper pulled Peter back into his arms.

"Becky," whispered Peter.

"She can handle herself. She'll make it."

"We've achieved nothing."

"Shh."

"But we haven't."

Cooper kissed the back of Peter's neck. But he didn't say anything to contradict him and a thousand thoughts tumbled out of the darkness. It was freezing and they needed to head back to check that Becky had made it to Dad. Peter gently pushed down on Cooper's arms to release him when he felt the weight of someone watching him and swung round.

Two figures stood over them. Cooper's hand reached instinctively for the empty sheath, but something told Peter they didn't need to be scared. They were strangers though. Everyone on the lake looked dirty in winter on account of all the fur pelts, mud and dried blood or a mixture of all three of those things, but not these two. Peter looked down at the pair of skis the two were wearing. Red hooded ski jackets and goggles shielded their faces. He couldn't see their eyes behind the tinted glass to gauge their intentions, but unlike the chaperone they didn't seem to radiate danger, just fascination.

The strangers looked at each other and nodded. One patted the other's back as if to suggest they'd done well. They seemed to come to some kind of agreement so the shortest one, a woman, drove her poles into the ice and stepped out of her skis. She swung her backpack down off her shoulders and yanked something out of the side pocket.

"Jim, we landed the helicopter safely," she said, talking into the black handset. "We found them."

"Well, I'll be…" said the voice down the other end. "Where were they?"

"A lake between the refuges at Yellowstone and Grand Teton. But there appears to be a whole island community we didn't even know about up here."

"How many Pale Wanderers?"

"Just one."

"Are you sure?"

"Yes," said the woman, looking at Cooper. "But he's not alone. He's with an uninfected boy. They're together."

"Very well," said the voice down the handset. "Just make sure you get them both back safely, ya hear me?"

The woman shoved the handset back in her jacket pocket and lifted the goggles to her forehead. She was older than Peter first thought. Middle-aged. Greying hair tied loose in a ponytail poked out the bottom of her hood. Lines scored her face as deeply as old driftwood left to crack in the sun. But her eyes were young, adventurous somehow.

"We lit the flare," said Peter.

The woman smiled. "Yeah. You and the cute blond one. We figured."

"No," said Cooper. "Pete did that. S'all Peter."

"Then you're lucky to have him."

"Rider heard your message on the radio," said Peter. "But I'm sorry – he didn't make it."

The woman indicated that she was sorry to hear that. But she didn't seem to know who they were talking about.

"Jonathan T. Rider," said Peter.

"I'm sorry," she said. "We don't know who that is."

"You're from Yellowstone?"

The woman frowned. "Yellowstone?"

She stopped herself from saying anything more and looked back at her colleague. The man drove his ski poles into the ice and removed his goggles. Long black hair, unbound, framed his bony features and spilled across his shoulders. His skin was pale. Like Cooper, he'd woken from death and his eyes carried the darkness of that journey inside them. But they weren't without kindness. He kneeled down in front of Cooper, and Peter watched that secret understanding hover in the space between them.

The man extended his hand. "Tokala."

"Cooper," he said, staring at the man's palm. "And this is Peter."

Peter shook the man's hand. "He's not real big on new people. But it's only because he doesn't think they're going to be big on him."

"That's not true," said Cooper, tucking his hair behind his ears.

"Well, it's kinda true."

The man smiled, but his thoughts were elsewhere. "Why did you think we're from Yellowstone?"

"Because that's where Rider said the radio message was coming from. The one calling out to any Pale Wanderers."

"Yes. We put that message out. But why would he think it came from Yellowstone?"

"Because he had allies there, friends who knew about the Returned."

"Because here is?"

"Wranglestone."

"Yes," said the man. "The lake, but—"

"A secret sanctuary for the Returned. It was built by a group of Returnees before the great evacuation, but without the government's knowledge so they could hide if the world wanted to hurt them."

The man crouched down in front of them. "Our people were among the general population even at the beginning?"

"Yes."

"And where's that group now?"

Peter held the man's gaze and said nothing.

"Peter?"

"Gone. They're all gone. Years ago. Our friend reached out to allies in Yellowstone to contact his family living there at the refuge. Gave away the coordinates for the lake too. But the ones that came first to check that everything was OK didn't like what they found here. By the time the rest of us stumbled out of the woods, looking for a new home, they, led by Henry, formed a new community and buried all knowledge of the Returned ever having been here."

"I don't understand," said the man. "How did this Henry prevent your community from discovering the truth about the Returnees?"

Peter gripped Cooper's hand tight and said nothing.

"How, Peter?"

"We led the bitten Lake Landers off the islands before anyone knew any different. Some were killed. Others were traded for provisions."

The strangers exchanged glances and the woman cleared her throat.

"We came from the refuge at Grand Teton National Park originally. But our community abandoned it over two years ago."

Peter shook his head. "But—"

"There's no need to be alarmed."

"But why did you abandon it?"

"Because it wasn't needed any more."

"Why?"

"We saw how you both made the herd swarm round the truck without Peter getting hurt just now," she said. "Well, over time we also became aware of the ones who come back and how they can cloak our loved ones from the Dead too. So we left the refuge."

Peter shook his head. "Why?"

"Because we could," said the woman as if the question was strange somehow.

"But where do you live?"

"In a town."

"Town?"

"West Wranglestone, yes. Thirty miles west of here."

"We know where that is," Cooper muttered.

"The streets were empty like Christmas Day the day we found it," said the woman. "The Dead most likely wandered on to the plains after a while, drawn out by lightning on the horizon perhaps, or wolves. But they left behind a perfect little ghost town. And as long as we walk in pairs, like Tokala and I, we're nothing but ghosts to them now."

Peter forced a smile. "You make that sound so easy."

The woman blinked once deeply as it to sympathize with Peter's pain. But she said nothing to contradict him.

"We would've come for you sooner," she said. "If we'd known you were out here."

Peter nodded. "Is it just you there?"

"No. The team from Yellowstone have joined us now. But our nearest neighbours after that are at Glacier over three hundred miles north so we've no idea how they're adapting. Beyond that to Yosemite, Death Valley, Grand Canyon? Who knows?"

Peter took Cooper's hand. "But our community's the only one that did this to the Returnees?"

"No, sweetheart," said the woman. "Not necessarily. We're concerned about a number of smaller backcountry communities who isolated themselves from the refuge program. They've resisted any outside interference until now. But that's about to change."

Peter shook his head. "Change?"

"Yes. You don't need to be out here alone any more."

Cooper sat forward. "Here ain't out of someplace else. It's our home."

"Well, yes, but—"

"And we ain't alone."

"No," said Peter. "There are more Returnees still needing our help out here. We've seen them. Perhaps we could find them. Welcome them on to the lake. Turn it back to the sanctuary it was meant to be. And, besides, we come with a horse and a dad who lives like a pig, so maybe we'll steer clear of your town and set up base camp here for a while."

The woman narrowed her eyes. "I'm sure you're in the best possible position to help them. It's just that the lake needn't be a sanctuary for anyone any more. None of the parks do."

Peter shook his head. "But why?"

The woman hesitated. Her eyes flickered with things left unsaid.

"That's enough for now," said the man, looking to the

fringes of the sky above the pines where the light was now glowing. "We can talk more on this later, but I'd like to stay a few days, longer if need be, and help. If you'd be kind enough to let me."

Peter looked at Cooper. He agreed and somehow a pact was made.

Across the lake, sunlight clipped the treetops, making the island's frosted spires glisten. Lamplight over at Cabins Creak went out. Peter stood, and soon his dad and Becky made it down to the foot of the island on to the jetty. They raised their hands to wave and one by one the remaining Lake Landers took to the ice and slowly made their way toward them.

"How did things even get this way?" Peter asked.

The man stood, drawing in the cold mountain air, and sighed. "Humankind has a history of turning people into disposable creatures."

"But why?"

"I suppose we simply forget the children we used to be."

Peter took Cooper's hand in his and when, sometime later, they set out back across the plains on horseback together in search of others in need of a place called Wranglestone, Peter hung the reins over the saddle's two bucking rolls and drew Cooper's arms round him.

"So what are we gonna watch if *Jaws* isn't showing?"

"Dunno," said Cooper. "*Back to the Future* maybe."

"OK. And what's that about?"

"It's about a kid who loves denim and skateboards cos it's 1985. But his ma and pa don't love each other so much no more so he goes back in time, in a car with wings that's really a time machine, to when they were young to make sure they do."

"We won't have to send somebody back to remind us, will we?"

"Nope," said Cooper. "I'll make real sure of it."

Peter leaned back into Cooper's chest and watched snow dust skittering across the surface of the plains.

In the distance, wolves loped the higher ground.

Snowball whinnied and somewhere over the mountains a wild bird flew.

I am here, it cried to anyone who would listen. *I am here*.

ACKNOWLEDGEMENTS

For taking this particular journey with me, my deepest thanks for your help go to you, Shirley and Daniel. Special thanks go to you Mark for setting the tone so beautifully for me with your original submission map design. And to you Hannah for being more than just a guiding mentor in this industry, but a friend.

To Stripes Publishing, for your belief in me and my work, my thanks go to Katie, Charlie, Ella, Elle, Mattie and Ruth. And to Pip and Jana, for giving my book its coat and visual identity so beautifully, my dearest thanks.

For helping a young boy on his way, my heartfelt gratitude goes to you, my school teachers, Sue Duncan, Ann Bullen and Sally Marchant. I didn't know it then, but you were looking after me in special ways, even when Section 28 prohibited you from saying so. Without your love and encouragement, I doubt these words would even exist.

Mum, thank you. You always let me be whoever I needed to be.

To Emily, Joseph, Zack, Eleanor, Joost, Frieso and Harry. Just look what you can do if you dream then put your mind to it!

And finally, special thanks go to you, Mike, Gemma, Dan, Claire and Laura, for simply being the best thing a person can have in life, old friends. I love you.

ABOUT THE AUTHOR

Darren Charlton lives in London with his
partner and works in the voluntary sector for a homeless
organization. His lifetime obsessions with the National Parks
of America, horror, film music and 80s kids' movies have
all worked their way into his writing.

For more information about Darren Charlton visit:
www.darrencharlton.com

Follow him on Twitter @DarrenRCharlton